SYMPATHY FOR THE DEVIL

I0664080

By

Skip Williams

Table of Contents

Prologue

Hitman Jake discovers betrayal, deceit, loyalty, and love while leaving a trail of destruction around the globe. The title and the chapter names are a homage to the Rolling Stones, and can also be used as the soundtrack to each chapter.

In a world often defined by shades of grey, some operate in the darkest corners, men and women who navigate a shadowy realm where morality is flexible, loyalty is fleeting, and survival depends on a razor-sharp wit and unwavering resolve. This is the world of Jake and Julianna.

From the first chapter, *Sympathy for the Devil* plunges you into a relentless journey, one that tests the boundaries of human resilience and the price of redemption. Jake, a seasoned contract killer with a hardened heart, and Julianna, his equal in skill and spirit, are characters born from a world few dare to explore, a world where trust is a luxury and betrayal lurks at every turn. Together, they challenge the notion of heroism, defying expectations with a moral code that is as ambiguous as it is intriguing.

This is not just a story about vengeance or survival, though both are woven into the fabric of every twist and turn. At its core, this book is about the complexities of human connection. Through bullets and betrayal, fire and fury, Jake and Julianna show us the raw, unfiltered power of loyalty and love, tested to the breaking point and forged in the crucible of danger.

As you turn these pages, you'll find yourself immersed in a high-stakes world of mob bosses, crooked politicians, and secret alliances. You'll travel to gritty cities and forgotten corners of the globe, navigating the chaos alongside two of the most compelling antiheroes you'll ever meet. The tension is palpable, the stakes are personal, and every chapter forces you to ask yourself: How far would you go to protect the one person who truly matters?

For those who crave action, suspense, and characters who feel as real as the world they inhabit, *Sympathy for the Devil* is a story that will grip you by the collar and refuse to let go. It's a tale of shadows, light, betrayal, and redemption, where even the devil deserves a little sympathy, or perhaps, just enough to keep him human.

Welcome to the story. Buckle up. You're in for a ride.

Intro – Start Me Up

When it comes to lines of work, some people hate their jobs, others tolerate them, and a rare few love them too much. In my line of work, loving it too much isn't just a problem. It's a warning sign. The ones who love it too much? They savor every contract like it's their personal art project, dragging things out for their own twisted satisfaction.

Me? I'm not here for the thrill. I'm here because I'm good at it. The money's solid, and the travel keeps life interesting, even if the destinations are more gutter than glamour. And there's a certain pride in doing things right. Not everyone can handle the precision it takes to succeed in my business, but that's where I thrive: in the details and the execution. The job itself? Anticlimactic, if I'm being honest. It's the planning that gets me going, thinking it through, crafting a flawless strategy, and then watching it unfold without a hitch.

Some of my peers draw the line at women and kids. Not me. I figure if someone's willing to pay, there's a reason. The mark's hands aren't clean, and neither are mine. To survive in this business, you need more than just skills; you need a code, a set of rules you don't break. Mine's simple: plan meticulously, execute cleanly, and never let the noise get to you.

And there's plenty of noise, politics, backstabbers, and the occasional idiot who thinks they can stiff me. Take this one guy, a big shot who figured he could skip out on paying. By the time I was done, he was begging to pay double. Lesson learned: I don't take crap from anyone. Never have, never will.

Today, my name is Jake. Tomorrow? Could be anything. But for now, this is my story. Take it or leave it.

Chapter 1: You Got Me Rocking

Jake adjusted his gloves, the cool leather snug against his fingers. The rooftop garden was silent except for the faint rustle of leaves in the evening breeze. Below him, the city hummed with oblivious energy: honking horns, the occasional wail of a distant siren, and the murmur of lives being lived. Jake stood still, scanning the luxury apartment terrace just a few floors down, with his light blue eyes. He felt the familiar calm settle over him, a practiced detachment that had become second nature.

This was a high-stakes job, the kind he preferred. No room for error, and no messy loose ends. His target, a mid-level mobster named Dominic Vezzi, had made his share of enemies and knew too many secrets. Tonight, Dominic's secrets would die with him.

Jake's light pack rested against his back, containing everything he needed: a silenced pistol, a coil of climbing rope, and a pair of night-vision goggles. He crouched, peering through the scope of his rifle as Dominic strolled onto the terrace, drink in hand. The man was smug, his rotund frame draped in an expensive robe, and he sipped from a tumbler like he owned the world.

Jake let the crosshairs settle on Dominic's chest, exhaling slowly to steady his aim. A faint pang of something, maybe pity, maybe disgust, flickered in his mind. He pushed it aside.

You don't play with your food, Jake, he reminded himself. He squeezed the trigger.

The silenced rifle emitted a muffled cough. Dominic's glass slipped from his hand, shattering on the tiles as his body jerked and crumpled to the ground. Jake didn't flinch, watching the scene for a full thirty seconds to ensure there were no unexpected movements or sounds. Dominic wasn't getting up again.

Jake disassembled the rifle with practiced efficiency, packing it away as his earpiece crackled to life. A woman's voice, smooth and confident, came through.

"Is it done?" Her tone was casual, but Jake knew better. She wouldn't ask if she wasn't certain.

"Clean hit," Jake replied. "No complications."

"Good. The client will be pleased. Anything else you noticed?"

Jake hesitated for a moment, then said, "He was alone. Either his people don't care about him, or they underestimate the threat. Their mistake. My payday."

The faint hum of a helicopter interrupted the night's stillness. Jake's eyes darted upward. A black chopper loomed in the distance, circling toward the building. His calm remained, but his muscles tensed.

"Looks like I've got company," he said into the earpiece.

"Extraction team?" she asked, her voice tightening.

"Most likely." Jake pulled a pair of binoculars from his pack and scanned the approaching helicopter. The markings on its side confirmed his suspicions.

"Mercs," he muttered. "Dominic must have paid for some insurance."

Jake slung his pack over his shoulder and moved swiftly across the rooftop, his boots silent against the concrete. He reached the edge where his grappling line was anchored. The city spread out below him like a glittering maze, a dozen escape routes flashing through his mind.

The chopper was closing in. Jake pulled a small device from his pocket, a remote detonator. He pressed a button, and a series of small explosions erupted on the terrace below. Nothing large enough to cause serious damage, but enough to create confusion and obscure the scene.

The helicopter hovered above the chaos, its spotlight swinging wildly as men in tactical gear rappelled down ropes. Jake was already on his way down the side of the building, the rope whistling softly through his gloves. When his boots hit the alley below, he unclipped the line and melted into the shadows.

The adrenaline coursed through him, sharpening his senses as he moved quickly but deliberately toward the extraction point. His escape vehicle, a nondescript black sedan, waited two blocks away.

Jake slid into the driver's seat. He started the engine, the low rumble a comforting sound. "Tell the client it's done."

"Copy that," the voice in his ear replied. "You know where to meet me."

Jake nodded to himself and pulled into the street, blending into the flow of traffic. His heart rate was steady, his hands relaxed on the wheel. Another job finished. Another night where he could slip back into anonymity.

As he drove, Jake allowed himself a brief moment of reflection. The job had gone smoothly, as it always did. But a small part of him wondered how long he could keep it up. He wasn't invincible, and he knew it.

He pushed the thought away. There was no room for doubt in his line of work. You did the job, and you moved on. Everything else was a distraction.

The city lights faded in his rearview mirror as Jake vanished into the night, leaving no trace of the chaos behind.

Chapter 2: Mother's Little Helper

The bus pulled into the Port Authority terminal just as the first streaks of dawn painted the sky. Jake stepped off, his duffel bag slung over one shoulder and paused to take in the city. New York was alive, even at this hour. Street vendors were setting up their carts, cab drivers leaned on their horns, and the air was thick with the smell of exhaust and hot pretzels.

He adjusted the strap of his bag and started walking. The neighborhoods shifted as he moved further downtown. Gleaming office buildings gave way to cracked sidewalks and graffiti-covered walls. Trash littered the streets, and the occasional flicker of a neon sign cast jagged shadows on the pavement.

Jake preferred it this way. The grime felt honest, a far cry from the sanitized facades he often encountered in other cities. He turned a corner and spotted the diner up ahead, its flickering "Open 24 Hours" sign buzzing faintly in the morning light.

Inside, the place was as rundown as he expected. The smell of burnt coffee and stale grease hit him the moment he walked through the door. A waitress with tired eyes and a pencil tucked behind her ear gave him a half-hearted nod as he slid into a booth near the back.

A few minutes later, Eddie walked in. The broker's cheap suit was wrinkled, and a faint sheen of sweat glistened on his forehead despite the cool morning air. He spotted Jake and made his way over, sliding into the booth across from him.

"You're early," Eddie muttered, pulling a crumpled napkin from the dispenser and dabbing at his brow.

"You're late," Jake replied, his tone flat.

Eddie didn't argue. Instead, he reached into his bag and pulled out a manila envelope, sliding it across the table. Jake opened it, revealing a stack of photos and a neatly typed schedule.

"She's got a kid," Eddie said, his voice barely above a whisper. "You sure about this one?"

Jake ignored the question, flipping through the photos. The woman in the pictures seemed early forties, with sharp features softened by dark curls. The next photo showed her walking hand-in-hand with a little girl, no older than six.

"You've got her routine?" Jake asked without looking up.

Eddie nodded quickly. "School drop-offs, work schedule, the whole nine yards. It's all there."

Jake slid the photos back into the envelope and closed it. "You'll get your cut when it's done."

Eddie swallowed hard, nodding again. Jake stood, leaving a few bills on the table for the coffee he hadn't touched. Without another word, he walked out, stepping into the chaos of the city.

A few days later the suburban streets were quieter than Jake preferred, but that only made the job more interesting. No neon distractions here, just the soft hum of streetlights and the occasional bark of a dog. The target drove a navy sedan, the kind of car that blended into the background. Jake followed at a respectable distance, his headlights off to avoid suspicion.

The woman behind the wheel, early forties, with sharp features softened by weariness, glanced at the rear-view mirror but never lingered. She had no reason to suspect she was being followed. Jake had spent two days learning her schedule: school drop-offs, a quick coffee run, and hours at her office job before picking up her daughter from soccer practice. Predictable. Efficient. Easy to shadow.

The plan was already in motion. Jake noted the turn she took onto a dimly lit side street. Her usual route home. The perfect place. He adjusted his speed, keeping her taillights in view as she slowed at a stop sign.

The child in the back seat caught his eye. Dark curls framed a face lit by the soft glow of a tablet screen. Jake's gaze lingered just a moment before returning to the road. He wondered if something was wrong with him for not caring, but it didn't matter. None of it mattered. The contract was clear.

He signaled a turn, taking a parallel street to avoid being seen. The timing was everything. At the next intersection, he'd be waiting. The alley was narrow, lined with dumpsters, and shadowed by overgrown trees. He'd scouted it earlier, no cameras, no pedestrians, and mostly, no complications. Just how he liked it.

When the navy Sedan appeared, Jake's car was already idling, half-concealed by shadows. He waited until she passed, then pulled out, blocking her path. The woman braked hard, the Sedan's tires screeching against the asphalt. Jake stepped out, calm and deliberate, his gloved hand resting on the doorframe as he approached her window.

The conversation was brief. A few words were exchanged, her tone shifting from confused to alarmed. Jake's voice remained steady, almost soothing. She didn't scream. She didn't have time.

When he returned to his car, the street was silent once more. The navy Sedan sat empty; its doors ajar. Jake drove off without a glance in the rearview mirror. Somewhere in the distance, the faint wail of a siren began to rise, but it wouldn't matter. By the time anyone arrived, Jake would be gone, and the scene would tell its own story.

The child's tablet lay discarded on the back seat, its screen still glowing. Jake didn't think about it. He never did. The contract was complete, and that was all that mattered.

Chapter 3: Under My Thumb

The train rattled into the Hlavni train station just as the morning fog began to lift, revealing the sharp spires of the old city against a gray sky. Jake stepped off the platform, his single suitcase in 2hand, and immediately felt the damp chill seep through his jacket. Prague always seemed to wear a veil of melancholy, but that suited him fine. It was a city built for shadows.

The streets outside the station were a mix of faded grandeur and modern grit. Tourists clutched maps and cameras, oblivious to the locals who slipped past them with practiced indifference. Jake hailed a cab and handed the driver a scrap of paper with the address of his hotel. No small talk. Just a nod and the lurch of the cab as it merged into the flow of traffic.

The hotel was as unimpressive as the online photos had promised. A post-communist relic, sandwiched between a shuttered storefront and a bakery faintly reeking of yeast and despair. The lobby's dim lighting did little to mask the peeling wallpaper or the receptionist's disinterest as she handed over the key. Jake took the stairs to his room on the third floor, the faint squeak of each step echoing in the stairwell.

Inside, the room was sparse: a single bed with a faded duvet, a desk with a wobbly chair, and a television that looked older than he was. He locked the door behind him and set the suitcase on the bed. From the outside, it looked like an ordinary traveler's bag, but Jake's meticulous nature extended to his luggage. Hidden compartments housed tools of his trade: a set of burner phones, a small laptop, forged identification, and other essentials.

Jake unpacked methodically, arranging his items on the desk. The laptop booted up, its encrypted files coming to life with the press of a few keys. He opened the folder labeled *Project Vltava*, and the screen was filled with maps, schedules, and photographs of his target.

The man was a mid-level financier with ties to a burgeoning criminal syndicate, the type who thought his status made him untouchable. Jake had spent weeks studying him. His schedule was precise, his routines predictable, a pattern begging to be disrupted.

Jake leaned back in the creaky chair, studying the target's predictable routine. But predictability didn't mean easy. Prague's narrow streets and watchful locals offered little room for error, and he couldn't shake the feeling that even meticulous plans could unravel in seconds.

He studied the map of Prague, his finger tracing the financier's daily route. From his home in a leafy suburb to the modern glass office building in the city center, then to the private gym, where he spent his evenings. The man's meticulous habits were almost a mirror of Jake's own.

It was a routine waiting to be shattered, that the man likely found comforting, a certainty Jake couldn't afford in his own life. His routines were shadows, whispers, and the occasional echo of a conscience he buried long ago.

The plan had already begun to take shape. He'd scouted the city virtually and had three viable locations for the approach. Tomorrow, he'd walk those routes in person, identifying vantage points, blind spots, and potential escape paths. Jake's work wasn't glamorous, but it was thorough. That was why he was still alive.

It was time, the rain drummed softly against the windshield, blurring the neon haze of the city. Jake sat motionless in the driver's seat; his fingers wrapped loosely around the steering wheel. Across the street, the target emerged from a dimly lit diner, the kind of place that smelled of burnt coffee and indifference. He moved casually; a man unaware of the end that was tailing him. He wasn't oblivious to his surroundings, but he walked with a false sense of security.

Jake had been watching him for days, mapping his routines down to the second. From the late-night poker games to the midday rendezvous with the blonde in the red heels, every detail was cataloged, every variable accounted for. That was the difference between an amateur and a professional: discipline.

Through the rain, Jake caught the faint gleam of the man's watch as he waved for a cab. That was his signal. Jake's hand moved to the gearshift, the engine purring to life as he followed at a safe distance. Not too close, not too far. Just a ghost on the road.

The plan was simple but elegant. It always was. Jake didn't rely on theatrics or over-complicated schemes; clean, efficient, and untraceable was the goal. He'd scouted the alley where it would happen, an intersection of isolation and anonymity. No cameras, no witnesses, and no loose ends.

As the cab turned onto a desolate street, Jake allowed himself a small smirk. He was in control. He always was. For him, the thrill wasn't in what came next; it was in the precision, the knowledge that he'd orchestrated every moment to perfection.

The cab stopped, the target stepped out, and Jake's smirk faded. It was time to work.

Moments later, Jake walked away, his stride unhurried. The street behind him was quiet, save for the soft patter of rain. Everything was as it should be, every trace meticulously erased. The city carried on, oblivious. Just the way he liked it.

Chapter 4: Take It or Leave It

Was Jake the Devil? He often wondered himself. He didn't think so. Sure, he was tough, and he could be ruthless when the situation called for it, but he thought of himself as a soldier, not a monster. A man doing his duty, not one who enjoyed the taking of lives. Each mission was a means to an end, a transaction carried out with precision. Enjoyment wasn't part of the equation.

At 5 feet 11 inches, Jake's presence was more unassuming than imposing. He was fit, with a wiry strength that belied his years, but he didn't boast the overly muscular frame of a man who spent his life in a gym. His light blue eyes had an unsettling quality, capable of shifting from calm to steely in an instant, particularly when the light caught them just right. They were the kind of eyes that could pierce through a lie or silence a room with a glance. His face, square-jawed and perpetually shadowed by a stubbly beard, was framed by graying dirty-blond hair that spoke years of experience.

Jake was in his early 50s now, though his movements still carried the agility and sharpness of a man much younger. He'd been in the business since his late 20s, transitioning from a decorated career in the military into something far less honorable, at least by society's standards. In the army, he had been a sniper, a damn good one at that, known for his steady hand and uncanny ability to calculate the minute variables that determined success or failure. Explosives had been another specialty, a skill he'd picked up out of necessity and honed into an art form.

Almost thirty years in the business afforded him a wide network of safe houses, bus terminal lockers, storage units, and weapons dealers that allowed him to have whatever tools he needed, wherever he needed them, almost anywhere in the world.

Some might call him the Devil, but Jake preferred to think of himself as a necessary instrument in an evil world. Violence existed long before he did and would continue long after he was gone. He simply navigated it with more precision and discipline than most.

Fast thinking had always been one of Jake's strengths, but he preferred not to rely on instinct alone. Planning was where he truly thrived, crafting strategies with painstaking detail to ensure flawless execution. Mistakes weren't just unacceptable; they were dangerous. Over the years, he'd cultivated a strict process, one that left no room for error and allowed him to stay a step ahead of those who would like to see him fail.

Jake's life had been a series of calculated risks and moral compromises. He'd seen the worst humanity had to offer and had often been forced to be a part of it. But through it all, he maintained his own code. It wasn't written down or even spoken aloud, but it governed every decision he made. To him, it was the difference between being a soldier and being a savage.

There were moments, fleeting and rare when Jake allowed himself to wonder what life might have been like if he'd chosen a different path. Suppose he hadn't taken that first contract if he'd turned left instead of right. But such thoughts were dangerous, leading to doubt and hesitation, luxuries he couldn't afford. At this point, Jake sought the job that would secure his future. He wanted to be the best, but also the best-kept secret. He wasn't looking for fame, he was aspiring for perfection. Perhaps his next call from Eddie would be the one that tested his tenacity, the one that allowed him to prove himself.

Jake wasn't the Devil. He was something else entirely. Perhaps a shadow that moved in the spaces between right and wrong, a man who lived in the gray but carried the weight of his choices with quiet resolve.

Chapter 5: Mixed Emotions

The sun was high in the sky, glaring down on the sprawling chaos of Los Angeles as Jake stepped into Eddie's office. The broker's space was as cluttered as ever. Papers and folders were stacked on every available surface, the smell of stale coffee hanging in the air. Eddie looked up from his desk, a greasy grin spreading across his face.

Eddie leaned back in his chair, lighting a cigar with an air of exaggerated nonchalance. "Jake, my man. My favorite freelancer. Let's make some magic, huh? I've got a juicy one for you. High stakes, high reward."

Jake crossed the room and dropped into the chair opposite him. "Let's hear it."

Eddie slid a folder across the desk. Jake opened it, revealing two photos: One photo showed a hulking man with a penchant for velvet suits and ostentatious jewelry. His nightclub was a fortress of neon lights and bouncers with itchy trigger fingers. The other was wiry and sharp-eyed, his safe house a nondescript building hidden behind layers of fake businesses. The dossier included addresses, routines, and business dealings. Both men were mob bosses of rival Russian outfits, their operations straining under a fragile truce.

"They're both trouble," Eddie said, exhaling his cigar. "But take them out, and we've got a power vacuum. Makes it easier for... let's say, interested parties to step in and streamline things."

Jake narrowed his eyes at the folder. "You're stirring up a hornet's nest. You sure this is worth the fallout?"

Eddie shrugged. "Someone's gotta do it. These guys are holding back progress. You handle this cleanly, and there's a nice bonus in it for you. Just remember, Jake," Eddie said, tapping the ash off his cigar. "This is business, nothing personal. But business is messy."

Eddie always managed to make Jake's skin crawl, though he didn't show it. Jake continued to study the folder, flipping through the pages. The targets' routines were laid out in meticulous detail. Eddie had done his homework, but there was always more to uncover. Jake never relied solely on someone else's intel.

"When?" Jake asked.

"As soon as you're ready. The sooner, the better," Eddie replied. "You know how these things go, timing is everything."

Jake stood; folder tucked under his arm. "I'll be in touch." Jake left the office without another word, the folder tucked under his arm. Outside, the sun was setting, casting long shadows on the cracked pavement. He paused, flipping through the dossier again. Every job has its risks, but this one? This one felt like a powder keg waiting for a spark.

The first target's estate was a fortress, complete with high walls topped with razor wire and patrolling guards armed to the teeth. Jake observed from a wooded ridge for two days, studying the guards' movements and noting the target's late-night routine. Each night at 11:45, a black SUV brought him home from his nightclub. He would spend 15 minutes in the pool house before heading inside. That was Jake's window.

Dressed in black tactical gear, Jake infiltrated the estate under the cover of darkness, slipping through a gap in the laser sensors he had scoped earlier. Every step was deliberate, every sound muted as he moved with surgical precision toward the pool house.

Through the glass door, he saw his target reclining in a lounger, a cigar glowing faintly in his hand, and a phone pressed to his ear. Jake drew his silenced pistol, his breath steady. As he ended the call, Jake slid the door open. The soft hiss of the rubber seal caught the mark's attention, but by the time he turned, Jake had already fired.

The bullet struck his left temple, the muffled pop of the gunshot swallowed by the hum of the pool heater. When he slumped over, the cigar falling into the water with a soft sizzle, Jake exited, the estate was as silent as when he arrived. He didn't look back as he slipped into the shadows, leaving the guards oblivious to the corpse cooling in the pool house.

The second target had a penthouse that was a far cry from the last fortress, but it came with its own challenges. Perched atop a high-rise in downtown Los Angeles, the penthouse was accessible only via a private elevator guarded around the clock. Jake knew subtlety wouldn't work here. He needed a distraction.

At 3 A.M., a stolen van crashed into a transformer across the street, plunging the block into darkness. As the guards scrambled to assess the situation, Jake made his move. Using a magnetic climber, he scaled the side of the building, his night-vision goggles illuminating the path ahead.

Through the penthouse window, he saw his target seated at his desk, lit by the dim glow of his laptop. Jake used a diamond tool to cut the glass, the piece falling away silently with a suction cup. He slipped inside, his footsteps muffled by the thick carpet.

Jake crept up behind the mark, who was too engrossed in his laptop screen to notice. In one swift motion, Jake looped a garrote around the neck, pulling it tight. The man struggled, clawing at the wire, but Jake held firm, his grip unwavering until the body went limp.

He laid him on the floor, positioning him as if he'd collapsed naturally. Then, Jake accessed the laptop, downloading incriminating files onto a USB drive. Before leaving, he planted evidence suggesting a rival gang's involvement.

The next morning's headlines would attribute the death to the escalating mob war, but Jake was already hundreds of miles away, erasing any trace of his presence.

By the time Eddie received Jake's call, the groundwork for chaos in the Los Angeles underworld had been laid. Eddie's voice was smug over the line. "Knew I could count on you, Jake."

Jake hung up without a word. Something about Eddie's tone lingered, a faint itch in the back of his mind. But for now, the job was done. And in Jake's world, that was all that mattered.

Jake checked his bank account. The payment was there, the full amount, transferred as promised. On the surface, it seemed fine.

Professional. Reliable. But Jake's instincts told him otherwise. Eddie's eagerness, the way he'd glossed over details, the smug satisfaction in his voice, it all felt too convenient.

Sitting in his car, Jake opened the folder Eddie had given him one more time. The targets, the routines, the intel, it was too clean, too precise, almost as if it had been tailored to ensure success. But why? Eddie wasn't known for making things this easy.

Jake glanced at his phone, scrolling through his encrypted notes. Every detail checked out, but the sinking feeling in his gut didn't fade. Eddie's voice replayed in his mind: *"Knew I could count on you."* It wasn't the words themselves, but the way Eddie had said them, as he'd already won some game Jake wasn't privy to.

Trust wasn't a currency Jake traded lightly, and Eddie had been reliable so far. But in this business, even a whisper of doubt was enough to warrant caution. Jake stared out at the Los Angeles skyline, the city's lights shimmering in the distance. He'd done the jobs. The payment was there. On paper, everything was fine.

And yet, Jake knew better than to ignore his gut. He'd seen it before, the calm before a storm, the setup before the double cross. He couldn't prove anything yet, but he'd start digging. Quietly. Patiently. If Eddie thought he could pull something over on Jake, he was in for a surprise.

Perhaps the newly acquired USB drive would have the answers. The encryption wasn't difficult, but the data did not provide any answers that he needed to allay his fears. Jake closed his laptop, the glow of the screen fading to black. Whatever Eddie was playing at, Jake would find out. And when he did, there wouldn't be any second chances.

Chapter 6: Jumpin' Jack Flash

A sharp knock rattled the hotel room door. Jake froze, his instincts flaring. The rhythm was wrong, too forceful, too deliberate. Not housekeeping. No room service.

He reached for his bag, his fingers grazing the cold steel inside. The adjoining door to the next room, already unlocked as part of his usual precautions, beckoned like an escape hatch. Jake moved silently, slipping through and easing it shut just as the first door splintered under the force of a heavy boot.

Muffled voices filtered through the thin walls, three of them, at least. Their words were curt and professional. Jake pressed his back against the adjoining door, his heartbeat steady despite the tension.

"Where is he?" one voice growled, followed by the crash of overturned furniture.

Jake clenched his jaw. Eddie's doing. It had to be.

He pulled his go-bag from under the bed, its familiar weight reassuring. In one hand, he gripped the bag; in the other, his gun. His eyes darted to the window as he weighed his options. The adjoining door shuddered as someone tested the handle.

"He's gotta be close," said another voice. "Check the next room."

The lock gave way with a gunshot, and the door burst open. Jake didn't wait. He bolted for the window, throwing it open just as the second door to the next room slammed against the wall. He swung himself out onto the fire escape, his movements practiced and fluid.

From above, a shout went up, followed by the metallic clang of boots on the fire escape, their frantic rhythm sending a chill down his spine. A shot rang out, striking the railing near Jake's hand. He ignored it, descending the creaking metal stairs two at a time. The fire escape was slick with rain, the cold metal biting against Jake's hands. His boots hit the pavement with a controlled thud, and he rolled to absorb the impact.

The alley was narrow, dimly lit, and smelled of week-old garbage, the perfect cover for a clean getaway. As Jake sprinted through the alley, his mind churned with anger. Eddie hadn't just crossed him; he'd underestimated him. That was his first mistake. His last

As Jake moved toward the street, the idling silhouette of a nondescript sedan caught his eye. The driver, a wiry man with a cigarette dangling from his lips, looked toward the alley just as Jake emerged. The driver's eyes widened, his cigarette falling into his lap as Jake lunged. The driver's hand darted toward the glove compartment, but Jake was faster. A single, bone-crushing punch sent the man sprawling onto the sidewalk. Jake shoved his bag onto the passenger seat, climbed into the car, and slammed the door.

As he tore down the street, tires screeching, Jake's mind raced. Eddie thought he could outmaneuver Jake, but the pieces didn't fit. This betrayal felt orchestrated, too clean. Someone else was pulling the strings.

For the first time in years, Jake felt off balance. He wasn't playing his usual game of meticulous strategy. This wasn't Bach or Mozart, it was Charlie Parker: improvisation, chaos and the wild unknown.

And yet, even as the city blurred past him, Jake couldn't help but feel the thrill. Eddie had made his move. Now it was Jake's turn.

Chapter 7: Harlem Shuffle

The sedan screeched to a halt at the edge of the LAX drop-off zone. Jake stepped out without hesitation. He grabbed his bag and stepped out, blending seamlessly into the flow of harried travelers. His gun and any other telltale equipment were stashed in a dumpster two blocks back. For now, anonymity was his best weapon.

Inside the airport, chaos reigned. Crying babies pierced through the muffled drone of announcements, and the sharp clatter of luggage wheels on polished floors blended into the cacophony. Jake moved like a ghost through the crowd, his eyes scanning for signs of trouble. At a kiosk, he purchased a last-minute ticket to Houston under an alias, his movements deliberate and unhurried despite the tension coiling in his chest.

The flight was uneventful. Jake kept to himself, flipping through an in-flight magazine he wasn't reading. His mind was already moving forward, recalibrating his next steps. The betrayal had shaken him, but it hadn't broken him. If anything, it had crystallized his resolve.

Jake touched down in Houston just after midnight, the humid air wrapping around him like a damp blanket. He picked up a rental car but didn't keep it long. The vehicle was a disposable asset, ditched a few miles away in a gritty neighborhood, where he found an equally gritty pickup truck, unattended and nondescript.

Jake drove through the night, the pickup truck's engine a steady hum against the quiet of the highway. Each stop for fuel and caffeine felt like a gamble, his eyes scanning every face, every shadow for signs of pursuit. The interstate stretched endlessly ahead, a ribbon of headlights and asphalt. As the miles ticked by, his mind worked relentlessly, piecing together the next moves while suppressing the nagging sense that someone might already be closing in.

In Dallas, he parked the truck in a long-term lot with harsh lighting, and retrieved another identity from his bag: a different name, a different passport. This time, he bought a ticket to Buenos Aires. South

America was far enough to disappear for a while, a chance to regroup and figure out his next play.

The flight to Buenos Aires was long. The cabin lights dimmed as passengers drifted into restless sleep. Jake leaned back in his seat, staring out the window at the endless expanse of darkness.

Eddie's betrayal gnawed at Jake, festering like an open wound. He'd always known Eddie was a snake, but he hadn't expected the venom to run so deep. Was it greed that drove him? Ambition? Or was this personal, some grudge Jake hadn't seen coming? But Eddie wasn't smart enough to pull this off alone... was he? Someone else must be pulling the strings, and Jake needed to find out who.

The questions churned in his mind, but one thought stood out above the rest: Eddie had underestimated him. That would be his fatal mistake.

Jake knew he couldn't stay in the shadows forever. Eddie had made his move, and now Jake had to make his. The trick was to strike back without giving Eddie another opening. This wasn't just about survival anymore; it was about reclaiming control.

The seatbelt light dinged on as the plane hit a patch of turbulence. Jake barely noticed. His mind was elsewhere, sketching out possibilities, weighing risks, and planning his return.

Somewhere below, the lights of South America began to glitter against the horizon. A new city, a new stage. Jake cracked his knuckles, his lips curling into a faint smirk.

Eddie thought he'd won. He was wrong.

Chapter 8: Gimme Shelter

The Buenos Aires night clung to Jake like a second skin, cool, heavy, and imbued with memories of past lives. His safe house in San Telmo was a nondescript relic tucked between the cobblestone streets and faded colonial facades. Its peeling shutters and ivy-draped walls whispered of a forgotten charm, blending effortlessly into the neighborhood's bohemian haze. For Jake, it was a refuge, a fortress wrapped in shadows and routine. The reinforced door locked with a satisfying click as he stepped inside. The air tinged with the faint musk of aged wood, leather, and long-extinguished cigars.

Jake dropped his bag by the door and took a deep breath. Everything was as he left it, no signs of tampering — no misplaced furniture. The walls still hid his cache of weapons, passports, and cash. He locked the door, poured himself a glass of wine from the half-empty bottle of Malbec he'd left behind months ago, and settled into the armchair by the window.

He let his mind wander for a moment, taking in the rhythmic hum of the city. But beneath the comfort, a storm brewed. Eddie's betrayal gnawed at him, and though Buenos Aires was far from Los Angeles, he wasn't naïve enough to think distance alone would keep him safe.

Morning seeped into the room on the scent of fresh bread and coffee, mingling with the muted hum of street vendors setting up stalls not far from his bedroom window. Jake stirred at the knock on his door, a sharp rhythm that cut through his light sleep like a blade. His hand instinctively found the pistol under the pillow, his body tensing as he moved silently toward the door.

A glance through the peephole brought a flicker of relief but not enough to let his guard down. Julianna stood on the other side, her lips quirked in that half-smile that was equal parts mischief and trouble. She wore a loose sundress, her dark curls catching the morning light, but it was her eyes that held Jake's attention, sharp, observant, always assessing.

Jake tucked the gun into the waistband of his pants and opened the door.

"Well, look who's back," she said, stepping inside without waiting for an invitation. Her voice carried the faint lilt of someone who could shift languages mid-sentence without missing a beat.

"Morning, Julianna," Jake said, shutting the door behind her.

"Business or pleasure?" she asked, her tone playful but her gaze calculating.

Jake smirked, running a hand through his hair. "Haven't decided yet."

She tilted her head, giving him a long once-over. "You look like you've been through it."

"You could say that."

Julianna wandered around the room, her fingers brushing the edge of the desk where Jake had spread out a map of Los Angeles and a burner phone. She knew better than to pry, directly, anyway.

"I saw the light on last night," she said casually. "Figured you might need some company."

Jake leaned against the counter, watching her. They'd worked together before, when the lines between business and personal had blurred in ways both exhilarating and dangerous. Julianna had always been as skilled as she was unpredictable, a wildcard with a penchant for precision when it counted.

"You here to check on the house or on me?" he asked.

"Maybe both." She turned to face him, arms crossed. "You're not exactly subtle when you're lying low, Jake."

"I didn't think I had to be, not here."

She stepped closer, her voice dropping slightly. "Maybe not. But things have a way of catching up, even here."

For a moment, the room felt charged, their shared history hanging between them like an unfinished sentence.

Julianna broke the tension with a smirk. "Come on. You look like you could use some real food."

Jake hesitated, then nodded. He grabbed his keys and followed her out into the street. The neighborhood was alive with morning activity: vendors setting up stalls, neighbors chatting in rapid Spanish, and the occasional motorbike weaving through traffic.

They fell into step as they wandered through San Telmo's lively streets, the air thick with the chatter of vendors hawking their wares and the hum of motorbikes weaving through the narrow roads. Julianna led him to a café tucked between two aging storefronts, its chipped blue awning flapping lazily in the morning breeze.

The scent of fresh pastries and espresso greeted them as they stepped inside. Jake chose a corner table, his back to the wall, while Julianna ordered with effortless confidence, her Spanish flowing like the melody of a tango. She'd always had a way of commanding attention without seeming to try.

"So," Julianna said, draping one arm over the back of her chair, "Are you going to tell me what kind of trouble you've brought to my city, or do I have to guess?"

Jake smirked, stirring his coffee slowly. "Maybe, I'm just here for the croissants."

She snorted. "Please. You don't show up anywhere without a reason, and I'm betting this isn't a vacation."

"Your instincts are as sharp as ever," he admitted, leaning back in his chair.

"Damn right," she said, her tone softening. "You're lucky I'm around, Jake." She leaned forward, her expression turning serious. "Whatever mess you're in, just remember, this city's not as forgiving as it looks."

Jake's smirk faltered, her words striking deeper than he let on. For all her charm and playfulness, Julianna had a knack for cutting to the heart of things. As she sipped her coffee, her gaze drifting out to the street, Jake let his mind wander to a different time, a time when their paths first crossed, when she'd proven just how dangerous and invaluable she could be.

Chapter 9: Emotional Rescue

The hum of Vespa engines weaved through the labyrinth of Florence's cobblestone streets, mingling with the lilting strains of an accordion that drifted from a distant corner café. Jake emerged from the shadow of a narrow alley; his every step calculated. The piazza before him bustled with life: tourists snapping photos of the Duomo, street performers captivating small crowds, and locals weaving effortlessly through the chaos. Jake adjusted the strap of his duffel bag and slipped into the current, becoming just another face in the vibrant mosaic of the city.

This wasn't Jake's first time in Italy, but it was the first time he'd been sent here with such a specific mission: extract an operative who had gone dark mid-job and complete her assignment. The details were murky, as they often were. He wasn't sure if he was working for a criminal organization or a government agency. All he knew was her code name: Mariposa.

The contact file had included a grainy photo of a woman with dark hair and an unforgettable smile, her brown eyes sparkling even in the low-quality image. The mission brief was more clinical: South American origins, experienced field operative, currently undercover to intercept sensitive intelligence from a high-ranking arms dealer operating out of Florence. Jake's job was to locate her, figure out what went wrong, and clean up the mess, whatever that entailed.

Jake spotted her through the amber haze of a trattoria's dim lighting, her figure framed by the flickering glow of a single candle on the table. Tucked away in the far corner, she exuded a deceptive calm, her posture poised but her eyes betraying her vigilance as they flicked toward the entrance every few seconds. The low murmur of the room faded as Jake approached, his footsteps muffled by the worn tiles beneath him.

She was smaller than he'd imagined, around 5 foot 6, her brown hair swept casually over one shoulder. She wasn't the kind of beauty that stopped traffic, but there was something arresting about her presence, a quiet confidence and an easy, natural grace.

He approached cautiously, his hands in his pockets to appear non-threatening.

"Mariposa?" he said softly as he reached her table.

Her eyes flicked to his, and for a moment, there was no recognition. Then her expression shifted, and she gave him a faint smile. "You're late," she said, her voice carrying a faint accent, the lilting cadence of her South American roots tempered by years of working globally.

Jake sat across from her, keeping his movements slow. "Had to make sure I wasn't walking into something messy."

Her smile widened, and for a brief moment, it felt genuine. "Too late. You're already in it."

The mess she referred to became apparent within hours. The arms dealer, a paranoid man named Conti, had sniffed out her cover. Mariposa as Jake still thought of her then, had narrowly escaped with her life but had been forced to abandon her equipment and the intelligence she'd gathered.

"He'll be at the villa tonight," she told Jake as they crouched in the shadows of an ancient stone bridge later that evening. "That's where the files are. But he's doubled his security."

Jake studied her as she spoke, noting the tension in her shoulders and the faint tremor in her hands. Despite her calm demeanor, it was clear the close call had shaken her. Yet there was no trace of fear in her voice, only determination.

"We'll get it back," he said simply, and her eyes softened as she looked at him.

The villa rose like a fortress against the velvet backdrop of the Tuscan night, its ivy-covered walls casting long shadows under the moonlight. Jake's plan had been precise, with every detail accounted for. But Conti's guards proved more disciplined than he'd anticipated. What began as a calculated infiltration devolved into a deadly game of cat and mouse.

The hallways echoed with the sharp bark of orders and the rhythmic stomp of boots. Jake and Julianna moved like ghosts, weaving through the chaos, their synchronized movements a testament to their shared instincts.

"Why do you do this?" she whispered, her voice almost lost in the cacophony of distant footsteps and hurried orders. They were crouched behind a marble statue, the cool stone pressing against their backs.

Jake glanced at her, taken aback by the question. "Do what?"

"This," she said, gesturing vaguely around them. "Risk your life for missions that don't even belong to you."

He hesitated, unsure how to answer. "Someone has to."

She studied him for a moment, then nodded, as if that was all the explanation she needed.

Dawn broke over the rolling Tuscan hills, painting the sky in strokes of gold and lavender. Their escape had been frantic, but now the farmhouse offered a momentary reprieve. It was the kind of rustic retreat that city dwellers romanticized: terracotta roofs, weathered shutters, and a small patio overlooking endless rows of olive trees. But for Jake and Julianna, it was a sanctuary born of necessity, not charm. Julianna sat at the kitchen table, nursing a cup of strong Italian coffee as Jake cleaned a shallow cut on his arm.

"You're good at this," she said suddenly, her tone casual but her eyes serious.

Jake glanced at her. "At what?"

"At staying calm. At making me feel like everything's under control, even when it isn't."

He shrugged, a faint smile tugging at the corners of his mouth. "Part of the job."

"No," she said, shaking her head. "It's more than that. Most people in this line of work are all bravado or recklessness. You're… steady. It's a rare quality."

He didn't know how to respond, so he didn't. But her words stayed with him.

The chemistry between them had been simmering since that first meeting in the trattoria, but it wasn't until their third night together that the tension finally broke. They'd been lying low in a safe house arranged by one of Julianna's contacts, a cramped apartment overlooking a narrow Florentine street. The air was thick with the scent of rain and the distant hum of evening activity.

Julianna stood by the window; her silhouette illuminated by the warm glow of a street lamp. Jake watched her from the sofa, his gaze lingering on the curve of her shoulders and the way her hair fell loosely down her back.

"You keep staring at me like that," she said without turning around, "and I'm going to start thinking you're smitten."

He chuckled softly. "Maybe I am."

She turned then, her expression unreadable. Slowly, she crossed the room and sat beside him, her brown eyes searching his face. "You're full of surprises, Jake."

"So are you," he replied, his voice quiet.

The kiss was inevitable, a culmination of days filled with danger and unspoken connection. It was both tender and urgent, a moment of vulnerability in a world where neither could afford to let their guard down.

They completed the mission together, and by the time they parted ways, there was an unspoken understanding between them. Their paths might diverge, but they were bound by the memory of those days in Florence, and by the knowledge that they worked better together than either of them had ever worked alone.

The months after Florence were a blur of assignments and long stretches of silence. But every so often, Julianna would call. Her voice, calm and familiar, was a lifeline in the chaos of Jake's world.

"There's a place for sale next door to my house," she said during one such call. "It would make a great safe house."

"Oh, yeah?" Jake had replied, his curiosity piqued.

"You should come see it," she said, her tone teasing. "Consider it a vacation."

Jake chuckled but didn't commit. A few weeks later, circumstances conspired to make the decision for him. His latest mission had left too many bodies and too many questions. His handlers had suggested he lie low, and Buenos Aires sounded like as good a place as any.

Buenos Aires welcomed Jake with a riot of sensations. The jacaranda trees lining the wide boulevards spilled bursts of purple blossoms onto the streets, their vivid hues matched only by the energy of the city itself. Street performers captivated passersby with tangos that seemed to hold the pulse of the city, while vendors called out to sell empanadas and choripán from smoky grills. Jake took it all in as Julianna guided him through the city, her voice a mix of tour guide and confidante.

"This is Calle Caminito," she said, gesturing to the brightly painted houses lining the narrow street. "Tourists love it, but it's still one of my favorite spots."

They stopped at a small café for empanadas and coffee. Jake watched her as she spoke, her brown eyes alight with excitement as she described the city's history and culture. It was a side of her he hadn't seen in Florence, and he found himself drawn to her in a way he hadn't expected.

Later, she took him to the Recoleta Cemetery, its labyrinth of ornate mausoleums casting long shadows in the afternoon sun. "It's beautiful in a strange way, isn't it?" she said, her voice soft.

"Yeah," Jake replied, his gaze lingering on her rather than the surroundings. "Beautiful."

That evening, back at her house, she showed him the property next door. It was modest but secure, the kind of place that could disappear into the background while still offering a sanctuary.

"It's perfect," Jake said after a long look.

Julianna smiled. "I thought you'd say that."

By the end of the week, the paperwork was signed. Jake had a new safe house, and Julianna had a new neighbor. As they sat on her porch, sipping Malbec under the Southern Hemisphere's stars, Jake felt a rare sense of peace. For the first time in a long time, it felt like he wasn't running, he was just living.

Chapter 10: Brown Sugar

The café hummed with the lively clatter of cups and cutlery, a soundtrack of life that felt oddly out of place for two people so steeped in chaos. Jake and Julianna had fallen into an easy rhythm of banter and careful conversation, but Jake could feel the weight of her unspoken words. Her gaze lingered on him just a second too long, her smile tinged with something more thoughtful.

The midday sun bathed the cobblestone streets in golden light, the faint aroma of fresh empanadas wafting from a nearby vendor. As they walked, Julianna slipped her hand around Jake's arm, her touch deliberate and lingering. "Why don't we go back to your place?" she asked, her voice low, her lips curving into a playful smile. "Something tells me you could use a... distraction."

Jake hesitated for half a heartbeat, his instincts, and the walls he kept firmly in place warring with something softer. But Julianna's gaze wasn't just suggestive, it was knowing. She understood the weight he carried because she carried her own.

"Yeah," Jake said finally. "Let's go."

Back at Jake's safe house, the air was thick with an unspoken tension, charged like the moments before a storm. The familiar scent of aged wood and faint cigar smoke wrapped around them as Julianna slipped off her shoes and strolled into the living room. She moved with a feline grace, her dark curls catching the soft light filtering through the blinds.

"You've always been good at carrying the weight of the world," she said, turning to face him. "But even Atlas needs a break."

Jake didn't reply. He closed the door, the lock clicking into place with finality, and crossed the room. Whatever had simmered between them over breakfast, boiled over in an instant.

The connection between them was electric, a raw and unfiltered response to shared history, close calls, and a life lived constantly on the edge. It wasn't just chemistry, it was the understanding that, for all their calculated moves and survival instincts, there were moments where they simply needed to feel alive.

The world outside ceased to exist as they lost themselves in each other, a brief escape from the storm that raged around them.

Morning crept in, the soft rays of sunlight slipping through the half-closed blinds and pooling on the worn wooden floor. Jake lay on his back, his arm tucked behind his head, eyes fixed on the ceiling. Beside him, Julianna traced lazy patterns on his chest, her fingers warm against his skin.

"You've still got it," she murmured, a teasing smile tugging at her lips.

Jake smirked, his hand resting on her hip. "So do you."

For a while, they lay there in silence, the comfort of shared warmth settling between them. But Julianna's mind was clearly elsewhere.

"What's chasing you this time, Jake?" Julianna's voice was soft, almost teasing, but her eyes carried the weight of genuine concern as she propped herself up on one elbow.

Jake tensed slightly, his gaze shifting to the shadows on the ceiling. "Why do you assume I'm running?"

"Because I know you, Jake," she said, propping herself up on one elbow to look at him. "And because you're here. You never come to Buenos Aires unless something's chasing you, or unless you're chasing something yourself."

Her words hung in the air, heavy with implication. Jake hesitated, weighing his options. He'd trusted her before, in work, in bed, in moments like this, but the stakes felt higher now.

"Eddie set me up," Jake admitted after a long pause, his voice tight. "Job in L.A. went sideways, and he hung me out to dry. Now, I've got more enemies than I can count, and I need to figure out who's pulling the strings before they pull the trigger."

Julianna frowned, her fingers stilling against his skin. "Eddie's always been a snake," she said. "But setting you up? That's bold, even for him."

Jake turned his head to look at her, his expression unreadable. "He doesn't know about you, and that makes you my only safe option. I need someone I can trust, someone, who can help me figure out what he's planning."

Julianna held his gaze, her eyes sharp and searching. "And you trust me?"

"I trust you enough," Jake admitted.

She smirked, her confidence returning. "That's good enough for me. So, what's the plan?"

Jake exhaled, his mind already racing. "We start with Eddie. If he's the middleman, he's not working alone. I need to know who else is pulling the strings."

"And then?"

"Then," Jake said, his voice cold and certain, "I make sure they regret ever crossing me."

Julianna leaned in close, her lips brushing against his ear as she whispered, "Then let's make them regret it. Together." Her words carried a promise, one as dangerous as it was comforting.

Jake's grip tightened on her hip as the storm outside began to feel just a little more manageable.

Chapter 11: Paint It Black

Los Angeles was a city on the brink, its underworld a smoldering cauldron of rage and retribution. The tenuous truce between rival Russian factions had shattered like glass underfoot, leaving blood-soaked streets and fractured alliances in its wake. Eddie's plan was working, albeit with a grotesque level of collateral damage that even he might not have fully anticipated.

The city became a battleground. By daylight, the violence slithered in the shadows: whispers of sudden disappearances, quiet ambushes in nondescript parking lots, and corpses discarded in East LA's forgotten alleys. Nightfall stripped away the thin veneer of restraint. Streets became battlegrounds, with roaring engines and the staccato crack of gunfire shattering the uneasy silence of sleeping neighborhoods. News choppers buzzed overhead like vultures circling a carcass.

In West Hollywood, a serene bistro became a war zone. The evening buzz of clinking glasses and soft conversations was obliterated in seconds as gunmen stormed the restaurant, their automatic weapons spitting death into the dining room.

A rival crew, misled by Eddie's manipulations, targeted the wrong players. The windows of the bistro exploded in a rain of glass as gunmen stormed in, automatic weapons barking commands of death. Diners dove for cover, their terrified screams swallowed by the unrelenting cacophony of gunfire and shattering glass. By the time the attackers realized they'd hit the wrong group, it was too late. The counterattack came swiftly and brutally, leaving the restaurant riddled with bullet holes and red-streaked floors.

In a forgotten corner of downtown, a graffiti-streaked warehouse became the stage for yet another tragedy. Inside, a crew huddled over crude maps and crates of weapons, plotting revenge with grim determination. Unbeknownst to them, an informer had already leaked their location. As they huddled over maps and weapons, a van screeched to a halt outside, and masked men poured in. What followed was a slaughter, a grim punctuation to the escalating body count littering the city's dark underbelly.

The LAPD was drowning. Detectives scrambled from one crime scene to the next, chasing phantom leads. One moment, they thought they had a suspect in custody, a low-level enforcer from one faction. The next moment, he was dead in his cell, throat slit in a clear message from his enemies. The department's frustration mounted, and public pressure grew. Headlines screamed about the surge in violence, and city officials made promises they couldn't keep.

For those caught in the crossfire, life became a game of survival. Businesses shuttered early, streets emptied after sunset, and families huddled indoors, their nerves frayed by the omnipresent threat of violence. The media painted a vivid picture of anarchy: burning cars, shattered storefronts, and dazed witnesses recounting horror stories to reporters.

Eddie's office was a study in claustrophobic grime: peeling wallpaper, the flickering glow of an ancient desk lamp, and an ashtray overflowing with half-smoked cigars. His fingers drummed nervously on the worn wood of his desk. Eddie's outward bravado masked the undercurrent of unease roiling beneath his skin. He relished the chaos he'd ignited between the two warring Russian factions, but the elation was fleeting, swallowed by a gnawing sense of vulnerability. In the dim light, his eyes betrayed him, darting occasionally to the sleek, black phone resting in the middle of his desk.

It wasn't the mob war that unnerved him. No, Eddie relished the mayhem. It was the strings being pulled above him that weighed heavily on his mind. He wasn't the puppet master here; he was the puppet. And the hand controlling him belonged to someone with influence so vast and power so entrenched that Eddie didn't dare defy them. The phone sat in the center of his desk like a black hole, an unspoken symbol of his powerlessness. Its silence was louder than any ringtone, a chilling reminder of who truly pulled the strings in Eddie's precarious game.

The war was a distraction, a smokescreen, and a power play all at once. Eddie had his piece to move, but the game was being orchestrated far beyond his understanding. Whenever the temptation to seize control flickered in his mind, Eddie's thoughts snapped back to his last phone call. The voice on the other end had been calm, disarmingly so, but every measured word carried a weight that left Eddie drenched in cold sweat.

Eddie stubbed out his cigar, his hand trembling slightly. Leaning back in his chair, Eddie ran a hand through his thinning hair and muttered his plea under his breath. "Just keep it together. Play your part, Eddie. Don't screw this up."

But deep down, he knew he was expendable. In this game, everyone was.

Chapter 12: Let's Spend the Night Together

Jake lounged on the worn leather couch of his Buenos Aires safe house, the dim glow of a single lamp painting soft shadows on the cracked plaster walls. The faint aroma of leather and aged wood mingled with the cool evening air drifting through a partially open window. This wasn't just a hideout, it was a home away from home, a place where he had spent countless hours planning escapes and indulging in short reprieves from his chaotic life.

Julianna sat cross-legged on the floor beside the coffee table, a steaming cup of maté in her hands. Her expression was sharp yet contemplative, her mind clearly working through the layers of their predicament.

"So, what's the plan?" she asked, breaking the silence.

Jake took a deep breath. "First, we need to get to Eddie and figure out if he's really pulling all the strings. If he is, he's got to go. If he's not…"

"Then we need to find out who's holding his leash," Julianna finished, her voice steady.

Jake gave her a wry smile. "Exactly. And, of course, there's that minor issue of who sent those guys after me."

Julianna arched an eyebrow. "Ah, sí, the small matter of armed men who want you dead. A mere inconvenience," Julianna quipped, her lips curving into a wry smile.

Jake chuckled. Her dry humor was one of the reasons they worked so well together. "Right. That." After a moment he added, "It's not the trigger men that keep me up at night," Jake said, his voice low but resolute. "It's the shadow behind them. Cut off the head, and the body falls."

Julianna contemplates and adds, "Si, that makes sense, they are a temporary danger, but getting to the bosses is the key to your safety."

As they outlined their next steps, their conversation turned practical, contacts to leverage, disguises to prepare, routes to take. The hours melted away until it was time to leave.

The drive to Ezeiza Airport was uneventful, the city's vibrant pulse was reduced to a blur of graffiti-covered walls, glowing neon signs, and the rhythmic clatter of buses on uneven roads. The streets buzzed with life, but for Jake and Julianna, it was just background noise to their quiet determination. At Ezeiza International Airport, Jake ditched his weapons in a secured locker he'd long ago marked for emergencies. His duffel bag held only clothes and essentials, and their fake passports passed scrutiny with ease.

On the long flight to San Francisco, Julianna dozed off for a while, her head resting against Jake's shoulder. He stared out of the window, the dark ocean below giving him a blank canvas to plan his next move.

By the time they landed, Jake's mind was sharper, his thoughts more cohesive. They picked up a rental car under false identities and began their drive down the California coast.

The California coastline was a striking counterpoint to Buenos Aires' gritty urban sprawl. Towering cliffs framed the endless expanse of the Pacific, waves crashing against jagged rocks in a timeless symphony. The car's windows were down, letting in the crisp, salty breeze.

"Beautiful, isn't it?" Julianna said, her eyes fixed on the horizon.

Jake nodded, his fingers drumming on the steering wheel. For a fleeting moment, Jake let his guard down, the salt-laced breeze and the hypnotic rhythm of the ocean lulling him into a rare state of calm. But the calm only served to sharpen his focus on the storm ahead.

As the miles passed, the atmosphere between them shifted. Julianna rested her hand on Jake's thigh, her touch lingering. He glanced at her, and she met his gaze with a sly smile.

"We've got some time," she said softly.

Jake smirked, spotting the faint glow of a neon motel sign cutting through the twilight. "Looks like as good a place as any," he said, steering the car into the gravel lot.

The motel room was modest, its whitewashed walls bare except for a cheap print of a seascape above the bed. The faint scent of lavender drifted from a sachet tucked beneath the pillows, a strange touch of serenity amid their whirlwind lives.

Julianna pushed Jake onto the bed, her laughter mingling with the hum of the air conditioning. For a brief, blissful reprieve, the weight of their mission melted away. In the quiet intimacy of the small room, their connection reignited, raw and undeniable, a reminder of the fragile humanity beneath their hardened exteriors.

Later, as they lay tangled together, the weight of their mission crept back in.

"How can I help?" Julianna asked, tracing a finger along Jake's arm.

Jake considered the question carefully. Trust didn't come easily to him, but if there was one person he could rely on, it was Julianna. "Just stay sharp. When we get to Eddie, we'll need to be ready for anything."

Morning sunlight filtered through the worn motel curtains, pooling on the small table where their arsenal was meticulously arranged. Burner phones, maps scrawled with notes, and an array of weapons painted a stark picture of their dangerous reality.

Julianna flipped through their notes, her brow furrowed in concentration, while Jake methodically inspected each weapon, the metallic clinks, and clicks punctuating the room's tense quiet. The sun filtered through the curtains, casting warm light on their determined faces.

By the time they got back into the car, the coast was a distant memory. As Los Angeles loomed ahead, the city's sprawling chaos promised that their return would be anything but peaceful.

Chapter 13: Steel Wheels

Los Angeles sprawled beneath the night sky, a chaotic mosaic of flickering lights and restless energy. As Jake and Julianna maneuvered through the cramped alleys of East Hollywood, the city felt alive, its pulse quickened by the violence simmering beneath its glittering surface. The city's relentless energy was a hum in the background, but their focus was singular: capture both Russian crime bosses without tipping off their organizations.

The plan was bold, almost reckless, but they had no other option. Time was running out, and the chaos Eddie had sparked was quickly spiraling out of control.

Jake adjusted his earpiece, glancing around as he steered the van into an alley behind the dive bar. "You in position?"

"Already inside," Julianna replied, her voice crackling slightly. "Our friend is nursing his vodka in the VIP lounge. Shouldn't be long now."

Jake eased the faded gray van into the shadowy alley behind the bar, its dull exterior blending seamlessly with the city's grime. He stepped out, the soft creak of his leather gloves breaking the silence as he adjusted his gear. A silenced pistol, a vial of chloroform, and zip ties, tools for precision, not mess.

Julianna was already working her magic. She glided through the crowded bar like a predator in disguise, her sleek black dress an armor of allure. Heads turned as she passed, but her focus remained on Sergei Ivanov, the bleary-eyed man nursing his vodka in the VIP lounge. She slid into the booth beside Sergei Ivanov, one of the two Russian bosses they were targeting.

"Well, isn't this a surprise," she said smoothly, her lips curling into a smile that carried equal parts charm and menace.

Sergei glanced up, squinting as he tried to focus. "Do I know you?"

"Not yet." She leaned in, her tone low and conspiratorial. "But I know you've been looking for someone to help you even the score with your rivals."

Sergei's eyes sharpened slightly, suspicion mixing with interest. "You're well-informed."

Julianna leaned closer, her hand brushing against his arm. "Let's just say, I have a vested interest in your success."

Before Sergei could respond, Jake emerged from the shadows like a phantom, his movements calculated and silent. In one swift motion, he pressed the chloroform-soaked cloth to Sergei's face, muffling the man's surprised grunt. The man struggled briefly, his protests muffled, before slumping forward.

"Nap time," Jake muttered under his breath, catching Sergei's limp form before it could hit the table. With practiced efficiency, he slung the unconscious man over his shoulder and melted into the shadows of the rear exit.

Meanwhile, across town in a gaudy penthouse suite, Nikolai Petrov was enjoying his nightly routine of cheap whiskey and expensive escorts. Julianna had scoped out the location earlier, noting the building's security flaws and the predictable rotations of its guards.

Jake rolled into the underground garage; his every sense sharpened by the adrenaline coursing through his veins. The van hummed softly as he parked, its engine barely a whisper in the cavernous space. The elevator ride to the penthouse was uneventful, and the stolen access card worked perfectly.

Nikolai barely had time to register the shift in the room's atmosphere before Jake emerged from the shadows like a ghost. With a single, precise strike, Nikolai crumpled to the floor, the glass of whiskey slipping from his hand and shattering on the marble tiles. Jake worked swiftly, securing Nikolai's hands and feet with zip ties before gagging him.

"You're coming with me," Jake said, dragging the unconscious boss toward the elevator.

As Jake loaded Nikolai into the back of his van, a sharp whistle echoed through the garage. Jake turned to see two armed guards sprinting toward him, weapons drawn.

"Move!" Julianna's voice barked through the earpiece.

Jake didn't hesitate. He slammed the van's rear doors shut and jumped into the driver's seat. The tires squealed as he sped out of the garage, the guards' bullets ricocheting off the walls behind him.

Julianna, in her own van with Sergei, was already a few blocks ahead. "They're onto us," she said. "You okay?"

"Fine," Jake replied, weaving through traffic. "Just keep moving. We'll meet at the warehouse."

The streets of Los Angeles turned into a chaotic maze of sharp turns and close calls. At one point, a black SUV joined the pursuit, its headlights glaring in Jake's rearview mirror.

"Company," he muttered, accelerating through a red light.

Julianna's voice came through again. "Lose them. I've got a clean route."

Jake yanked the wheel, steering the van into a narrow alley. The tires scraped against the uneven pavement, the sound echoing off the surrounding walls as the black SUV barreled after him. Jake slammed on the brakes, causing the SUV to rear-end him. The SUV clipped the van's rear bumper with a jarring crunch, but Jake seized the moment. He slammed on the gas, the van lurching forward with a roar, leaving the damaged pursuer behind in a haze of exhaust and desperation.

Jake pulled into the graffiti-covered warehouse; his nerves frayed but his resolve steely. The dim light from a single hanging bulb cast long shadows across the concrete floor, adding to the oppressive air of the place. Julianna was already there, her van parked inside the cavernous space.

She stepped out, brushing her hair back as she approached Jake. "Everything goes smoothly?"

"As smooth as breaking into a penthouse and dodging bullets can get," Jake quipped, swinging open the van's rear doors to reveal Nikolai's bound and slumped figure.

Julianna smirked. "Now for part two."

Together, they unloaded their captives and secured them to two chairs in the center of the warehouse.

Jake leaned against a support beam; his arms crossed. "Ready for the fun part?"

Julianna nodded; her expression serious. "Time to find out who's really pulling the strings."

Chapter 14: Undercover of the Night

The warehouse reeked of mildew and oil, the faint hum of an overhead bulb casting jagged shadows across the concrete walls. Jake stood in the center of the room, his leather gloves creaking softly as he adjusted his grip on the pistol at his side. The cold air bit at his skin, but his focus was unflinching, his presence radiating quiet menace.

Bound to wooden chairs in the center of the dimly lit room, Sergei Ivanov and Nikolai Petrov, once feared crime bosses, now looked like cornered animals. The gags stifled their protests, but their eyes burned with anger and suspicion. Sergei, red-faced and barrel-chested, shifted uncomfortably, while Nikolai's wiry frame leaned forward as if poised to pounce despite his restraints.

Before they became feared mob bosses commanding loyalty and bloodshed, Sergei and Nikolai had been inseparable, two boys navigating the gritty streets of East Los Angeles with boundless energy and reckless ambition. Back then, they weren't rivals but brothers in mischief, sharing smokes stolen from corner stores and dreams of one day clawing their way out of the gutters.

In junior high school, Sergei and Nikolai were thick as thieves, roaming the streets with the kind of boundless energy and reckless curiosity only teenagers could muster. They shared everything back then: smokes stolen from corner stores, late-night mischief by the strip mall parking lots, and dreams of becoming powerful men in a world where power was a rare and coveted thing. Together, they were unstoppable, causing chaos in the streets and drawing equal measures of ire and admiration from their peers. Teachers despaired of their antics, but their loyalty to each other was unshakable.

High school marked the beginning of the divide. Nikolai, born into a made family, had his path paved with privilege and power. Sergei, the son of blue-collar immigrants, had to fight for every scrap. While Nikolai attended exclusive gatherings and honed his cunning among the children of the elite, Sergei roamed the streets, hustling and building a crew from scratch. By junior year, Sergei had dropped out entirely, trading textbooks for turf wars. Sergei had a knack for leadership, and his crew quickly gained influence.

Though they were no longer close, Sergei and Nikolai maintained mutual respect during those early years. They were like two sides of the same coin, Nikolai, polished and poised, climbing the ranks of the established order; Sergei, rough and relentless, carving out his own path through sheer force of will. For a time, their paths rarely crossed. They operated in different circles, each building his empire in his own way.

But as the years passed, their respective territories began to overlap, and old friendships were no longer enough to stave off conflict. The respect they once had for each other turned to rivalry, and that rivalry eventually hardened into enmity. The recent chaos had only deepened the divide. Each man blamed the other for the escalating violence, neither willing to consider that the true enemy might lie elsewhere.

Now, years of enmity and spilled blood had brought them here, tied to chairs in a shadow-drenched warehouse. For the first time in decades, Sergei and Nikolai found themselves on the same side of a fight, or, at the very least, sharing the same enemy. Jake stood before them, his piercing gaze shifting between the two like a blade hovering over a coin toss.

Despite their years of animosity, there was a flicker of recognition in their eyes as they glanced at each other. For a brief moment, it was as if they were back on the streets of East Los Angeles, two boys with the world at their feet, unaware of the paths they would one day tread. But the moment passed quickly, swallowed by the harsh reality of their current predicament.

Julianna observed from the shadows, silent and unseen. She was a ghost in the room, ready to step in if things got out of hand.

Jake paced in front of the captives, his boots echoing ominously against the floor. "Listen carefully," Jake began, his tone low and deliberate, each word cutting through the tense silence like a scalpel. "I know the two of you would rather rip each other apart than sit here and listen to me. Frankly, I couldn't care less. But before you resume your little war, there's something you need to hear. Something neither of you saw coming."

He stopped and faced them, his piercing gaze cutting through their groggy confusion. "This whole war, this chaos in your ranks, it didn't happen by accident," Jake said, stepping closer. His voice dropped to a growl. "You've both been played. And the man pulling the strings is someone you know. Eddie Moreno."

The moment the name left Jake's lips; chaos erupted. Sergei's muffled growl of rage turned into a venomous string of curses, directed squarely at Nikolai. Nikolai, his face a mask of fury, lunged forward as far as his bindings would allow, spitting accusations right back. The warehouse filled with their overlapping shouts, each man's voice a cocktail of fury and betrayal.

"You bastard!" Sergei spat at Nikolai. "You paid this man to kill Dimitri!"

"Lies!" Nikolai roared back. "It was you who wanted Yuri dead! Admit it!"

Jake raised his pistol and fired a single shot into the ceiling. The deafening crack echoed off the concrete walls, silencing the room like the abrupt halt of a storm. Both men froze, their fury replaced with wide-eyed fear as they stared at Jake. "Shut up!" he barked, his voice reverberating through the warehouse.

The bosses fell silent, their eyes wide with fear and fury.

"I don't know much, but what I do know is that this wasn't started by either of your organizations." He paused and said, "Here's the deal," his tone cold and commanding. "I don't know if Eddie's pulling the strings or if someone else is controlling him. But I'm going to find out. And this is where you two come in."

He began to pace again, his words measured. "I need whatever intel you've got on Eddie, contacts, deals, everything. Then I need you to hire me to take care of him. Permanently."

The bosses exchanged wary glances; their skepticism evident. Sergei was the first to speak. "Why the hell should we trust you?"

Jake smirked. "You don't have to trust me. But think about this, if Eddie's just a pawn in someone else's game, killing him outright won't solve your problem. You'll still be at each other's throats, while whoever's behind this watches and laughs."

Nikolai grunted. "And what makes you think we can't handle this ourselves?"

Jake shrugged. "Sure, you could try. But let's be real, you two cooperating? That's a disaster in the making. I'm offering you a clean solution. No messy alliances, no backstabbing. Just results."

The room fell silent as the bosses mulled over his words. Finally, Sergei broke the silence. "How much?"

"Twenty million," Jake said flatly, letting the number hang in the air like a guillotine blade. "Ten for me, ten for my partner. Half upfront, the rest when the job's done."

Their jaws dropped. Nikolai sputtered, "Twenty million? Are you insane?"

Jake crossed his arms, his expression unyielding. "This job will burn every bridge we've got. When it's done, we're out of the game for good. Think of it as an investment in your survival," Jake continued, his tone hard and unyielding. "This war has already cost you more than twenty million in blood, men, and territory. Compared to that, this is a bargain. And when I'm done, it'll all be over."

The bosses exchanged a long, reluctant look. Finally, Sergei grunted. "Fine. But if you fail…"

Jake cut him off. "I don't fail."

Within minutes, both bosses accessed their accounts via their phones, transferring five million each to Jake's offshore account. He verified the transactions and then pocketed his phone.

"Pleasure doing business," Jake said with a smirk.

As he and Julianna prepared to leave, Jake turned back to the bosses. "Your phones are in your pockets. Call your people and get out of here. And remember, this war ends now. If I hear otherwise, I'll be back. And you won't like that."

Jake and Julianna disappeared into the night; the warehouse doors creaking shut behind them. Inside, Sergei and Nikolai sat in stunned silence, their mutual hatred momentarily eclipsed by the grim realization of who they'd just dealt with. For the first time in years, their lives weren't in their own hands, and that terrified them.

Chapter 15: Love Is Strong

The tension in the car was palpable as Jake and Julianna sped down the darkened highway. Neither spoke, the silence broken only by the hum of the engine and the rhythmic thrum of tires on asphalt. Jake's knuckles gripped the steering wheel, unrelenting. Beside him, Julianna leaned back against the headrest, her chest rising and falling as she worked to steady her breath.

The silence stretched on until Julianna finally spoke, her voice breaking through the stillness. "That went better than I expected."

Jake nodded but didn't relax. "Yeah, but we've still got a wild card in play."

"The Joker in the deck?" Julianna teased, a faint glimmer of mischief cutting through the somber atmosphere. She leaned toward him, brushing a quick, playful kiss against his cheek. "Relax, Jake. You pulled it off, again."

Jake's lips twitched into the shadow of a smile, but his eyes never left the road. "Yeah. For now." He allowed a small smile to form but didn't fully let down his guard. "You're right. Let's get out of town, lay low for a bit, and figure out our next move."

Julianna leaned forward, grabbing Jake's phone from the center console. Her fingers danced across the screen, her tone crisp and efficient. "I'm rerouting the funds to our shadow accounts, cycling them through a few extra shells just to be safe."

Jake cast her a sidelong glance, his focus flicking between her and the road. "Good thinking. Make sure the trace points are clean. I want them chasing ghosts, if they even try."

"Already on it," she replied with a smirk, not looking up from the screen.

As they merged onto the 405, the Los Angeles skyline began to fade behind them, replaced by the sprawling suburbs and industrial parks of Southern California. The sun dipped lower in the sky, casting long shadows over the freeway. Julianna glanced out the window, watching as the chaos of the city gave way to the relative calm of open stretches of highway.

The hum of the road filled the silence as they merged onto the I-5, the sprawling chaos of Los Angeles fading into the rearview mirror. The open highway stretched before them; a dark ribbon bordered by the distant shimmer of the Pacific. The salty tang of ocean air crept through the car's vents, softening the edge of tension between them.

Julianna leaned her head against the window, her voice soft but determined. "Jake, what's the plan for Eddie? If he's the one pulling the strings, this ends with him. But if someone else is in control..."

Jake tightened his grip on the wheel. "If someone else is calling the shots, we'll figure it out. But Eddie's our starting point. He's not walking away from this either way."

They drove on in comfortable silence for a while, the tension between them easing slightly. As they neared Oceanside, the view opened up to reveal the Pacific Ocean, its surface shimmering under the pale moonlight. The coastal cliffs were dotted with small homes and hotels, their lights twinkling like fireflies against the dark landscape.

"We'll stop here," Jake said, his voice calm but firm as he guided the car off the highway onto a winding coastal road. The headlights swept across a small hillside hotel perched above the cliffs, its modest stucco exterior glowing faintly under the moonlight. The crash of waves against the rocks below echoed in the stillness, a soothing rhythm that belied the storm brewing in their minds.

The hotel was clean and modest, its stucco exterior was painted a warm beige that blended with the surrounding landscape. Jake parked the car and stepped out, stretching his legs. The sound of crashing waves reached them, mingling with the distant hum of traffic.

Inside the room, Julianna moved with practiced efficiency, setting their duffel bags on the bed before methodically checking the locks on the windows and door. The faint scent of ocean air seeped through the cracks in the old frame, mingling with the freshness of the linens.

Jake sank into the chair by the window, his silhouette cast in the pale glow of moonlight through the curtains. He stared out at the restless ocean, his mind replaying the events of the day and plotting the moves yet to come.

Julianna crossed the room and placed her hands gently on Jake's shoulders. "One step at a time," she murmured, her voice a quiet balm against the storm raging in his head.

Jake reached up, his calloused hand covering hers, letting out a long, measured breath. For the first time that night, his shoulders eased slightly. "I know," he said, his tone softer now. "I just can't shake the feeling that we're walking a tightrope over fire."

"You've never fallen yet," she said, her lips curving into a faint smile. "And if you do, we'll fall together."

As the night wore on, they sat together, reviewing what lay ahead. Their partnership had weathered storms before, but this time, the stakes felt impossibly higher. Every move they made now was a gamble, and every breath carried the weight of lives hanging in the balance. As they sat together, the steady crash of waves outside their window seemed to echo their unspoken vow: no matter what came next, they would face it together.

Chapter 16: (I Can't Get No) Satisfaction

The morning light seeped through the thin curtains, painting the room in soft gold and revealing the tangle of sheets on the bed. Jake stirred first, the faint creak of the mattress breaking the stillness. His hand brushed against Julianna's, warm and familiar. She turned toward him, her dark hair spilling across the pillow like ink on parchment.

"Morning, stranger," she murmured, her lips curving into a sleepy smile. "Don't tell me you're actually letting yourself rest for once."

Jake chuckled; his voice rough from sleep. "Even I need a break sometimes." He pulled her closer, his voice dropping. "But don't get used to it."

Jake chuckled, pulling her into a passionate embrace. Their laughter faded into soft whispers and stolen kisses; the tension of their mission was momentarily forgotten.

The laughter and warmth eventually gave way to quiet determination. Jake leaned against the headboard, his hand absently brushing through Julianna's hair. "We start tonight," he said, his tone steady but grim.

Julianna propped herself up on one elbow, her gaze sharp and inquisitive. "Alright. Let's hear it."

Jake outlined his plan, each step deliberate and precise. Julianna listened intently, occasionally interjecting with suggestions or pointing out potential pitfalls.

"That's a solid start," she said, "but what about the security cameras? We'll need to disable them, before we make our move."

"Good point," Jake admitted. "We'll handle that first thing."

They spent the day in a rare moment of peace, savoring the calm before the storm. Over brunch at a sunlit café, they let their guard down just enough to enjoy the crisp air and the sound of waves crashing in the distance. Later, as they strolled along the beach, the salt spray mingling with the breeze, Julianna kicked off her shoes and walked barefoot in the sand.

"You know," she mused, looking out at the endless horizon, "it's moments like this that almost make me forget what we do for a living."

Jake smirked, slipping his hands into his pockets. "Almost."

By mid-afternoon, they were back on the road, heading north toward Los Angeles. The coastal scenery was a patchwork of rugged cliffs, sandy beaches, and sprawling estates, a stark contrast to the gritty cityscape they were returning to.

As dusk settled over the city, they arrived at Eddie's office building. Parking a few blocks away, they waited patiently, watching as the last of the building's occupants trickled out. When the final light on Eddie's floor went dark, they moved.

Slipping into the lobby, they bypassed the security system with practiced ease and took the elevator to Eddie's office. The office was a stark contrast to the lively city below. The blinds were half-drawn, casting sharp lines of shadow and light across the cluttered desk. The faint glow of the Los Angeles skyline seeped through the cracks, offering just enough illumination to work by. They wasted no time, rummaging through papers on his desk and drawers, searching for anything that might reveal Eddie's secrets.

"Of course," Julianna muttered, pulling a strip of tape from the bottom of Eddie's keyboard. Scrawled on it in smudged ink was the password: *Eddie123*. "Amateur hour," she said, shaking her head as her fingers danced over the keys.

Within seconds, the screen blinked to life, revealing a labyrinth of folders and encrypted files. They sifted through them methodically, uncovering damning evidence piece by piece. Julianna's sharp intake of breath broke the silence.

"Jake, you need to see this," she said, pointing to the screen.

"Jake," Julianna said, her voice cutting through the quiet like a knife. "You need to see this."

Jake leaned over her shoulder, his brow furrowing as he read the document on the screen: a Confidential Informant Agreement, complete with Eddie's signature and that of a DEA agent, named Fred Alton.

"Fred Alton," Jake muttered, the name leaving a sour taste in his mouth. Julianna clicked through more files, her expression darkening with each revelation. Correspondence with Los Zetas. Payment logs. Coordinates.

"This guy's running a double game," Jake said, his voice low. "DEA on one side, Los Zetas on the other. He's been playing puppet master while the rest of us dance on his strings."

They worked through the night, gathering as much intel as possible. As dawn approached and the building stirred to life, they each found hiding spots in the office. With earpieces in place, they whispered to each other, their banter a mix of lighthearted teasing and serious strategy.

"Think he'll show up on time?" Julianna asked.

"Eddie? Punctuality isn't his strong suit," Jake replied, smirking. "But he'll come."

When Eddie finally arrived, they watched from the shadows as he settled at his desk. Moments later, Eddie's phone buzzed, its vibration cutting through the quiet room like a warning. He answered on the second ring, his voice deferential.

"Yes, sir... No, sir... I understand," Eddie said, his tone a mix of nervousness and feigned confidence. His fingers drummed against the desk as he listened, each tap echoing in the stillness.

And then, the glass shattered.

The single crack of a high-powered rifle broke through the quiet, and Eddie's body jolted forward. Blood splattered across the desk and the empty shelves behind him as his phone clattered to the ground, the line still open.

"Stop!" Julianna hissed through the earpiece. "Let the shooter leave before we move."

They waited in tense silence, counting down the minutes. When they were certain the coast was clear, they emerged from their hiding spots, quickly grabbing Eddie's laptop and cell phone. Jake and Julianna moved like shadows, silent and calculated. They slipped through the office door and opted for the stairwell, descending quickly but cautiously. Every creak of the metal steps made their hearts race, but neither spoke.

Outside, the city began to wake, the early morning light reflecting off the glass facades of nearby buildings. They blended seamlessly into the crowd of commuters, their steps measured, their expressions calm. Behind them, Eddie's office stood as a silent witness to the chaos they were leaving behind.

Chapter 17: Wild Horses

The early morning air was sharp and still, amplifying every sound as Jake and Julianna crossed the quiet street. Julianna moved with purpose, her stride quick but composed, and slid into the driver's seat of the waiting car without hesitation. "I'm driving," she announced, her tone brooking no argument. Jake didn't protest, slipping into the passenger seat and slamming the door shut.

The engine roared to life, and within moments, they were speeding through the sleeping city. The streets of Los Angeles blurred past in streaks of orange and gold from the streetlights, but the tension in the car remained heavy.

The cityscape blurred past them as they sped through Los Angeles, her focus split between the road and the rearview mirror. "Who do you think sent the shooter?" she asked, her voice steady despite the adrenaline coursing through her veins.

Jake pulled out his phone and typed a quick message to Sergei and Nikolai, the Russian mob bosses: *Eddie's down. Now looking for the next domino.* He hit send and leaned back in his seat. "Let's see how they respond to that," he said. "Might tell us if one of them was behind it."

The city faded behind them as Julianna merged onto the highway heading east, the concrete jungle giving way to the sprawling desert. Jake opened Eddie's cell phone, scrolling through messages and contacts, while Julianna kept her eyes on the road.

"You find anything?" she asked.

"Not yet," Jake replied, frowning at the cryptic text exchanges. "But I'm just getting started."

The sun began to rise, casting long shadows over the empty highway as they neared the city limits. Julianna's sharp eyes darted to the rearview mirror. A single car, too far back to seem suspicious at first, had stayed with them through several turns.

"We've got company," she said, her voice steady but laced with an edge. Her grip on the steering wheel tightened as the reality of the situation sank in.

Jake glanced over his shoulder, spotting the faint silhouette of the car against the morning light. "Persistent little bastard," he muttered.

A car lingered several lengths back, its headlights faint against the horizon. "You think it's the shooter?" she asked as she checked the mirrors to subtly map out the scenario in her head.

"Very likely," Jake said, closing the laptop and sitting up straighter. "Take the next exit. Let's see if he follows."

Julianna nodded, guiding the car off the freeway and onto a smaller highway leading toward the I-40. For a moment, it seemed they had lost the tail, but then Jake spotted the car, still hanging back.

"He's still with us," Jake muttered. "Find the next rest area or pull out. We need to deal with this."

A few minutes later, Julianna spotted a dirt pull-out off the highway. She turned in smoothly, the car kicking up a cloud of dust as it came to a stop. Jake grabbed a small device from his bag of tricks and slipped out of the car, finding cover behind a cluster of large rocks and desert brush. Julianna remained in the driver's seat, her earpiece crackling to life.

"What's he doing?" she whispered.

The trailing car crept to a halt a few hundred yards down, its engine cutting off in the stillness. From his cover behind a cluster of boulders, Jake watched as the driver stepped out, tall and lean, his movements purposeful. The faint metallic glint of a rifle case in his hand made Jake's jaw tighten.

"He's got a rifle," Jake whispered into his earpiece. "Looks like he's gonna set up shop on that ridge."

Julianna's voice crackled softly in response. "What's he doing? Is he aiming for the car?"

"Not yet," Jake replied. "But if he gets that rifle set up, you'll be in his crosshairs before you can blink."

Julianna exhaled sharply. "What's the plan?"

"Here's what we're going to do," Jake said, his tone calm but decisive. He outlined the plan quickly, then began moving toward the shooter's car, keeping low, and using the rocks and desert brush as cover.

When he reached the vehicle, he slid into the passenger seat, careful not to make a sound. "Julianna," he whispered into the earpiece, "he's found his position. Looks like he's setting up. Get ready to take off before he has time to assemble his rifle."

Crouching low, Jake slipped into the shooter's car, the faint scent of motor oil and cigarette smoke hanging in the air. His fingers brushed against the keys still dangling in the ignition. Perfect. He twisted them slightly, the engine groaning softly but not roaring to life.

"Julianna," he said, his voice calm despite the adrenaline coursing through him, "on my signal, hit the gas. Make as much noise as you can. He'll take the bait."

"Ready," Julianna replied.

"Go, now!" Jake commanded.

Julianna slammed on the accelerator, and the car roared to life, tires spinning in the dirt before catching. A cloud of dust rose in her wake, obscuring the car as it hurtled back onto the highway.

The shooter spun around at the sound, his rifle half-assembled and cursed loudly. He abandoned his position and began sprinting toward his makeshift perch, hoping to take aim before she vanished.

Jake didn't give him the chance. He cranked the ignition, the car jolting forward with a growl.

Over the earpiece, Julianna laughed. "So much for Vegas, baby."

"I'll take you there some other time," Jake replied. "Drive ten to fifteen miles, and we'll find a good exit to ditch this car, so I can join you."

"Yeah, but how's dickhead going to get home?" Julianna asked, her voice tinged with amusement.

Jake chuckled. "That's his problem."

A few miles later, Julianna veered onto a deserted exit ramp, the glow of the sun casting long shadows over the barren desert landscape. Her car idled, the engine ticking softly as she scanned the horizon for signs of pursuit.

Moments later, Jake rolled up beside her in the shooter's car, skidding to a halt in the gravel. He climbed out, his face flushed but triumphant, and tossed the car keys into the open expanse of scrub and sand.

"Well?" Julianna asked, raising an eyebrow.

"He won't be following us anytime soon," Jake replied, sliding into the passenger seat of her car.

"Which way, now?" Julianna asked, her tone sobering as they merged back onto the highway.

Jake considered for a moment. "South or west to Palm Springs and Vegas is too predictable. We either turn around and head back to LA or go toward Fresno."

He paused, a smirk forming. "Wait, I have the perfect place. Head north toward Baker, take the back way through Shoshone, and we'll end up in Pahrump."

"Pahrump?" Julianna repeated, one brow arching skeptically.

"It's no Vegas," Jake said, smirking. "But it's out of the way, and nobody will be looking for us there. Plus, I hear they've got casinos. And brothels, if you're into that sort of thing."

Julianna rolled her eyes, suppressing a smile as she shifted gears and pulled back onto the highway. "You really know how to pick the romantic spots, Jake."

He chuckled, leaning back in his seat. "I aim to please."

Julianna shook her head, laughing softly as she turned the car north. By the time they reached a small hotel on the outskirts of Pahrump, the exhaustion of the day had caught up with them. They checked in, flopping onto the bed in their room without even bothering to undress.

Lying on their backs, staring at the ceiling, they both let out simultaneous sighs of relief.

"Long day," Julianna muttered.

"Just another day at the office," Jake replied, his voice laced with tired humor.

Chapter 18: Casino Boogie

The aroma of strong coffee and fresh pastries greeted Jake as his eyes fluttered open. Warm sunlight filtered through the thin curtains, casting golden stripes across the room's modest décor. He turned his head, spotting Julianna perched at the small desk, Eddie's laptop glowing faintly in front of her. Her dark hair was pulled into a loose knot, and her focus was razor-sharp as her fingers danced across the keyboard.

"Morning, sunshine," she said without looking up, her tone equal parts teasing and focused.

Jake groaned, rubbing his face with one hand as he sat up. "You always this chipper at dawn?" he muttered, reaching for the steaming cup on the nightstand. The rich, bitter brew jolted his senses to life.

"Find anything?" he asked after his first sip, his voice still gravelly with sleep.

Julianna didn't pause her typing. "I still think our best two leads are this DEA agent, Fred Alton and the Los Zetas cartel," she replied. "But here's something. Not sure what it means yet, but it looks like Fred Alton is no longer working for the DEA. He's been a private citizen for about two or three months now."

Jake straightened, setting the coffee cup down. "Private citizen, my ass," he muttered. "What kind of agent was he? Any commendations?"

Julianna's brows furrowed as she squinted at the screen. "Quite the opposite," she said. "He was recently accused of taking bribes, but they couldn't prove anything. That's probably why he decided to get out of the DEA."

Jake scratched his stubbled jaw. "Pushed out, I'd wager," he said grimly. "Someone like that, doesn't just retire. He's playing for someone else now, or himself. Safe bet is that Fred was using Eddie to find professionals. And now, he is covering his tracks by trying to eliminate Eddie, and probably me as well."

Julianna nodded, her fingers flying across the keys as she delved deeper into the files. Jake leaned back against the headboard, sipping his coffee as he mulled over their next move. The weight of their mission pressed on him, but the calm efficiency with which Julianna worked was oddly comforting.

After they finished their coffee and Danish, Jake stretched and headed to the bathroom. Jake leaned against the cool tiled wall, letting the warm spray of the shower cascade over him. It was a rare moment of solitude, the water washing away the weight of their escape and the lingering tension that clung to him like a second skin.

He closed his eyes, exhaling deeply when he heard the shower door slide open. "Mind if I join?" Julianna's playful tone broke through the sound of running water.

Jake opened his eyes, taking in her mischievous smile as she stepped inside, steam curling around her like an embrace. "You don't play fair, do you?" he said, smirking.

She shrugged, stepping closer. "Where's the fun in that?" Her hands found his shoulders, and for a moment, the world outside the fogged glass didn't exist.

Jake turned to face her, the steam curling around them. "I think we make a pretty good team," she said, her tone both playful and sincere.

Jake placed his hands on her hips, his eyes locking with hers. "If I have to be in this," he said softly, "I'm glad you have my back."

Julianna smirked and spun him around, grabbing the soap. "I'll always have your back," she said, her hands moving methodically as she began to wash his shoulders.

The steam enveloped them, muffling the outside world as they stood together, the warmth of the water and their shared purpose forging an unspoken bond. The moment ended in a deep embrace, their foreheads touching as the water ran over them, carrying away the weight of the past few days.

As Jake and Julianna exited the hotel, they tossed their bags into the trunk of their car. The morning sun glinted off the windshield as they slid into their seats, Julianna taking the driver's side this time.

"Over the mountain and down to Vegas," Jake remarked, fastening his seatbelt.

The road from Pahrump to Vegas stretched out like a ribbon of asphalt through the barren desert. The stark beauty of the landscape surrounded them, jagged mountains rising in the distance, their edges softened by the morning haze. The sun climbed higher, bathing the desert in a harsh, golden light.

Julianna drummed her fingers on the steering wheel as they cruised down the empty highway. "You think anyone's noticed, we're not where we're supposed to be?" she asked her tone light but her eyes scanning the rearview mirror.

Jake leaned back; his arms crossed. "They'll figure it out eventually, but by then, we'll be long gone. Vegas is just a pit stop."

"Pit stop, huh?" Julianna quirked an eyebrow, a teasing smile playing on her lips. "Sounds like someone owes me a proper trip to Sin City when all this is over."

Jake chuckled, the corners of his mouth curving into a grin. "Add it to the list, sweetheart. First, we survive."

As they approached the city, the skyline of the Strip began to take shape in the distance. The towering hotels and casinos stood like beacons against the stark desert backdrop.

They parked the car in the crowded lot of a major casino, careful to choose a spot away from cameras and easy to blend into the masses. Julianna grabbed her bag and locked the car, tossing the keys onto the dashboard.

"Think anyone will notice it's abandoned?" Jake asked, slinging his duffel over his shoulder.

"Not until we're long gone," Julianna replied, leading the way into the casino.

The casino floor was a kaleidoscope of lights and sound, a symphony of clinking coins, shuffling cards, and the occasional triumphant cheer. Rows of slot machines blinked in rhythmic patterns, their mechanical chimes vying for attention against the low hum of conversation.

Jake and Julianna moved through the crowd with purpose, their presence blending seamlessly into the throng of tourists and gamblers. The mirrored walls and endless rows of tables created an illusion of space, but Jake's sharp eyes took in every detail, from the uniformed security guards near the exits to the discreet cameras perched in every corner.

"Ever get the feeling you're being watched?" Julianna murmured, leaning closer to Jake as they passed a row of roulette tables.

He smirked, keeping his gaze forward. "Always. Let's make sure, they don't remember us."

"There's the exit to the taxi stand," Julianna said, pointing ahead.

They slipped out of the casino unnoticed, hailing a cab for a short ride to the airport. Once inside, they moved quickly through security, their forged IDs holding up under scrutiny. Within an hour, they were seated on a flight to Mexico City.

The steady hum of the plane's engines provided a strange sense of calm, a temporary reprieve from the chaos that seemed to follow them like a shadow. Jake gazed out the window, watching as the sprawling desert gave way to clusters of city lights far below.

Julianna leaned against his shoulder, her head resting lightly as she dozed. The softness of the moment was at odds with the tension that hung in the air, a fleeting reminder of normalcy in their otherwise tumultuous lives.

As she stirred slightly, Jake glanced down at her, a faint smile playing on his lips. "You always this peaceful in your sleep?" he teased softly.

Reopening her eyes, Julianna smirked. "Only when I'm not dreaming of you." And added, "We've come a long way in a short time," her voice low enough not to carry.

Jake nodded. "Too far to turn back now. But what about after this? Ever thought about what comes next?"

Julianna tilted her head thoughtfully. "Sometimes. But right now, this is what matters. We've got threads to pull and people to stop."

He gave her a small smile, appreciating her clarity and resolve. They spent the rest of the flight alternating between discussing their strategy and falling into companionable silence.

When they landed in Mexico City, the vibrant energy of the airport hit them immediately. The airport was alive with energy, a vibrant mix of hurried travelers, rapid-fire Spanish announcements, and the rich aroma of freshly brewed coffee wafting from nearby kiosks. Bright signs in bold colors guided passengers through the maze of terminals, a sensory overload that reflected the pulse of Mexico City itself.

Jake and Julianna moved through the crowd with purpose, their bags slung over their shoulders. They spoke little, their shared glances communicating everything they needed. They made a quick stop at a storage locker where Jake removed a medium-sized leather bag with a few tools of the trade inside and they were on their way.

Outside, the city greeted them with its chaotic charm. Traffic was a symphony of honking horns and revving engines, and the streets teemed with life. The taxi they hailed wove through the maze of bustling avenues, the driver narrating landmarks with a mix of pride and humor.

A taxi ride through the bustling streets brought them to the Gran Hotel Ciudad de México. The building was a marvel, its art nouveau façade standing as a testament to an era of grandeur. As they stepped inside, the opulence of the interior took their breath away. The stained-glass ceiling bathed the lobby in a kaleidoscope of colors, and intricate wrought-iron railings spiraled gracefully around a central atrium. Chandeliers cast a warm glow over the polished marble floors.

"Impressive," Jake murmured, his gaze sweeping the space.

"Fit for a couple of fugitives," Julianna quipped, a sly grin on her lips.

The concierge greeted them warmly, handing over their room key with practiced efficiency. Once inside their suite, they dropped their bags and took a moment to take in the view. The sprawling Zócalo plaza lay below, alive with activity. The contrast between their turbulent journey and the serenity of the scene was not lost on them.

Julianna sank onto the plush bed, kicking off her shoes. "We should enjoy this while we can. Who knows what's waiting for us next."

Jake leaned against the window frame, his eyes on the city. "We'll find out soon enough."

Chapter 19: Time is on My Side

Sunlight filtered through the sheer curtains, painting warm streaks across the hotel room's polished floors. Jake stirred, stretching his sore muscles as the aroma of freshly brewed coffee teased him awake. Across the room, Julianna sat at the desk, bathed in the morning glow, her dark hair loosely tied back. The faint clatter of her fingers on the laptop keyboard broke the silence.

"Morning," she said without looking up, her tone brisk but laced with familiarity.

Jake grunted, pulling himself upright. "You're always the early bird," he muttered, reaching for the steaming cup she'd left on the nightstand. "You still poking around Eddie's files?"

"More like untangling them," Julianna replied, her gaze focused on the screen. "There's a lot to unpack. Los Zetas, encrypted communications," as she clicked something and leaned closer, "some interesting phone logs tied to our friend, Fred Alton."

Jake moved to her side, peering at the screen. Together, they combed through the digital files, a mix of spreadsheets, correspondence, and encrypted logs. One file caught their attention: a list of major U.S. cities with code names listed beside them.

"Hitmen?" Jake guessed, pointing to the cryptic names.

"Most likely," Julianna replied. She minimized the file and opened another. "There's a lot here about Los Zetas. I'm going to make some calls to my contacts in Mexico, and see if I can shake anything loose."

Jake nodded. "Good idea. I'll start digging into Fred Alton. I want to know where he's been, and who he's been talking to."

They spent the next hour working in tandem. Julianna dialed a series of numbers, speaking in rapid Spanish with an air of authority. Jake, meanwhile, used one of his secure lines to contact an old friend with access to phone records. Within minutes, he had a list of Fred Alton's recent locations and calls.

"Looks like Alton's been hopping around," Jake said, jotting down notes. "Last known whereabouts were Houston, Denver, and Tijuana. That's an interesting mix."

"Interesting and suspicious," Julianna replied, covering the receiver of her phone for a moment. "Los Zetas have been active in all those areas recently."

Jake leaned back in his chair, rubbing his temples. "This guy's deep in it. We're going to have to tread carefully."

As the morning stretched into late hours, Jake decided to take a break. He stood and stretched. "I'm going to hit the shower. Let me know if you find anything big."

"Will do," Julianna said, her focus still on her laptop.

The sound of running water filled the room as Jake stepped into the bathroom. Julianna continued her work, her eyes scanning lines of text and her fingers flying over the keyboard. A sudden knock at the door broke her concentration.

The knock on the door broke the stillness. Julianna's instincts kicked in instantly, her body tensing as her hand shot toward the desk drawer where she'd stashed her gun. "Room service," a voice called from the hallway, calm and professional.

"Jake?" she called, her voice low. The sound of the shower running offered no reply.

She approached the door cautiously, every sense on high alert. Peeking through the spyhole, she saw a uniformed server with a cart of trays. It looked harmless enough, but appearances could be deceiving. Her fingers tightened around the grip of her gun as she cracked the door open just wide enough to speak.

The server greeted her with a polite smile. "Your breakfast, ma'am," he said, his tone pleasant but detached.

Julianna stepped aside, allowing him to roll the cart in while keeping a careful eye on his movements. Her other hand stayed near her waistband, where the gun rested, ready to draw if needed.

When the door clicked shut behind him, Julianna exhaled, only partially relaxing.

Jake emerged from the bathroom, droplets of water clinging to his shoulders as he wrapped a towel loosely around his waist. "What's going on?" he asked, catching the sharp edge in Julianna's posture.

"I almost shot the poor guy," Julianna said, crossing her arms and glaring at him.

Jake blinked, then smirked. "Room service?"

"Yeah," she said, shaking her head. "And you didn't think to tell me?"

"Sorry, babe," he said with mock contrition, stepping closer. "Let me make it up to you."

Julianna rolled her eyes but let him pull her into an embrace. "You're lucky, I didn't shoot you instead."

"Noted," Jake replied with a grin before kissing her lightly. "But, next time, let's skip the life-or-death moment and just have breakfast."

Over the clatter of silverware and the soft hum of the city outside, Jake and Julianna pieced together their findings.

"Fred Alton's movements are all over the place," Jake said, pointing to the notes scrawled in his notebook. "Houston, Denver, Tijuana. Every single one of those cities is a known hotspot for Los Zetas activity."

Julianna tapped her laptop screen. "It's worse than that. One of my contacts says Alton's been working with them directly, facilitating supply chains and even coordinating safe houses for their operatives."

Jake leaned back, frowning. "So, he's gone full rogue. DEA agent turned cartel facilitator. Makes sense, given his sudden retirement."

"Retirement," Julianna scoffed, her tone dripping with sarcasm. "Let's call it what it is. He's neck-deep in this mess. And it gets better." She turned her laptop toward Jake, showing an email thread between Eddie and Alton. "This confirms Eddie was acting as a broker for Alton, connecting him to professionals for… projects."

Jake's eyes narrowed as he read. "Hitmen. Supply chain coordinators. Probably even explosives experts." He shook his head. "This guy's not just a middleman. He's a damn kingpin in training."

Julianna leaned back in her chair; her expression grim. "But here's the scary thing: one of my contacts says, Fred Alton is getting help from a Washington politician."

Jake frowned. "A politician? That's not just scary, that's a game-changer. So, how do we put this all together, and what do we do next?"

They sat and discussed the situation for a while, the puzzle pieces slowly taking shape. After some deliberation, Jake decided to call the two mob bosses in LA to bring them up to speed.

The call with Sergei and Nikolai started like a typical mob negotiation: curt words, a few veiled threats, and a lot of posturing. But Jake's bombshell about Alton shifted the tone.

"We've called a truce," Sergei admitted finally, his voice gruff but sincere.

Jake raised an eyebrow. "You two? Working together? Hell must've frozen over."

"Don't push your luck," Nikolai interjected, his tone sharp but laced with humor. "We're not friends. We're... pragmatic."

Sergei grunted in agreement. "This war cost us too much already. We both see the bigger picture now."

Jake exchanged a look with Julianna, who mouthed the word "unexpected" with a smirk. Turning back to the phone, he said, "Well, if you two can bury the hatchet, maybe there's hope for humanity, after all."

The call ended with tentative plans to coordinate efforts. Jake set his phone down and looked at Julianna. "Looks like we've got allies now. Strange bedfellows, but I'll take it."

Julianna smirked. "Allies, chaos, and a U.S. politician in the mix. What could possibly go wrong?"

Chapter 20: Midnight Rambler

The dim light from a single desk lamp cast long shadows across the ornate walls of their hotel room at the Gran Hotel Ciudad de México. Jake stood near the window; his silhouette framed against the sprawling nightscape of the city below. Julianna sat at the small table, her laptop glowing faintly as she scrolled through files. The room's grandeur, stained glass, and antique furnishings felt oddly at odds with the storm brewing between them and their enemies.

"We've stirred up a lot of trouble," Jake muttered, running a hand through his hair. "It's only a matter of time before someone comes looking for us."

Julianna glanced up, her expression calm but firm. "Then let's make sure they regret it," she said, closing her laptop. "We need a backup plan. Let's extend our stay and set up across the hall."

Jake nodded. "Good thinking. I'll handle the setup in the first room. We'll leave enough clues to make it look like we're still staying there, and a little surprise as well," he said while holding up a grenade.

By mid-afternoon, their preparations were complete. The second room across the hall was rented under an alias, stripped of anything personal, and outfitted with a makeshift command center. A hidden camera, cleverly tucked into the room's decorative molding, provided them a clear view of their original room's entrance.

Jake sat at the edge of the bed in the decoy room, assembling a simple but effective tripwire explosive from a grenade near the front door. He held up the small device, grinning at Julianna. "Nothing fancy, but it'll get the job done."

Julianna, watching the hallway feed on her laptop, smirked. "I'm just hoping these guys are as predictable as we think."

The hours dragged on, tension mounting as the city outside transitioned from the golden hues of evening to the inky black of night. Jake leaned back in a chair; eyes fixed on the laptop screen. "Nothing yet. You think they'll show tonight?"

"If they're coming, it'll be late," Julianna replied. "They'll want the cover of darkness and quiet halls."

The clock ticked past midnight when Jake stiffened in his chair, his eyes locked on the laptop screen. Three men stepped out of the elevator, clad in dark clothing that blended seamlessly with the shadows. Their movements were sharp, coordinated, and professional.

"Showtime," Jake murmured, his voice low.

Julianna joined him at the screen, her expression hardening. "Three of them. Armed, and not here to make friends."

On the feed, the men approached the decoy room, one pulling out a lock-picking kit. Jake and Julianna exchanged a glance, the unspoken communication of seasoned partners.

The faint *click* of the lock opening carried through the quiet hallway, followed seconds later by a muffled explosion. The screen went static as the camera's feed cut out. The explosion rocked the building, making the lights flicker. Jake and Julianna were on their feet in an instant, guns drawn as they listened for any further commotion.

Jake was already moving, gun in hand, whispering, "IED took out two for sure."

They stepped into the hallway, moving swiftly and silently. Inside the first room, the scene was a grim tableau: two of the attackers lay motionless near the entrance, their bodies riddled with shrapnel. The third man lay on the floor, groaning and clutching his head, blood trickling down his temple.

"We don't have time for questions," Jake said, his voice edged with regret as he checked the man's jacket for ID. "The police will be here soon."

Julianna nodded, rifling through the pockets of another man and pulling out a phone. She noticed the earpieces still in place on each of them. "Comms.," she said. "Someone might be listening."

Jake's expression. "Then we need to move, now. Grab the phone and let's go."

The distant wail of sirens urged them into action. Jake and Julianna grabbed their go-bags, their movements; fluid and synchronized, and slipped into the stairwell. Every creak of the metal stairs felt amplified as they descended, the adrenaline sharpening their senses.

On the ground floor, Jake cracked open the door to the alley. The cool night air hit them like a slap, carrying the faint buzz of the city's nightlife. He scanned the empty street, his hand resting on the holstered pistol at his side.

"Clear," he murmured, motioning Julianna forward.

The streets were quieter than Jake liked, the stillness amplifying every sound. Julianna stuck close to him, her eyes scanning the area for any signs of pursuit.

"The airport will be watched," Julianna said, her voice steady despite the adrenaline coursing through her veins. "Where do we go?"

Jake glanced down the street, his mind racing. "Sticking around might have been a mistake," he admitted. "We can't afford mistakes, not now. Let's find somewhere to lay low, regroup, and figure out our next move."

Julianna gave a curt nod. "I know a place, a safe house not far from here. It's quiet, off the grid."

Jake trusted her instincts and followed her lead, their footsteps quick but measured. The adrenaline still coursing through them kept their senses sharp, every shadow and noise scrutinized as they disappeared into the labyrinth of Mexico City's backstreets.

The grand hacienda on the outskirts of Puebla stood as a fortress of opulence. High walls and iron gates shielded its sprawling grounds, while armed guards patrolled the perimeter. Inside, in a room lit only by a flickering chandelier and the glow of a roaring fireplace, Manuel Torres paced like a caged predator.

"¡Qué pendejos!" he roared, slamming his fist onto the mahogany table. The room fell silent, his men standing rigidly at attention, their faces pale under his seething glare.

Manuel's sharp eyes darted to a scarred subordinate, his voice dropping to a deadly calm. "Three of my best men, dead. Do you know what that means? It means they're laughing at us. At me."

The subordinate hesitated, but Manuel's rising fury cut him off before he could speak. "I don't want excuses. I want blood. Call Hector and Luis. Tell them to bring the Sicarios."

His confidants stood silently, heads bowed, as Manuel paced back and forth. "Do you know how much those bastards cost me?" he snarled. "And now they're making a mockery of us. This Jake and his little girlfriend think they can humiliate me? Think they can escape? No. They'll pay."

One of his men, a wiry figure with a scar running down his cheek, ventured cautiously, "Senior, they are professionals. Perhaps we need…"

"Silence!" Manuel cut him off, his eyes blazing. "We don't need more professionals. We need brute force. Relentless force. Send the Sicarios."

The room fell into a heavy silence. Everyone present knew what that meant. The Sicarios were a breed completely apart; ruthless and untethered by codes or protocols. They were not like Jake or Julianna, whose precision and calculated moves resembled a chess game. The Sicarios were blunt instruments, agents of chaos unleashed to burn everything in their path.

Manuel's lips curled into a dark smile as he envisioned their next move. "Send them into the city," he commanded. "I want Jake and that woman hunted like animals. No subtlety, no mercy. Burn everything in their path if you must."

His men nodded and retreated from the room, leaving Manuel alone with his simmering rage. He turned toward the fire, the orange flames reflecting in his eyes.

"You think you can outsmart me, Jake?" he muttered under his breath. "Let's see how far your clever plans get you, when the Sicarios are on your heels."

Chapter 21: Play with Fire

Miles away, Jake and Julianna continued to weave through the maze of Mexico City's alleys, oblivious to the storm now unleashed upon them. But the instincts that had kept them alive this long told them one thing: the hunt was far from over.

Jake and Julianna slipped through the shadowed alleyways; their footsteps muffled against the cracked pavement. The air was thick with the scent of exhaust and damp stone, every shadow a potential threat. Just as they rounded a corner, Julianna's phone buzzed in her pocket, breaking the tense silence.

She glanced at the screen, recognizing the number immediately. Without hesitation, she answered. "Talk to me."

The voice on the other end was low, trembling with fear. "Julianna... I'm so sorry. I didn't have a choice. Don Manuel... he forced me to tell him where you were."

Julianna's pulse quickened, but her voice remained calm. "It's okay," she said softly, masking her frustration. "You did what you had to do. Did you hear anything else?"

"Yes," the voice whispered, urgency dripping from every word. "He's sent the Sicarios. They're coming for you."

The weight of the warning settled heavily on her chest. "Thank you," Julianna said, her voice barely above a whisper. "Get somewhere safe. Now."

As the call ended, she turned to Jake, her eyes sharp but shadowed with worry. "We've been burned. Sicarios are on their way."

Without hesitation, she tossed her phone into the bed of a passing pickup truck. "They've been tracking us. Phones are compromised."

Jake followed suit immediately, throwing his own phone onto another moving vehicle. His jaw tightened as he met Julianna's gaze. "Looks like the dogs are loose," he said grimly.

Julianna nodded, her face set. "We can't go to the safe house. We need to change direction and regroup."

They ducked into a small, dimly lit park tucked between two towering apartment blocks. The distant hum of traffic and muffled chatter from nearby windows created a surreal calm, but their nerves were razor-sharp.

Julianna perched on the edge of a weathered bench, eyes scanning the shifting shadows. Jake paced in front of her, the gears of his mind visibly turning.

"What's the play?" Julianna asked, her voice steady despite the adrenaline surging through her veins.

Jake stopped pacing and locked eyes with hers. "We turn the tables," he said, his tone low but decisive. "If they want to hunt us, fine. But we'll be the ones setting the traps."

Julianna smirked faintly, her admiration for him cutting through the tension. "Good," she said. "Let's make them regret it."

Julianna scanned the shadows, her instincts honed and ready. "Then we better figure it out fast. Because they're not going to stop until we're dead."

From his bag, Jake retrieved a burner phone, its cheap plastic casing glinting faintly under the park's solitary streetlamp. He dialed Sergei's number, his fingers steady despite the weight of the call.

The line connected after two rings. Sergei's voice came through, rough and impatient. "What do you want, Jake?"

"Manuel Torres," Jake said without preamble. "Is he top brass in Los Zetas?"

Sergei chuckled darkly. "Not even close. He's ambitious, but he's a mid-level player at best. Why?"

Jake's voice hardened. "Because he sent the Sicarios after us."

There was a pause, then a low growl on the other end. "Sicarios? That's a bold move for someone like Manuel. He's punching above his weight class."

"Then take him out of the equation," Jake said flatly. "You deal with him. We'll handle the Sicarios."

Sergei's laughter was cold like ice cracking under pressure. "Consider it done. Just make sure you stay alive long enough to finish this game."

Sergei leaned back in his leather chair, swirling a glass of vodka in his hand. A sinister smile spread across his face as he picked up another phone, a direct line to someone who could reach Los Zetas' leader, El Patrón.

"Tell your boss, Manuel's been overstepping," Sergei said smoothly, his tone laced with amusement. "Sicarios in Mexico City? Unauthorized moves against my associates? He's making you all look sloppy."

The message traveled quickly, reaching El Patrón in his lavish estate within hours. The cartel leader, a man whose word carried the weight of life and death, was seething by the time he heard the details.

"Manuel," El Patrón growled, his voice heavy with menace, "thinks he can play his own games? That ends tonight. Send a message. Let him know what happens to those who cross me."

Chapter 22: Rock and a Hard Place

The night was quiet around Manuel Torres' sprawling hacienda, its manicured lawns and marble fountains lit by the soft glow of strategically placed floodlights. Inside, Manuel enjoyed a rare moment of calm, swirling a glass of whiskey as he plotted his next move. The peace was short-lived.

The stillness of the night around Manuel Torres' hacienda shattered as twelve men, shadows against the manicured gardens, moved with lethal precision. Clad in black tactical gear and armed with high-powered rifles, they navigated the property's perimeter like wolves stalking their prey. Their movements were synchronized, each man playing his part in the coordinated assault.

A faint rustle in the bushes alerted one of Manuel's guards. His flashlight beam cut through the darkness, briefly catching a glimpse of a gloved hand. The guard barely had time to yell, "¡Alerta!" before a silenced shot dropped him where he stood.

The alarm spread like wildfire, and within seconds, chaos erupted. The sharp staccato of gunfire cracked through the night, punctuated by the deep booms of grenades.

Inside the grand office, Manuel Torres jolted upright at the first distant crack of gunfire, the crystal glass of whiskey slipping from his fingers and shattering against the polished tile. His pulse pounded in his ears as he reached for the pistol stashed in his desk drawer.

"¡Idiotas! Defiéndanme!" he bellowed, his voice rising above the cacophony.

Manuel's guards, disoriented but fiercely loyal, scrambled to fortify their positions. The sound of bullets ricocheting off walls mixed with the pained cries of wounded men. Manuel moved to the window, peeking through the heavy curtains. His manicured lawn, once pristine, was now a warzone. Flames licked at the edges of a toppled vehicle, and bodies littered the ground like discarded chess pieces.

Outside, the attackers pressed forward. Two of El Patrón's men fell, clutching their wounds as the others continued their advance. A grenade exploded near the main gate, sending shards of iron and stone flying. One of Manuel's guards screamed as he was thrown back by the blast.

The battle raged on, both sides suffering casualties. The once-pristine lawn was now a battlefield, littered with bodies and stained with blood. Finally, three of the attackers breached the main house, their weapons sweeping the dimly lit interior.

Manuel raised his pistol with trembling hands, firing blindly at the shadowy figures advancing through the house. The first shot went wide, embedding itself into the ornate wood paneling. The second grazed one of the intruders, who barely flinched before delivering a brutal blow to Manuel's temple with the butt of his rifle.

Manuel staggered, his vision blurring as he crumpled to the floor. Before he could recover, rough hands hauled him to his feet. His arms were wrenched behind his back, and the cold steel of a gun barrel pressed against the base of his skull.

"Manuel Torres," one of the men growled, his voice low and venomous. "Your time has come. El Patrón sends his regards."

Manuel struggled, his face contorted with fury and fear. "You have no idea what you're doing! He'll…"

"Quiet," the man snapped, jamming the barrel against Manuel's temple. "Walk."

Under the cover of sporadic gunfire, the three men escorted Manuel out of the house. The remaining defenders, witnessing their boss's capture, began to retreat or surrender. The attackers melted into the shadows; their mission was complete.

As they disappeared into the night, Manuel's muffled curses faded into silence. The once-grand hacienda stood in ruins, a testament to the brutal efficiency of El Patrón's wrath.

By dawn, Manuel Torres was dragged into the opulent grand hall of El Patrón's mansion. The room was a stark contrast to the chaos of the previous night: polished marble floors gleamed under the light of gilded chandeliers, and the heavy scent of cigar smoke mixed with the faint aroma of freshly polished wood.

At the head of a long mahogany table sat El Patrón, a man whose presence demanded silence. His tailored suit fit him like armor, and his dark eyes burned with controlled fury. Behind him, a massive portrait of a jaguar loomed, a predator watching over its domain.

"Manuel," El Patrón said, his voice a dangerous whisper. "Do you know why you are here?"

Manuel, his wrists bound and his pride shattered, stood flanked by two armed guards. Sweat beaded on his forehead, and his bravado had been replaced by raw fear. "Patrón, I… I can explain."

"Manuel," El Patrón interrupted, his voice a low growl. "How could you betray me?"

Manuel, wrists bound, stood flanked by two armed guards. He swallowed hard, his bravado from the night before replaced with fear. "Patrón, I didn't betray you. I was expanding opportunities"

"Expanding opportunities?" El Patrón interrupted, slamming his fist on the table. "You were lining your pockets and jeopardizing my operations. Do you take me for a fool?"

Manuel shook his head desperately. "No, Patrón. I swear. It was a deal…"

"What deal?" El Patrón demanded. "Speak."

Manuel hesitated; his throat dry as he searched for words. The guard to his right raised his pistol, the barrel cold against Manuel's temple. "Talk," the guard ordered, his tone devoid of mercy.

Manuel stammered, his voice cracking under the weight of the moment. "It was… it was the Aryan Circle. They approached me. They wanted our product to establish dominance in the southern cities. They paid well, very well."

El Patrón's expression darkened, his hand curling into a fist. "The Aryan Circle," he repeated, his voice dripping with disdain. "You allied with white supremacists? Betrayed my organization for their blood money?"

"It wasn't betrayal!" Manuel protested. "It was… business. Their methods were effective. They helped secure territory quickly."

"Quickly," El Patrón said, standing slowly. The air in the room seemed to shift as his towering presence loomed over Manuel. "And how much of this blood money did you skim for yourself, Manuel?"

Manuel stammered, but the guards behind him yanked him back by the collar. "Speak!" one of them barked.

Chapter 23: Street Fighting Man

As Jake stirred his coffee absently, the realization hit him like a punch to the gut. Sitting at the café table with Julianna, he couldn't shake the weight of his mistake. They had broken the cardinal rule of their trade: plan, strike, and vanish. Instead, they had lingered, giving their enemies time to regroup and close in.

"We stayed too long," Jake muttered, his voice low, more to himself than to Julianna. He glanced at her, her calm demeanor belying the tension simmering beneath the surface. "We've trapped ourselves here until we finish this war."

Julianna tilted her head slightly, her sharp eyes studying him. "Then let's finish it," she said simply, her tone steady and resolute.

Jake leaned forward in his chair, stretching his elbows back in preparation for the next step. "Do you think we can track the phone you tossed earlier?" he asked Julianna.

She smirked, opening her laptop and typing quickly. "Of course. GPS should still be active unless someone's tampered with it." A map flickered to life on the screen, a blinking dot marking the phone's location. "Here it is, pinging from where I dropped it all the way to where it is now."

Jake's eyes narrowed as he studied the map. "Let's stake it out. Better we chase them, than the other way around."

Julianna grinned; her sharp features alight with anticipation. "You always know how to make a girl's day."

An hour later, they were parked in a dusty gray sedan that Jake had hotwired without breaking a sweat. The car, with its peeling paint and cigarette burns in the upholstery, was perfect for disappearing into the city's patchwork of forgotten neighborhoods.

The blinking dot on Julianna's laptop screen marked their target's location, less than a block away. Jake leaned back in the driver's seat, scanning the quiet street through the rearview mirror. "Not exactly the Beverly Hills," he said, his tone dry.

Julianna smirked; her eyes fixed on the screen. "No, but it's where the trouble is."

Jake added. "Yeah, perfect for keeping a low profile."

The hours passed slowly. They passed the time with idle chatter and burritos from a nearby food truck, their senses sharp despite the calm. The air inside the car grew heavy with the scent of spicy meat and diesel fumes.

"Do you ever think about doing something else?" Julianna asked suddenly, her voice softer than usual.

Jake raised an eyebrow. "Something else? Like what? Accountant? Librarian?"

She smirked. "You'd make a terrible librarian."

"True," Jake said, grinning. "What about you?"

Her smile faded slightly. "I've thought about it. But what's the point? This life… it's all I know."

Jake was about to reply when he noticed a pair of headlights creeping slowly down the street. He sat up straighter, his muscles tensing. "Hold that thought."

The car crawled past them; its occupants hidden behind dark-tinted windows. Jake and Julianna exchanged a glance but said nothing. Minutes later, the car looped back around, parking in front of the house where Julianna's phone was located. Two men stepped out, their movements deliberate and unhurried.

"That's them," Jake murmured, sliding out of the passenger seat. "Stay here and be ready to move."

Julianna nodded, her eyes following Jake as he crouched low and moved toward the rear of their car. From the shadows, he rested his rifle across the trunk, steadying his aim. The two men walked toward the house, their postures rigid, almost mechanical.

Jake exhaled slowly, his pulse steadying as he lined up his shot. His rifle rested on the car's trunk; its scope locked on one of the two men walking toward the house. The faint sound of their boots crunching against gravel carried through the still night.

When he squeezed the trigger, the rifle's muffled crack shattered the silence. The bullet struck true, and the man staggered backward before crumpling to the ground.

The second man spun around instantly; his pistol drawn. Muzzle flashes lit up the darkness as he fired wildly, the shots sparking off the car and sending Jake diving for cover.

"Get ready to move!" Jake yelled over his shoulder.

Julianna didn't hesitate. She slammed the car into gear, the tires squealing as they tore away from the curb. Jake barely managed to slide into the passenger seat, the door slamming shut behind him as bullets ricocheted off the rear bumper.

"They're still shooting!" Julianna yelled, gripping the wheel tightly.

"Yeah, I noticed," Jake replied, his voice dry, despite the adrenaline coursing through him. He twisted in his seat, watching the figures recede in the distance. "Keep going. They won't be catching up anytime soon."

Julianna glanced at him; her knuckles white against the steering wheel. "So much for a quiet stakeout."

Jake laughed, the tension easing slightly. "Yeah, not exactly by the book."

Jake rubbed his temples, thinking fast. "We don't have time to regroup. Quick, let's find another car and circle back."

Julianna nodded; her gaze focused on the road ahead. "Let's hope they're licking their wounds and not ready for battle."

Jake's lips curved; his smile grim. "They may be relentless, but they'll regret coming after us."

As they rounded a corner, Julianna's sharp gaze landed on a battered 4X4 pickup truck sitting beneath a flickering streetlight. She hit the brakes, the sedan skidding slightly as she pointed to the vehicle. "That one," she said, already calculating how quickly Jake could get it running.

Jake jumped out, darting toward the truck with practiced efficiency. Within moments, the door was open, wires exposed, and the engine growled to life. Julianna pulled up beside him, tossing their gear into the truck bed before sliding into the passenger seat.

"Let's see if our friends are still around," Jake steered the truck back toward the scene of the shootout. The pickup's engine growled as they navigated the quiet streets, tension crackling between them.

When they arrived, the neighborhood was eerily silent. Jake parked in the shadows of an alley, his eyes scanning the area. "There," he whispered, pointing, and added, "You drive, I'll take shotgun."

A sedan was parked in front of the house. One of the Sicarios was helping his injured partner into the passenger seat, their movements hurried but purposeful. The sound of distant sirens pierced the air, growing louder with each passing second.

"The cops are on their way," Julianna said, her voice low. "What's the play?"

Jake's eyes narrowed. "Just play it cool and follow them. Let's see where they lead us."

Julianna nodded, pulling the truck onto the road. She took a side street, circling back with a right turn and then two lefts until they were comfortably behind the sedan. The Sicarios wove through the city streets, their route erratic but with a clear destination in mind.

The neighborhood began to change as they moved deeper into the city. The lights grew dimmer, the roads rougher. Graffiti-covered walls and abandoned buildings loomed on either side. Julianna tightened her grip on the wheel, her jaw set. "This isn't exactly the scenic route."

"No," Jake agreed. "But it's exactly where I'd expect them to go."

The Sedan finally slowed, pulling into the cracked driveway of a dimly lit veterinary clinic. The neon sign buzzed weakly, its letters flickering and casting an eerie green hue over the scene. The building was small and decrepit, its windows barred and its paint peeling.

Jake parked the truck a block away, tucked into the shadows of an abandoned warehouse. He turned to Julianna, his expression serious. "We've got them cornered. Let's make it count."

"I'll take the high ground," Jake said, grabbing his rifle from the back. "You stay here and cover the entrance. Let's make sure they don't leave."

Julianna nodded, retrieving her hunting rifle and settling into the back seat of the truck. Her heart pounded as she adjusted her scope, her breaths coming slow and steady.

Jake moved silently through the factory, finding a broken window with a clear line of sight to the clinic. He spoke into his earpiece, his voice calm but firm. "Let me take the first shot on the uninjured one. You finish what I didn't with the wounded guy."

"Got it," Julianna replied, her tone steady despite the tension coiling in her chest.

Through his scope, Jake watched the uninjured Sicario placed near the entrance, his hand resting on a pistol. The injured man remained slumped in the passenger seat, his head leaning back against the headrest. Jake's finger hovered over the trigger; his mind razor-focused.

"Steady," he muttered to himself, exhaling slowly. The crosshairs aligned with the target's chest.

Julianna's voice crackled in his ear. "Whenever you're ready."

Jake squeezed the trigger. The bullet hit its mark, spraying blood across the clinic's front door. The previously uninjured Sicario crumpled instantly, his body collapsing onto the pavement.

Julianna shifted her focus, expecting the first wounded Sicario to exit the sedan and check on his partner. Instead, he slid across the seat into the driver's position and started the engine, the car lurching forward with erratic, jerky movements.

"Damn it!" Julianna hissed, steadying her aim. She fired twice, the shots ringing through the night, but the car fishtailed violently, throwing off her trajectory. Sparks flew as the sedan sideswiped a parked car, its rear bumper hanging precariously.

Jake, still in the factory, attempted another shot, but the wounded Sicario swerved the car sharply, disappearing into the narrow side street.

"He's getting away!" Julianna called through the earpiece; her voice tight with frustration. She climbed back into the driver's seat of their truck, gripping the wheel. "Get your ass down here, Jake. Now!"

"Already on my way," Jake replied, his voice calm despite the rush of adrenaline surging through him. Jake sprinted down the factory stairs, rifle slung over his shoulder. As he reached the truck, Julianna had already started rolling forward. Jake swung the passenger door open and dove inside.

"Go, go!" he shouted, slamming the door as Julianna floored the gas. The huge pickup truck's engine roared to life, almost catapulting them down the street instantly. Julianna gripped the wheel tightly as they went sideways around the corner, the tires squealing in protest.

The pursuit was on. Every nerve in Jake's body was electric, his mind racing with calculations. He glanced at Julianna, her jaw tight and her eyes locked on the road ahead.

"We can't lose him," she said through gritted teeth, weaving the truck through the streets in pursuit of the battered sedan.

"We won't," Jake assured her, loading a fresh clip into his rifle. "Not tonight."

"There!" Jake's voice cut through the tense silence as he spotted the battered sedan limping further down the street, its rear bumper dragging sparks against the asphalt.

Julianna gritted her teeth, her knuckles white against the steering wheel. "Let's finish this."

She pressed the accelerator, the truck's engine roaring as they closed the gap. The sedan swerved erratically, the injured driver struggling to maintain control.

As the chase barreled toward a busy intersection, Jake's sharp eyes caught the telltale flash of a garbage truck's headlights from the left. "Julianna…"

"Got it," she snapped, her focus razor-sharp.

With precision honed by years of high-stakes escapes, Julianna slammed the truck into the back of the sedan, the force sending the smaller car skidding into the intersection. The garbage truck had no time to stop. It plowed into the sedan, the sound of crunching metal and shattering glass filling the air.

Julianna quickly veered right, guiding the truck into the morning traffic and blending seamlessly with the commuters. Jake glanced back, the wreckage receding into the distance.

"Well," he said, his voice tinged with dark humor, "that's one way to take out the trash."

Julianna smirked, but her eyes remained on the road. "Let's hope they don't have backup."

Chapter 24: Gimme Shelter

The silence inside the truck was heavy, punctuated only by the rhythmic hum of the tires on the asphalt. Julianna kept her eyes on the road, her jaw set in concentration, while Jake occasionally glanced her way. The adrenaline that had propelled them through their escape was wearing thin, leaving behind an almost palpable exhaustion. As they drove further, the rough edges of the city began to soften, the barrios giving way to tree-lined streets and modest homes with tidy lawns.

Jake noticed Julianna's right hand resting on the wheel, her left hand doing most of the work. She rubbed her wrist absentmindedly, her movements tense.

"Did you get hurt?" Jake asked, his voice cutting through the quiet.

Julianna flexed her fingers and winced. "I think I sprained it pretty bad in that collision."

Jake frowned. "Pull over, let me drive."

"I'm fine," she snapped, then softened her tone. "We're almost there anyway."

He didn't push further, though his eyes lingered on her wrist, now visibly swollen. They turned onto a quiet cul-de-sac, the houses modest but well-kept. The safe house, an unassuming one-story home with a red-tiled roof and ivy climbing the front facade, came into view.

The truck rolled to a stop in the driveway, the engine ticking as it cooled. Julianna gripped the wheel for a moment longer than necessary, her fingers trembling slightly. The ivy-covered house stood quiet and unassuming, the promise of safety within its modest walls beckoning them.

Jake noticed the tension in her shoulders as she exhaled sharply, the exhaustion of the night finally catching up to her. "We made it," he said softly, his voice carrying a note of reassurance.

Julianna nodded, but when she reached back for the duffel bag, her injured wrist betrayed her, shaking under the strain.

"Stop," Jake said firmly, stepping out of the truck and coming around to her side. "I've got it. You're done for tonight."

She hesitated, pride warring with practicality, before conceding. "Fine. But don't start acting like you're in charge," she muttered, her tone half-heartedly sharp.

Jake smirked, shouldering the gear. "Wouldn't dream of it."

She glared at him, her pride evident in the tightness of her jaw, but relented, stepping aside as Jake hefted the bags over his shoulder. She fished the keys from her pocket and moved to unlock the front door. The key slipped from her fingers and clattered to the ground.

"Damn it," she hissed, bending down awkwardly to retrieve it. Her hand shook as she tried to slot the key into the lock, her movements clumsy and pained.

"Here," Jake said, taking the keys gently from her. "Just get inside."

He opened the door and carried the bags in, setting them down in the living room. Julianna sank into a worn but comfortable armchair, cradling her injured wrist. Jake returned from the kitchen with a makeshift ice pack, condensation already forming on the dish towel. He knelt beside Julianna, gently taking her hand in his. "This will help with the swelling," he said, his voice unusually tender.

She winced as he placed the ice on her wrist, but a faint smile tugged at her lips. "You know, for someone who spends most of his time breaking things, you're surprisingly good at fixing them."

Jake chuckled. "Don't get used to it. This is a one-time deal."

Julianna leaned back, closing her eyes as the ice numbed the pain. "You're a liar," she murmured, a teasing lilt in her voice.

"And you're stubborn, you know that?" Jake said, a hint of a smile tugging at the corner of his mouth.

"Takes one to know one," she shot back, though her words were tinged with fatigue.

Jake stood, stretching his back. "I'm going to go ditch the truck and grab some supplies. Do you need anything?"

Julianna opened her eyes, the corners crinkling slightly as she gave a tired smile. "More ice. And coffee. Lots of coffee."

"Got it," he said, grabbing a second set of keys from the counter. "Rest. I'll be back soon."

As the front door clicked shut behind him, Julianna exhaled slowly, leaning further back in the chair. The dull throb in her wrist was growing more insistent, each pulse a reminder of their chaotic escape. She glanced around the room, taking in the familiar surroundings of the safe house. It had been a refuge for her before, and now a place where they could catch their breath, plan their next moves, and feel, if only temporarily, removed from the dangers that constantly shadowed them.

But tonight, the sense of safety felt tenuous. Every creak of the house, every distant car engine, set her nerves on edge. Her hand throbbed, but she barely noticed as her mind drifted back to the events of the evening, the chase, the gunfire, the tension. She closed her eyes again, willing herself to relax, but sleep wouldn't come easily.

Jake parked the truck three blocks away, his movements methodical as he wiped down the interior and handles with a rag. Every action was calculated, a routine etched into muscle memory. As he locked the truck, he took one last look at the vehicle before vanishing into the shadows.

At the corner tienda, Jake moved swiftly, grabbing bandages, painkillers, and a few staples to tide them over. The fluorescent lights buzzed overhead, casting a harsh glow over the neatly packed shelves. The cashier barely glanced at him, accustomed to late-night visitors with hurried steps and quiet voices.

When Jake returned to the house, Julianna was slumped in the chair, her head tilted to one side. Her chest rose and fell in the steady rhythm of sleep. The bag of ice had slipped from her wrist, melting into a damp spot on the fabric of the armchair. Jake smiled faintly, shaking his head. Even stubbornness had its limits.

He set the groceries on the kitchen counter and began unpacking, his movements deliberate and quiet. The kitchen was small but functional, with a chipped tile backsplash and mismatched wooden cabinets. A single overhead light cast a warm glow over the room, softening its worn edges. Jake pulled out a frying pan and set it on the stove, the clatter making Julianna stir slightly but not wake.

The rich aroma of garlic and onions sizzling in a pan wafted through the small house, mingling with the faint scent of rain on warm pavement drifting in through the open window. Julianna stirred in the armchair, blinking groggily as her senses caught up with her.

She stretched, wincing slightly at the pull in her wrist, and looked toward the kitchen. Jake stood at the stove; his movements uncharacteristically relaxed as he stirred the pan. "You're full of surprises," she murmured, her voice raspy with sleep.

Jake glanced over his shoulder, a faint smile playing on his lips. "Figured you could use a proper meal. Ice and coffee only get you so far."

Julianna smirked, then set up straight. "If this is your way of impressing me, you're off to a good start." She flexed her fingers experimentally, wincing. "It helps, I think. What are you cooking?"

Ignoring the question, Jake walked over with a glass of water and the pain pills. "Take two of these and let me wrap your wrist."

Julianna accepted the pills with a raised eyebrow, swallowing them quickly. She watched as Jake crouched beside her, carefully winding the ace bandage around her wrist. His touch was firm but gentle, his focus uncharacteristically tender.

"You're full of surprises," she said softly, her lips curving into a small smile. "Didn't know you had a nursemaid streak."

"Don't get used to it," Jake replied, though the corner of his mouth twitched upward. "You're lucky I'm a sucker for tough women."

She laughed quietly, the sound more a breath than a chuckle. "I'll take it."

Jake returned to the stove, stirring the contents of the pan while they talked about the last 24 hours. They replayed the chase, the gunfire, and the tension, their voices low and reflective. Julianna's fatigue caught up with her mid-sentence, her words trailing off as her head lolled back against the chair.

When Jake turned around, she was sound asleep again, her wrist resting on her lap, now securely bandaged. He shook his head, a mixture of amusement and affection softening his expression. Gently, he lifted her into his arms, her body warm and pliant against him.

The bedroom was small, its furnishings sparse but clean. Jake laid her on the bed, tucking a blanket around her before brushing a stray strand of hair from her face. She murmured something unintelligible but didn't wake.

Back in the kitchen, Jake sat at the table with his plate of food, the room was quiet except for the faint hum of the refrigerator. He ate slowly, his thoughts churning. The events of the last day played out in his mind like a reel, each moment sharp and vivid. Despite the temporary respite, he knew the danger was far from over. But for now, he let the stillness wash over him, grounding him for the battles yet to come.

The next morning, Jake and Julianna both slept well into the day, their bodies demanding rest. It was Julianna who woke first, her wrist still tender but slightly less swollen. She padded quietly to the bathroom, wincing as she flexed her hand, then showered under the warm spray, letting the water wash away the grime and stress of the last two days.

After dressing and carefully re-wrapping her wrist, she made her way to the small kitchen. The house smelled faintly of the dinner Jake had made, now just a memory in the quiet morning. She brewed coffee, the rich aroma filling the space as she poured two steaming mugs. Balancing them carefully, she carried the cups back to the bedroom.

The morning light filtered through the curtains, casting soft patterns on the bedroom walls. Jake stirred as Julianna entered, her footsteps quiet but deliberate. She held two steaming mugs of coffee, the rich, dark aroma filling the room.

"Coffee delivery," she said with a sly smile, handing him one of the mugs.

Jake sat up, his hair mussed and his eyes still heavy with sleep. He took the mug, inhaling deeply before taking a sip. "You're spoiling me," he said, his voice low and rough.

"Don't get used to it," she replied, sitting on the edge of the bed.

Jake reached out, his hand curling around hers. His thumb brushed over the fresh bandage on her wrist. "How's the hand?"

"It's better," Julianna admitted. "Not great, but better."

Jake's gaze softened, and he tugged her closer, setting the mug aside. "You're tougher than you look, you know that?"

Julianna arched an eyebrow, a playful smile tugging at her lips. "I think you've mentioned that once or twice."

She laughed softly, her cheeks warming as they locked eyes. There was something unspoken between them, a shared understanding that went beyond words. The tension of the past days melted away as Jake pulled her into a firm embrace, their lips meeting in a deep, passionate kiss.

His expression softened further, and he brushed a strand of hair from her face. "Maybe, you bring out the best in me," he said simply.

Julianna leaned into Jake, resting her head against his chest. The steady rhythm of his heartbeat was a stark contrast to the chaos that had defined their recent days.

"You were incredible yesterday," Jake murmured, his fingers brushing a stray strand of hair from her face.

Julianna looked up at him, her eyes glinting with a mix of warmth and determination. "And you? You're a better partner than I give you credit for."

Jake's lips quirked into a small smile. "I'll take that as a compliment."

For a while, they sat in comfortable silence, the weight of the world temporarily held at bay. The danger was still out there, but for now, in this small, quiet house, they found a fleeting moment of peace.

Chapter 25: She Was Hot

Later that afternoon and evening, Jake and Julianna shared an unspoken agreement: they needed a break. The relentless chase, gunfire, and tension of the past days had taken their toll. For the rest of the day, they decided to shed the weight of their troubles and let the world outside their bubble fade, and Julianna needed time to heal.

Over the rim of her coffee mug, Julianna's gaze softened. "Let's play tourists today," she said, her tone almost wistful. "Take the day off. See the city like normal people."

Jake leaned back in his chair; one eyebrow raised. "Tourists, huh? You think strolling through the sights is going to fool anyone?"

Julianna smirked. "Sometimes, blending in means living like you belong. We could use a reset. Even you need a day off now and then."

Jake's lips quirked into a reluctant smile. "Fine. But no souvenir photos."

He understood the importance of a reset, and blending in was part of survival. They hired a cab driver for the day, a friendly middle-aged man named Raul, who spoke enough English to navigate their requests and delighted in sharing tidbits about his city.

The streets of Mexico City were a vibrant symphony of life, from the staccato honks of weaving taxis to the melodic calls of street vendors peddling tamales and trinkets. Raul, their cab driver for the day, navigated the chaos with the precision of a maestro, weaving through narrow lanes and gesturing to landmarks with practiced ease.

"That's the Palacio de Bellas Artes," Raul said, gesturing grandly toward the gleaming white building with its colorful domed roof. "Diego Rivera's murals are inside. A true masterpiece."

Julianna leaned closer to the window, her eyes lighting up. "It's beautiful," she murmured, her voice carrying a note of wonder.

Jake tilted his head, studying the architecture. "Not bad," he admitted, though his gaze never stopped sweeping for potential threats in the bustling crowd.

The cab slowed as they passed, allowing Jake and Julianna a better view. The architecture was a blend of neoclassical and art nouveau, its grandeur standing out even amid the bustling city. Raul continued his narration, leading them to the Zócalo, the main square.

"This is where history lives," Raul said. "The Catedral Metropolitans on one side, and the National Palace on the other."

They stepped out of the cab, and Julianna's eyes scanned the massive square. The Zócalo buzzed with activity, its massive square alive with the rhythm of Mexico City. Vendors hawked brightly colored crafts, their wares shimmering under the afternoon sun. The air was rich with the aroma of roasted corn and sugary churros, mingling with the faint strains of mariachi music drifting from a nearby street corner.

Julianna lingered near a stall selling handwoven textiles, her fingers tracing the intricate patterns. "Everything here feels alive," she said softly, more to herself than to Jake.

Jake, standing close enough to keep an eye on the crowd, chuckled. "That's one way to put it. But don't forget, alive also means unpredictable."

Julianna glanced at him, her lips curving into a knowing smile. "Relax, Jake. Not every crowd is a danger zone."

Jake huffed, but he couldn't entirely hide his amusement. "If you say so."

Once they were away from Raul's reach, Jake leaned close. "We need to talk about what's next. This break is nice, but we can't afford to lose focus."

Julianna nodded. "Agreed. Let's make the most of today, later tonight we plan."

Their next stop was Chapultepec Park, one of the largest city parks in the world. Raul drove them along avenues shaded by towering trees until they reached the entrance to Chapultepec Castle. Perched atop a hill, the castle looked like something out of a fairy tale, its turrets visible even from a distance.

As they climbed the winding path to Chapultepec Castle, the city stretched out below them in an endless sprawl of life and movement. The castle itself, perched like a crown atop its hill, exuded a regal charm that felt far removed from their reality.

Inside, sunlight filtered through stained glass windows, casting kaleidoscopic patterns on the polished marble floors. Julianna paused near a gilded banister, her fingers trailing over the intricate carvings. "It's hard to believe places like this exist," she said, her voice tinged with awe.

Jake stepped beside her, his gaze sweeping over the panoramic view beyond the windows. "A reminder of how far removed we are from a normal life," he muttered.

Julianna turned to him, her expression softening. "Or a glimpse of what we're fighting to get back to."

The castle's opulence seemed a world away from the tension they carried. Julianna ran her fingers over a carved banister, her thoughts momentarily lost in the elegance of another era. Jake's hand brushed hers, bringing her back. Their eyes met briefly, a silent acknowledgment of the precariousness of their momentary peace.

As the day progressed, Raul drove them to markets and hidden gems throughout the city. At La Ciutadella, an artisan market, Julianna admired vibrant textiles and hand-painted ceramics. The colors were almost overwhelming, a kaleidoscope of reds, blues, and yellows that spoke to the rich culture of the region. Jake purchased a leather-bound notebook, slipping it into his jacket pocket.

"For plans?" Julianna teased.

Jake smirked. "Something like that."

Lunch was street tacos near Mercado Roma, where they stood among locals savoring the flavors of freshly grilled meats, tangy salsas, and handmade tortillas. Raul recommended tamarind aguas frescas, which Julianna insisted they try. The sweet, tangy drink was refreshing, cutting through the heat of the day.

"So, what's the verdict?" Jake asked as Julianna took another sip.

"Delicious," she replied, holding up the cup. "Though I'm not sharing."

They both laughed a rare moment of levity in their otherwise fraught journey. The city around them seemed to pulse with life, the sounds of bustling markets and mariachi music weaving a vibrant tapestry. But beneath their laughter lay the unspoken understanding that their respite was temporary.

As the sun dipped below the horizon, Plaza Garibaldi came alive with music. Mariachi bands in ornate charro suits clustered together, their silver buttons gleaming under the streetlights. Trumpets blared, violins sang, and the rich baritone of a singer echoed across the square, drawing a small crowd.

Julianna clapped along; her grin infectious as a group launched into a spirited rendition of *"Cielito Lindo."* Jake stood beside her, his eyes scanning the crowd even as his lips twitched in a reluctant smile.

"You're supposed to enjoy this," Julianna teased, bumping his shoulder.

"I am," Jake replied, his voice low. "Just… multitasking."

When they returned to the taxi, Jake spoke softly. "We'll head back to the house soon. It's time to get back to work."

Julianna nodded; her expression serious now. "Agreed. Let's debrief and map out the next steps."

Their journey through the city had been a brief escape, a chance to remind themselves of the world outside their immediate danger. But as they made their way back, the weight of their reality began to settle once more. For Jake and Julianna, the day off was over; the fight was about to begin... again.

Back at the safe house, Jake stretched his arms over his head and dropped heavily into a chair. The evening air carried a cooling breeze through the open windows, rustling the curtains gently.

The quiet hum of the safe house enveloped them as they settled in for the night. Jake leaned back in his chair, his arms resting behind his head. "You know, I've been around the world. Seen a lot of cities," he said, his voice thoughtful. "But I've never actually *seen* them. Not like today."

Julianna sat cross-legged on the couch, her damp hair curling at the ends. "Yeah, today felt… different," she admitted. Her eyes drifted to the small leather-bound notebook Jake had bought earlier. "You planning on jotting down your travel highlights?"

Jake chuckled, reaching for the notebook. "More like mapping out our next moves. But who knows? Maybe I'll add a few notes about the best street tacos."

Julianna laughed softly, the sound filling the space between them. "Just don't forget to mention the tamarind drink. That was my favorite part."

Julianna smiled faintly, sinking into the couch across from him. "Yeah, that was nice. I haven't done much tourist stuff either." She sipped from a glass of water, her gaze thoughtful.

Jake let out a low chuckle. "I see people out there just living their lives. Makes you wonder what that would be like."

Julianna's smile faded slightly, and she leaned forward. "Don't go getting soft on me now," she teased, her voice steady. "We have miles to go before we sleep."

Her words brought a faint grin to Jake's face, though his eyes held a glimmer of something deeper. They spent the rest of the evening reviewing files and discussing their next steps. Their conversation grew quiet, almost cryptic, their plans forming in vague outlines that neither vocalized completely. The unspoken understanding hung between them like a taut wire, vibrating with tension.

As the night stretched on, Julianna flexed her wrist and gave Jake a small, triumphant smile. "It's feeling better," she said. "Not perfect, but better."

Jake nodded approvingly. "Good. We're going to need you at full strength soon enough."

With that, they decided to call it a night. Julianna rummaged through the cabinets, finding a half-empty bottle of tequila and two mismatched glasses. She poured them each a generous measure and raised her glass. She handed one to Jake and raised her own. "To survival," she said, her voice steady but laced with a faint smile.

Jake clinked his glass against hers, his expression softening. "To survival," he echoed. The tequila burned as it slid down, its warmth spreading through him like a small beacon in the dark.

For a moment, they sat in silence, the weight of the day balanced by the fragile peace of the evening. The distant hum of the city was a reminder that their fight was far from over, but for now, they allowed themselves this fleeting moment of reprieve.

As the bottle was returned to the cabinet, they made their way to the bedroom. The safe house grew silent save for the distant hum of the city outside, a rare moment of quiet before the storm they knew was coming.

Chapter 26: Strictly Memphis

The first rays of dawn crept through the blinds of the safe house, casting muted streaks of light across the floor. Jake and Julianna moved in practiced silence; the kind born of necessity. Their routine was precise: weapons secured, bags packed, and every detail double-checked.

Jake knelt by the floorboards, carefully sliding their weapons into a hidden compartment. "We'll come back for these, if we need to," he said, his voice low.

Julianna, standing near the door with her duffel bag, gave a dry smile. "With our luck? I'd bet on needing to."

They grabbed their bags and headed out to the waiting cab that would take them to the airport. As the city came alive around them, Jake leaned back in his seat, watching the streets of Mexico City pass by. Vendors set up their stalls, selling everything from freshly made tamales to trinkets for tourists. Julianna sat beside him, her gaze distant, likely turning over the plan in her head.

The flight to Miami was uneventful, the hours blending into a haze of airline announcements and the faint hum of the engines. Jake spent most of the time reviewing files on Julianna's laptop, while Julianna alternated between watching movies and napping. When they touched down, the humidity hit them like a wall as they stepped off the plane and into the terminal. They had a brief layover before catching their connecting flight to Memphis.

"Miami feels like a sauna," Julianna muttered, fanning herself with a travel brochure she'd grabbed from a kiosk.

"Better than dodging bullets," Jake replied, his eyes scanning their surroundings. He never truly relaxed, especially when in transit.

The golden hues of the setting sun bathed Memphis in a soft glow as their plane touched down. From the window, Julianna caught glimpses of the city's famed neon signs beginning to flicker to life, casting their vibrant colors against the darkening sky.

The rental car was deliberately nondescript, a silver sedan with enough scratches to blend seamlessly into any parking lot. As Jake drove, the hum of the engine was punctuated by the distant strains of blues music drifting from an open bar.

"Ever been to Graceland?" Julianna asked, breaking the silence.

Jake shook his head, eyes scanning the road. "Never found the time."

She smirked. "Maybe, after all this, we'll take a tour. You know, when we're not being hunted."

Jake chuckled softly. "Yeah, because nothing says 'relaxation' like Elvis memorabilia and fried peanut butter sandwiches."

Tracking Fred Alton's phone had been surprisingly simple once they accessed the right database. The signal led them to a modest motel near Graceland. The motel looked like it had been pulled straight out of a noir film. The flickering neon sign buzzed faintly, casting intermittent shadows across the cracked pavement. A few battered cars dotted the lot, their rusted frames silent witnesses to countless late-night arrivals and hasty departures.

Julianna placed a small camera on the dashboard, angling it toward the room Fred Alton's phone had led them to. "If he steps out, we'll see him," she said, adjusting the focus.

Jake leaned back, studying the social media photo of Fred on Julianna's phone. The man in the image had the kind of face that drew equal parts suspicion and disdain. "Doesn't look like someone who can stay off the radar," Jake remarked.

Time seemed to slow as the hours ticked by. The soft hum of the car's air conditioning and the distant sound of traffic filled the silence. Jake and Julianna alternated between scanning the motel and engaging in the kind of quiet conversation that only came in moments of waiting.

"You ever wonder, what a normal life would look like?" Julianna asked suddenly, her gaze fixed on the dimly lit motel room.

Jake glanced at her; his expression unreadable. "Sure. But normal doesn't come with an exit plan. You?"

She gave a small shrug. "Hard to imagine. I'm not sure I'd know how to sit still long enough to find out."

Jake chuckled lightly. "Guess we're in the right line of work then."

A truck rumbled past on the main road, its headlights briefly illuminating the motel's facade. Jake's eyes narrowed as he noticed movement near one of the rooms.

"There he is," Jake murmured, leaning forward to adjust the focus on his binoculars.

Julianna straightened in her seat. "Is it him?"

Jake studied the man stepping onto the motel balcony, the faint glow of a cigarette briefly illuminating his face. "Yeah, that's him," he confirmed, his voice low and steady.

Julianna exhaled slowly. "So, what's the plan?"

"We wait," Jake replied. "Let's see if he's meeting someone or just laying low."

Julianna leaned back in her seat, her fingers drumming lightly on the armrest. The air between them was charged with anticipation, each moment stretching longer than the last. Outside, the sounds of the city faded into the background as their focus narrowed to the man on the balcony.

The night was just beginning, and so was the hunt.

Fred eventually stubbed out his cigarette and disappeared back into his room. The hours dragged on, the only light in his window coming from the soft gray glow of a television. Julianna stretched, then rolled her shoulders and stifled a yawn. "Looks like we may be in for the night," she murmured.

Jake nodded. "Yeah. Why don't you try to get some sleep, while I keep watching?"

"Okay. Wake me in a few hours, and I'll take over," she said, adjusting the seat into a reclining position.

The stakeout settled into a rhythm of quiet vigilance. They took turns watching Fred's room, each stealing moments of restless sleep as the night stretched on. The cramped car offered little comfort, and the tension of the situation kept true rest just out of reach.

As the first rays of sunlight broke over the horizon, the motel parking lot began to stir. Jake and Julianna, bleary-eyed but sharp, watched as Fred stepped out of his room, a duffel slung over his shoulder.

Julianna perked up. "Looks like he's finally moving."

Jake started the car, keeping his distance as Fred climbed into a shiny black Cadillac SUV. The engine growled to life, and the vehicle eased out of the lot.

They followed cautiously, staying far enough back to avoid suspicion. "What are the odds he's leading us somewhere useful?" Julianna asked.

Jake smirked. "Considering how things usually go for us? About fifty-fifty."

"Well, so much for excitement," Jake said. "He's just grabbing breakfast."

Through the diner's grease-streaked window, Fred Alton sat at the counter, shoveling eggs and bacon into his mouth as he scanned his phone. He seemed oblivious, almost carefree, but Jake wasn't fooled.

She slipped out of the car and returned fifteen minutes later with two bags of fast-food breakfast and steaming cups of coffee. They ate in the car, the smell of greasy hash browns and egg sandwiches filling the cabin.

"He doesn't look like a man on the run," Julianna remarked, tearing into a fast-food breakfast sandwich.

"No," Jake agreed, his eyes never leaving Fred. "But everyone looks innocent, until they don't. But he has to be staying in this dump for a reason," Jake added, gesturing toward the motel as they watched Fred return. "If his business was finished, he'd be long gone."

Julianna nodded, sipping her coffee. "I guess we just settle in for a long surveillance then. He's our best lead at this point."

The hours dragged on, stretching into an uneasy rhythm. The black Cadillac remained parked in the motel lot, its presence a quiet reminder that Fred Alton wasn't going anywhere soon.

Julianna finished the last of her coffee, her sharp eyes flicking between the vehicle and the motel entrance. "He's hiding something. Nobody holes up in a place like this unless they're running from something or someone."

Jake nodded, his jaw set. "If he doesn't move soon, we'll have to make him."

As the sun climbed higher, the day ahead promised one thing: Fred Alton wouldn't be hiding for long.

Chapter 27: Out of Time

The oppressive afternoon heat seeped into the car, turning the cramped space into a makeshift oven. Jake adjusted the air conditioning, but it did little to combat the suffocating humidity. He leaned against the driver's seat, eyes trained on Fred Alton's door, while Julianna scrolled through her phone, her brow furrowed.

"Anything new?" Jake asked, breaking the silence.

Julianna shook her head. "No, but Fred's been sitting tight for too long. It's only a matter of time before something happens."

As if on cue, two motorcycles roared into the parking lot, their engines disrupting the quiet rhythm of the cicadas.

"Here we go," Julianna muttered, lowering her phone and sitting up straight.

Jake watched as two men dismounted, their leather jackets worn and patched with insignias that suggested allegiance to something larger. "Did you catch the patches?"

Julianna grabbed her phone, angling it for a few discreet photos. "Got them," she said. "I'll run these through a database once we're clear."

They watched as one of the men knocked on Fred's door. It opened after a moment, and the bikers stepped inside. The door shut with a faint thud, leaving Jake and Julianna to speculate in the silence.

"What do you think?" Julianna asked, leaning back in her seat.

"Could be a handoff. Could be trouble. Either way, we're not moving until we see what's in that room," Jake replied, his eyes fixed on Fred's door.

Time seemed to crawl while they waited. About twenty minutes later, the door opened again. The bikers stepped out, but now one of them carried a knapsack slung over his shoulder. It wasn't there when they arrived.

"Bingo," Julianna murmured. "Looks like a pickup or delivery."

Jake nodded. "Question is, do we stay here or follow them?"

"Let's see where they go," Julianna said, already starting the car.

The bikers left the motel with an air of casual confidence, the rumble of their engines fading as they hit the main road. Julianna started the car out of the parking lot, keeping a safe distance as she adjusted the rearview mirror.

"Think they're running something for Fred?" Julianna asked, her voice steady but curious.

"Could be. Or they're delivering something to him," Jake replied. "Either way, they've got answers we need."

The motorcycles led them onto the highway, weaving effortlessly through the light traffic. Julianna maintained her distance, blending into the flow of vehicles while keeping the bikers in sight. As the cityscape faded into the countryside, Julianna glanced out the window.

"Heading into no man's land," she remarked. "This feels like more than a casual meeting."

Jake nodded. "Wherever they're going, it's off the beaten path. Let's see where this leads."

The cityscape of Memphis gave way to open fields and dense clusters of trees as they crossed into Mississippi. The sun dipped lower, casting long shadows across the road. The air inside the car felt thick with anticipation.

"You know," Julianna said, breaking the silence, "if they're heading out this far, it's not for a social call. Whatever they're carrying is important."

Jake nodded in agreement. "Yeah. Let's hope it's worth the ride."

The paved roads gave way to narrow lanes lined with overgrown trees, their shadows stretching long in the fading light. Julianna gripped the wheel tighter, her eyes narrowing as the bikers slowed near a run-down honky-tonk bar. Neon beer signs buzzed faintly in the windows, their light casting eerie patterns on the cracked asphalt.

"They're stopping," Julianna said, pointing to the group of men loitering outside.

The bikers exchanged hand signals with the group as they passed, the gestures deliberate and familiar. Jake watched as the motorcycles continued down a dirt road, disappearing into the dense forest.

"That's it," Julianna muttered, pulling the car to the side of the road. "We can't follow them without tipping our hand."

Jake nodded, his gaze lingering on the bar. "But we know the kind of people they're running with. That's a start."

The ride back to Memphis was steeped in quiet tension, the hum of the tires on the asphalt filling the space between them. Jake rested his head against the window, the neon lights of passing diners and gas stations casting fleeting patterns across her face.

"You think Fred's in bed with these guys?" she asked finally, breaking the silence.

Jake glanced at her; his hands steady on the wheel. "If he's not, he's playing close enough to get burned. And if they're working with Los Zetas… this thing's bigger than we thought."

Julianna let out a slow breath. "Aryan Circle and Los Zetas. Strange alliance, but the motive's clear. Money and control."

Jake's expression darkened. "And Fred's the key to tying it all together. He knows more than he's letting on."

Back at the motel, the air in the rental car was heavy with frustration. Julianna flipped open her laptop, her fingers flying across the keyboard as she uploaded the photos of the bikers' patches.

Jake leaned against the window, his gaze flicking to Fred's room. The curtains were drawn tight, the faint glow of a television visible through the fabric.

Julianna's sharp intake of breath snapped Jake's attention back to her. "What is it?"

She turned the screen toward him, her face grim. "Aryan Circle," she said. "White supremacist gang. Known for drug running, violence, and expanding into new territories. And Tupelo's right in their wheelhouse."

Jake's jaw tightened. "Aryan Circle and Los Zetas teaming up. That's a new one."

"It's not just drugs," Julianna continued, scrolling through an article. "They're looking for power plays."

Jake exhaled sharply. "That would track with what we already know. If they're tied to this, it's not a coincidence."

Julianna nodded. "And there's more. They used to be known to work as enforcers or couriers, but this is new territory for them. If they're in bed with Fred Alton, we're looking at a whole new level of danger."

Jake nodded thoughtfully. "Makes sense. We're going to have to tread carefully. This is bigger than just a bad deal gone sideways."

Julianna leaned back in her seat, her fatigue showing. "So, what now?"

Jake leaned back in his seat; his gaze fixed on the flickering neon sign of the motel. "Fred's staying here for a reason," he said, his voice quiet but resolute. "And we're going to find out why."

Julianna shut her laptop, exhaustion creeping into her voice. "But if he doesn't move soon, I might drag him out myself. I'm not built for stakeouts this long."

Jake smirked, the tension easing slightly. "Patience, Jules. If there's one thing I've learned, it's that people like Fred always make a move. We just have to wait for the right moment."

As the night deepened, they settled into their vigil once more, the weight of their mission pressing down on them. They were running out of time, but neither was willing to back down.

Julianna sighed but didn't argue. "Alright. But if he gets breakfast tomorrow without us eating first, I'm storming that diner myself."

Jake smirked, the tension easing just slightly. "Deal. Let's hope he makes a move soon."

Chapter 28: Honky, Tonk Women

The dashboard clock blinked at 9:02 PM as the door to Fred Alton's motel room creaked open. A faint slice of light cut across the dim parking lot, followed by Fred's shadowed figure stepping out. Jake straightened in his seat, his fingers brushing the ignition key out of instinct.

"There he is," Julianna murmured, her gaze sharp as she closed her laptop. "Finally."

Fred climbed into his black SUV, the low rumble of the engine breaking the silence. He pulled out of the lot without hesitation, merging onto the main road.

"Heading south?" Jake guessed as he started their car.

"Probably back to Tupelo," Julianna said, tightening her seatbelt. "Let's stick close but keep it subtle. He's not stupid."

They followed at a safe distance, the glow of Fred's taillights fading in and out as he navigated the Memphis streets and merged onto the highway heading south. For the first twenty minutes, the ride was uneventful. Jake kept their car far enough back to avoid suspicion, but close enough to maintain visual contact.

After about 45 minutes on the road, Fred pulled into a gas station. Jake slowed as they approached, watching as Fred stepped out to pump gas. Julianna leaned forward. "Let's not sit here like sitting ducks. We should pull over somewhere and let him go ahead."

Jake hesitated, considering the gamble. "Yeah, that might work. But we'll have to time it just right."

They drove another twenty-five miles before pulling into a brightly lit convenience store parking lot. The air was thick with humidity, and the hum of fluorescent lights buzzed overhead. They sat in silence for a few minutes, the tension palpable.

"There he is," Julianna said suddenly, pointing as Fred's SUV sped past them on the highway.

Jake started the engine and pulled out carefully, slipping into the flow of traffic. "Game on."

The glow of Fred's taillights flickered as his SUV veered onto the same dusty side road they'd scouted earlier. Jake slowed the car, keeping a safe distance as the darkened stretch of road gave way to a narrow gravel path.

The familiar neon lights of the honky-tonk bar emerged through the trees, their garish colors slicing through the night. Outside, a row of motorcycles gleamed under the buzzing signs, and clusters of men loitered by the entrance, their postures rigid and watchful.

Julianna leaned forward, her voice barely above a whisper. "Looks even worse after dark."

Jake's jaw tightened as he pulled off the road, parking under the cover of trees. "This isn't a drop-off. This is a meeting," he muttered, eyes scanning the crowd outside the bar.

Up ahead, Fred pulled into the gravel parking lot of the honky-tonk bar they'd seen earlier. Men loitered by the entrance, their postures tense and watchful.

"What do you think this means?" Julianna asked, whispering.

Jake's jaw tightened. "I don't like the looks of this place at night."

Jake shifted the car into reverse, his movements deliberate as he tried to back away, unnoticed. "We're too exposed here," he murmured. "We'll regroup down the road."

But before they could retreat, two shadows emerged from the trees, stepping into their path. The glint of metal in their hands was unmistakable. One man carried a shotgun held low but ready, while the other flanked the passenger side, his weapon trained on Julianna's window.

"We've got company," Jake said under his breath, his hand hovering over the gearshift.

The man in front raised his hand, signaling for them to stop. "Don't even think about it," he barked, his voice sharp in the still night.

Jake's grip tightened on the wheel, his mind racing. "What's the plan?" Julianna asked, her voice steady but low.

"Stay calm," Jake replied. "We don't have room for mistakes here."

The second man stepped closer; his shotgun raised. Without warning, the deafening crack of a shot shattered the air, and the car lurched as the front tire exploded.

"Damn it!" Jake cursed, slamming on the brakes as the car tilted unevenly. The man on the passenger side yanked open Julianna's door.

"Out," he growled, his tone leaving no room for negotiation. "Both of you. Now."

Jake exchanged a quick glance with Julianna. Her eyes were wide, but her expression was steely. Slowly, they stepped out of the car, keeping their hands visible. The cool night air did little to mask the heat of the moment, the tension crackling like static electricity.

The two men herded Jake and Julianna toward the center of the gravel lot, their weapons raised. The sharp crunch of boots against the ground filled the silence.

"Who the hell are you, and what are you doing here?" the man with the shotgun barked, his eyes narrowing as he studied them.

Jake raised his hands slightly, keeping his voice calm. "Just passing through. Got turned around. Didn't mean to end up here."

The man sneered. "Bullshit. We've seen your car hanging around all day. You're not lost. You're snooping."

Julianna clenched her jaw, but Jake shot her a warning glance before taking a small step forward. "We don't want trouble," he said evenly. "Let us go, and you'll never see us again."

The man's laugh was harsh, cutting through the tension. "You've already got trouble, pal."

The honky-tonk door creaked open, and more figures emerged, their silhouettes backlit by the garish neon glow. One of them, a burly man with a grizzled beard and an air of authority, strode forward.

"What the hell's going on?" he demanded, his gravelly voice carrying across the lot.

Jake kept his voice calm and measured. "Just passing through. Didn't mean to intrude."

The man sneered, his gaze flicking between Jake and Julianna. "Bullshit. You've been snooping around all day. Thought we wouldn't notice?"

The man on the porch, clearly in charge, strode closer, his boots crunching on the gravel. He stopped near Fred, who had been standing by his SUV, watching the scene unfold. "You know these two characters?" the man asked, jerking his thumb toward Jake and Julianna. "Looks like they were following you."

Fred squinted through the darkness; his expression cautious. He hesitated for a moment, before shaking his head. "Nope. Never seen 'em before."

The grizzled man, Sarge, judging by the murmurs of the others, approached, his sharp gaze sweeping over Jake and Julianna. "Who are they?" he asked the man with the shotgun.

"Caught them creeping around," the man replied. "Looks like they've been tailing Fred."

Sarge rubbed his beard thoughtfully, his expression darkening. "Well, that complicates things. We can't have loose ends."

He snapped his fingers, and the two armed men grabbed Jake and Julianna, shoving them toward the back of the lot. "Take them to the barn," Sarge ordered. "Search their car, strip it for anything useful, and get rid of it. Make sure there's nothing left behind."

Jake's mind raced as he and Julianna were marched toward the shadows. Her sharp intake of breath told him she was just as tense. He caught her eye briefly, their silent communication clear: stay calm, wait for the right moment.

As they disappeared into the darkness, the faint hum of the honky-tonk music faded behind them, replaced by the crunch of gravel and the ominous creak of the barn door swinging open.

Chapter 29: Don't You Lie to Me

The barn was suffused with a thick darkness, the faint moonlight seeping through cracks in the warped wood. Jake hung from the rafters, his arms pulled taut above his head, the coarse ropes biting into his wrists. His boots barely grazed the dusty floor, offering little relief from the weight pressing on his shoulders. Beside him, Julianna hung in a similar predicament, her chest rising and falling in shallow breaths as she struggled to adjust her weight.

"Still with me?" Jake asked, his voice hoarse but steady.

Julianna turned her head, her lips curling into a faint smirk despite the pain etched across her face. "Yeah. Though this is far from my preferred way of spending time together."

Jake huffed a dry laugh. "Don't worry. When we get out of this, I'll find a place with less… rustic charm."

Julianna let her head rest against her arm, her voice dipping into wry humor. "No barns, no ropes. Got it."

Their brief levity was cut short by the opening of the barn door. A harsh beam of yellow light sliced through the darkness as Sarge entered, flanked by Fred and two goons. The faint crackle of a cattle prod announced their arrival, grating against the oppressive silence.

"Well, ain't this a picture," Sarge drawled, his gravelly voice tinged with mockery. "Two professionals strung up like piñatas. How the mighty have fallen."

Julianna's head lolled to one side; her brown eyes gleaming with defiance. "I've seen better piñatas," she said, her voice dry. "At least, they usually have candy."

Fred leaned against a rickety wooden table, his hand casually resting on Jake's rifle. "You know," he said, turning the weapon over like a prized artifact, "I always heard you were good, Jake. Precise. Ruthless. But seeing you like this? Doesn't quite match the legend."

Jake's gaze didn't waver, even as the goon with the cattle prod stepped closer, electricity sparking from its tip. "What's the plan here, Fred?" Jake asked evenly. "You going to kill us, or just bore us to death with your gloating?"

Fred's grin twisted into a sneer. "You know better than anyone, Jake. A job like this isn't about speed, it's about the payoff."

Sarge stepped forward, his boots crunching against the dirt floor. "We've got questions. You've got answers. The sooner you start talking, the easier this gets." He nodded to the goon, who jabbed the prod closer to Jake's side.

The crackling sound filled the barn, followed by a flash of light and the acrid scent of ozone. Jake's body jolted, muscles spasming as he clenched his jaw against the pain.

"Go to hell," he growled through gritted teeth.

Fred chuckled darkly. "You're halfway there, pal. Now, who sent you?"

As the questioning dragged on, the cattle prod alternating between Jake and Julianna, her patience finally snapped. She raised her head, her voice cutting through the barn like a whip. "Fred, we both know you're just the middleman. The real players? They're not here. They don't trust you, and for good reason."

Fred's smug expression faltered, and Sarge's head snapped toward her, his eyes narrowing. "Watch your mouth," Sarge growled.

"Why?" Julianna shot back; her voice laced with venom. "Afraid I'll say something true?"

The goon with the prod moved toward her, but Fred raised a hand, stopping him. He stepped closer to Julianna, his face inches from hers. "You've got guts, I'll give you that," he said, his tone low and dangerous. "But guts won't save you."

Julianna's lips curled into a defiant smile. "Neither will your boss when this all goes south."

Fred's grin twisted into a sneer. "Big words for someone hanging by a thread. Let's see how long that confidence lasts."

The goon jabbed the prod forward, and the barn was filled with a burst of light. Jake clenched his jaw, refusing to give Fred the satisfaction of a reaction. Beside him, Julianna's expression hardened, her mind racing as she tried to formulate a plan.

The barn fell silent again, save for the faint crackling of the cattle prod and the sound of heavy breathing. Sarge stepped closer, his eyes gleaming with a mix of curiosity and menace.

"Who are you working for?" Fred asked, nodding to the goon. The man jabbed the prod into Jake's side, sending another jolt through his body. Jake gasped, his muscles spasming as pain coursed through him. As the shock subsided, Jake's voice came through hoarse but defiant. "I was working for you, but you have a strange way of saying thank you."

Fred's eyes narrowed as he processed the words. His expression shifted, and a dark smile crept across his face. "That was you, wasn't it? The hitter Eddie hired. That was some nice work you did in LA. So, how'd you end up here?"

For the next couple of minutes, Fred and Sarge took turns questioning them. The goon's cattle prod punctuated each refusal to answer, each evasive reply. Bits and pieces of the story spilled out, enough to keep Fred intrigued but never the full truth. Jake's body hung limp, his head lolling forward, while Julianna clung to consciousness, her breathing shallow.

When Jake finally passed out and Julianna's head slumped against her chest, Fred stepped back, wiping sweat from his brow. "Take them down," he instructed the goons. "Tie them up against that post. I don't want them choking up there."

The two men complied, unhooking Jake and Julianna from the rafters and dragging their limp bodies to the barn's central support beam. Rope bound their wrists again, this time securing them to the wooden post. Julianna's head lolled to the side, and Jake's breaths came in shallow gasps.

Fred turned to Sarge. "I better call Barstow about this. We can continue later when they come to."

Sarge grunted in agreement. "You better. I don't like loose ends."

The group filed out of the barn, leaving Jake and Julianna slumped against the post, their bodies bruised and their breaths shallow. The heavy barn door creaked shut, plunging the space into silence once more.

Julianna stirred first, her voice barely a whisper. "Jake…"

"I'm here," he replied weakly, his head rolling against the post to meet her gaze.

She exhaled shakily, her defiance still flickering in her eyes. "We're not done yet. You know that, right?"

Jake managed a faint smile, his voice steady despite the pain. "Not even close."

Chapter 30: Gotta Get Away

Julianna slumped against the rough wooden post, her chest heaving with shallow breaths. The ropes cut into her wrists, raw and bruised from hours of struggle. "Jake," Julianna whispered, her throat dry and voice rasping. "Come on, Jake. Stay with me." Still nothing. Panic twisted in her chest as she shifted closer, her shoulder brushing against him. "Don't do this to me, Jake. We're not done yet. Wake up."

Jake lay crumpled on the dirt floor beside her, motionless. For a terrifying moment, she thought he was gone. "Jake!" she hissed, louder this time, nudging him with her shoulder. "Wake up, damn it!"

After what felt like an eternity, a faint groan escaped Jake's lips. His eyelids fluttered, barely lifting, and his voice was no more than a whisper. "Julianna... you okay?"

Relief flooded her, though the urgency of their predicament left no time to savor it. "Yeah, it's me," she said. "But we've got to move. They'll be back any second."

Jake blinked, his eyes struggling to focus. "What... what's the situation?"

"The ropes are brutal," Julianna muttered through clenched teeth, her voice shaking with effort. "But they're fraying... give me one more second."

"You've got this," Jake murmured, his strength slowly returning. "Just tell me what to do."

"Jake," she said again, her voice firmer now. "You've got to help me. Shake off the delirium. We've got to get out of here."

Jake's breathing deepened as he fought to pull himself together. He lifted his head slightly, grimacing as the motion sent a wave of pain through his body. "I'm trying," he said through gritted teeth. "What's the status?"

Her fingers, raw and trembling, finally found a weak point in the ropes. With one last surge of effort, she managed to free her right hand. "Got it," she whispered triumphantly, shaking off the rope and immediately moving to Jake. Ignoring the throbbing pain in her wrist, she reached over to Jake, fumbling with the ropes that held him. "Hold still."

Jake groaned, holding still despite the pain, his body sagging against the post. "You're a damn miracle worker," he muttered, his voice laced with pain.

Julianna didn't reply. Her focus was absolute as she worked at the ropes. Finally, they came loose, and she staggered to her feet, making her way to the table where their gear lay.

"We've got to hurry," she said, her voice urgent. "They could be back any second."

Jake rubbed his wrists as the ropes fell away, wincing at the raw skin beneath. He stumbled as he stood, but Julianna caught his arm, steadying him.

"Thanks," he muttered, his voice barely above a whisper. He took a deep breath, shaking his head as if trying to clear it. "What's the plan?"

Julianna hesitated, scanning the barn. "Not sure yet," she admitted. "But no matter what, we need to take our electronics. Everything else is replaceable."

Jake nodded; his movements sluggish but deliberate. He limped toward the table, his eyes scanning their gear. His fingers closed around a 9mm pistol, but when he checked the chamber, it was empty. "Figures," he muttered. He grabbed a couple of loaded magazines from the pile, sliding one into the gun and pulling the slide back with a satisfying click.

"Ready," he said, turning to Julianna. "How's your wrist?"

She gave a weak shrug. "It hurts like hell, but I'll manage. What about you? Are you good to move?"

Jake nodded slowly. "Not much choice, is there?" He straightened, his resolve hardening. Despite the pain etched across his face, his light blue eyes burned with determination.

Julianna handed him a small satchel with their essential electronics, then slipped her own pack over her shoulder. "Let's get out of here," she said, her voice firm.

As they moved toward the barn's side door, the sound of a pickup truck door slamming and boots crunching on gravel sent a jolt through both of them. Jake motioned for Julianna to stay low, his pistol ready. The footsteps grew louder, accompanied by faint voices. Two men were returning, their conversation growing clearer.

"I told you I heard something," one said.

"You're paranoid. They're not going anywhere," the other replied, but his tone held doubt.

Julianna looked at Jake; her eyes wide. He pointed to the ladder leading to the hayloft. She nodded and began to climb silently, her injured wrist screaming in protest. Jake followed; each movement deliberate to avoid creaking the old wood.

As the men entered the barn, Jake gestured for Julianna to keep moving. She reached the loft's edge, positioning herself above the men as Jake quietly unslung a length of rope he'd grabbed.

The two men stopped near the post where Jake and Julianna had been tied. "What the hell?" one of the men barked, stopping dead in his tracks. "They're gone!"

Before either could reach for their gun, Jake looped a length of rope over the first man's neck and yanked hard. The man thrashed, his gurgled choking breaking the tense silence, as Julianna dropped from the loft, driving her knee into the second man's ribs with a sickening crack.

Julianna stood over the bodies, breathing heavily. "Well," she muttered, "so much for subtle."

Jake gave her a faint smirk. "Subtle's overrated."

Kneeling beside the closest body, Julianna rifled through his pockets, her hands steady despite the adrenaline coursing through her veins. She pulled out a set of truck keys, holding them up with a grim expression.

"We're taking this." As she made her way to the truck Jake watched her go, his grip tightening on his pistol. When she was safely inside, he moved quickly to the weapons locker in the corner of the barn, scooping as many weapons as he could into a bag. As he sprinted toward the truck, the sound of a shout rang out, followed by the deafening crack of gunfire.

Bullets slammed into the truck's frame as Jake vaulted into the back. Without hesitation, he raised his rifle and fired, the recoil sharp against his shoulder. Two of their attackers dropped instantly, their weapons clattering to the ground.

The truck roared as Julianna punched the gas. The tires spun in the dirt before catching, fishtailing wildly. The abrupt motion swung the truck around, and Jake faced their attackers. When the truck stopped swinging from side to side, he steadied his aim, sighting Sarge through the scope. One clean shot and Sarge's head snapped back, his body crumpling to the ground.

"Nice shot," Julianna called over the roar of the engine as the truck lurched forward.

The vehicle again swayed violently, making it impossible for Jake to line up another shot. He braced himself, gripping the side of the truck as they barreled toward the compound's exit.

Up ahead, Julianna spotted a line of motorcycles parked near the fence. Without hesitation, she swerved, plowing through them. The sound of metal against metal, and plastic crunching filled the air as the bikes toppled like dominoes.

Jake clung to the truck bed; his knuckles white as bullets pinged off the metal around him. Returning fire when he could, he managed to take out another pickup truck and a motorcycle giving chase. But their pursuers were relentless, gaining ground despite his efforts.

Jake's hands sifted through the bag of weapons, his fingers closing around something familiar and heavy. A slow grin broke across his face as he held up a grenade.

"Hold steady!" he shouted to Julianna, lobbing the grenade toward the cluster of vehicles behind them. The explosion lit up the night, sending debris and bodies flying.

He didn't stop. Two more grenades followed in quick succession, each blast carving a path of destruction. The remaining pursuers faltered, their vehicles swerving to avoid the wreckage of twisted motorcycles and overturned vehicles.

"That'll hold them," Jake muttered, slumping against the truck bed as the compound faded into the distance. Julianna glanced back at him through the rear window, her expression a mix of relief and determination.

"Hang on," she said, her voice steady. "We're not out of this yet."

Chapter 31: Laugh, I Nearly Died

Julianna brought the truck to a grinding halt at the edge of the dirt road. Dust billowed up around them, briefly obscuring the view as Jake scrambled into the passenger seat. She jammed the accelerator, sending the truck lurching forward as the wheels clawed at the uneven surface.

Jake winced, settling into his seat and bracing one hand against the dashboard. "I'll say this much," Jake muttered, his voice rough with pain but tinged with admiration. "You've got a knack for this. Might have missed your calling as a getaway driver."

Julianna shot him a quick glance, a faint smile tugging at her lips. "Well, you're not exactly the easiest passenger. How're you holding up?"

Jake leaned back, resting his head against the seat as he closed his eyes. "I've had worse days," he admitted, his lips twitching into a faint grin. "Though this does rank pretty high on the 'worst dates ever' list."

They both tried to laugh, but the effort sent sharp pains through their battered bodies, and they fell silent for a moment, the tension broken only by the roar of the engine and the rattle of loose tools in the truck bed.

"Take a right at the end of the road," Jake said, his voice firm despite the exhaustion weighing on him. "I have a plan."

Julianna shot him a wary glance, her brow furrowing. "Memphis? Seriously? Feels like walking right into a trap."

Jake shook his head. "We're not going to Memphis," Jake said, shaking his head. His voice was cryptic but firm. As they neared the paved road, he added, "Pull into that church parking lot."

Before he could elaborate, Julianna slammed on the brakes, the truck skidding to a halt. She then parked it in the shadows of a row of trees. Without hesitation, she jumped out, sprinting toward an older sedan parked beneath a flickering streetlamp. Her movements were fluid and precise, even as pain etched lines of strain on her face.

Jake hauled their gear out of the truck, his muscles protesting. He dumped the bags into the back seat of the sedan just as Julianna worked her magic, bringing the engine sputtering to life.

"Remind me never to leave you unsupervised at a dealership," Jake quipped as he climbed into the passenger seat, his fingers brushing over the satchel of gear in his lap.

Julianna grinned, her breath coming in quick bursts. "You won't survive long in my line of work without learning a few tricks."

"Touché," Jake muttered, slamming the door as she pulled out of the lot. "Take a left."

Julianna's brow furrowed in confusion. "You mean back the way we came?"

"Exactly," Jake said, his tone steady despite the tension crackling in the air. "We're heading toward Birmingham. This way, we can see if anyone's following us."

The sedan sped down the darkened road, its headlights slicing through the inky blackness. Julianna's hands gripped the wheel tightly, her knuckles white against the faded leather. Every sound seemed amplified, the hum of the tires on asphalt, the faint whistle of wind through the cracked window, the rhythmic thud of Jake's heart pounding in his chest.

As they approached a bend in the road, the faint glow of headlights appeared in the distance, growing brighter with each passing second. Julianna's breath hitched as a convoy of motorcycles roared past them, their engines growling like a pack of wolves. Three trucks and SUVs followed closely, their headlights casting ominous shadows on the trees lining the road.

"That's them," Julianna murmured, her voice low as the convoy of motorcycles roared past, their engines growling like wolves on the hunt.

Jake's jaw tightened as his gaze fixed on the fading glow of taillights. "Heading west," he muttered, his tone measured but relieved. "They're looking in the wrong direction. We've got a little breathing room."

Julianna exhaled slowly, her grip on the wheel relaxing slightly. "For now," she said. Her voice carried a note of caution, but there was a spark of determination in her eyes.

Jake leaned back in his seat; his gaze fixed on the road ahead. "Let's not waste it. Keep going east. We'll find a place to regroup and figure out our next move."

The sedan hurtled through the night, carrying them farther from danger but deeper into the unknown. The tension in the air remained, a constant reminder of the predators lurking just out of sight. But for the first time in hours, Jake allowed himself a flicker of hope. They'd survived this far. With a little luck and a lot of determination, they'd find a way to survive the rest.

The lights of Birmingham shimmered in the distance as they pulled into a sprawling truck stop. The fluorescent glow from the overhead lamps illuminated the cracked asphalt, and the faint hum of a vending machine buzzed in the background. At this late hour, the lot was mostly deserted, with only a handful of semis idling in the trucker's section and a few scattered cars near the gas pumps.

Julianna maneuvered the car into the shadows on the edge of the lot. "I'll fill the tank," she said, her voice steady but strained. "You keep watch."

Jake gave a small nod, his sharp eyes sweeping over the nearly deserted lot as Julianna stepped out. The chill in the air gnawed at his bruised skin, but he welcomed the clarity it brought. While Julianna pumped gas, Jake's hand hovered near the pistol tucked into his waistband, ready for any sudden movement in the quiet lot.

Once the tank was full, they took turns in the restroom. Julianna went first, disappearing into the brightly lit building while Jake kept a vigilant watch by the car. When she returned, she handed Jake a plastic bag, the contents shifting noisily inside. "Clean shirts, first aid, and something to keep us going," she said, her smile faint but genuine. "Your turn."

Jake took his time in the restroom, splashing cold water on his face and scrubbing the grime from his hands. The reflection in the mirror looked worse than he felt: bruises darkened his jawline, and dried blood crusted at his temple. But his eyes, hard, determined, remained the same.

When he returned to the car, Julianna was sitting in the driver's seat, a bottle of water in one hand and her eyes scanning the road ahead. "Ready?" she asked.

"Let's go," Jake replied, sliding into the passenger seat. "Before we hit Birmingham, get on Highway 20 and head toward Atlanta."

Julianna raised an eyebrow but nodded. "Yeah, I think that's a good idea. Let's put some miles between us and Tupelo."

The hum of the tires on the highway filled the silence for several minutes. Finally, Julianna spoke, her tone thoughtful. "Did you hear Fred say something back in the barn?"

Jake frowned; the memory hazy. "What do you mean?"

"He said he had to call someone," she replied. "Or were you already passed out by then?"

Jake rubbed his temples, trying to piece the fragments together. "I knew there was something I needed to remember," he said, his voice tinged with frustration. "But my brain was too foggy. Actually, it's still a little foggy."

Julianna chuckled softly, her lips quirking into a smirk. "You and your foggy brain. He mentioned something... a name," Julianna said, frowning in thought. "Barstow. Could be a place or a contact. You remember anything about it?"

Jake shook his head. "I don't know. But it's a lead. We'll figure it out after we get some sleep."

Just before reaching Atlanta, they checked into a modest roadside motel, parking the stolen car across the street at another hotel.

As they crossed the lot, their meager belongings slung over their shoulders, the flickering neon sign bathed the cracked pavement in a dull, uneven glow. Inside their room, the walls were painted a muted beige, and the faint smell of cleaning supplies lingered in the air.

Jake dropped their bags near the bed, wincing as he stretched his sore muscles. Julianna opened the first aid kit, carefully cleaning and bandaging their wounds. Her movements were methodical, but Jake could see the exhaustion in her eyes.

"Get some sleep," Jake said quietly, his voice softer than Julianna was used to hearing. "Tomorrow, we figure out Barstow."

Julianna nodded, sinking onto the bed with a heavy sigh. "You too, Jake. We both need it."

As they settled in for the night, the weight of the day's events hung over them like a storm cloud. But for now, they had a brief moment of peace, a chance to regroup and prepare for whatever lay ahead.

Chapter 32: Shattered

Pale morning light crept through the thin motel curtains, dust motes swirling in the air like remnants of a restless night. Jake lay sprawled on the bed, his body a map of pain and exhaustion, every movement a reminder of the previous day's ordeal. His eyes, though heavy with fatigue, were fixed on Julianna. She was lying beside him, her breathing slow and even, her face partially buried in the pillow. Though bruises and cuts lined her skin like battle scars, Julianna exuded a defiant strength that made Jake marvel. Even in the stillness of sleep, she looked ready to take on the world.

He'd never met anyone like her, a woman who could match his resilience and grit. A faint smile tugged at the corners of his mouth as he said, "Julianna if I had half a tank of energy, I'd roll you over and take you from behind."

One of Julianna's eyes cracked open, her lips curving into a wry smile. "If I weren't feeling like a crash test dummy, I'd consider it."

They both laughed softly, the sound tinged with pain but laced with genuine affection. The laughter faded, leaving a comfortable silence between them as they lay there, battered but alive.

An hour later, Jake found the strength to push himself upright. He winced as he swung his legs over the edge of the bed, every movement a reminder of the previous day's chaos.

"I'm going to take a shower," he said, his voice hoarse but determined. "Maybe it'll make me feel human again."

Julianna murmured something incoherent, still half-asleep, as Jake shuffled into the bathroom, his movement stiff and deliberate. As the steaming water poured over him, the grime of the past twenty-four hours swirled down the drain, though the ache in his muscles remained stubbornly rooted. "Your turn," he said, helping Julianna sit up. "Trust me, it'll help. I promise."

She groaned as she swung her legs over the side of the bed, her movements slow and deliberate. "Fine, but if it doesn't work, I'm blaming you," she said with a weak smile.

Jake chuckled. "Deal." He guided her to the bathroom door, watching her carefully as she shuffled inside and closed the door behind her. Once she was out of sight, he grabbed his wallet and room key, slipping on his boots with a grimace. Every step to the motel's lobby was a lesson in perseverance, but the thought of food and coffee kept him moving.

The motel lobby was silent, broken only by the faint hum of an old coffee machine. The air was heavy with the mingling scents of burnt toast and over-brewed coffee, a blend that somehow felt comforting in its simplicity. Jake grabbed two coffees, a couple of breakfast sandwiches, and a small assortment of pastries, already thinking about how Julianna would react to the food. By the time he returned to the room, the coffee's warmth was seeping through the cardboard cups, offering a small measure of comfort against the morning chill.

Julianna was emerging from the bathroom as he stepped inside, her hair damp and a towel draped over her shoulders. She looked better, her posture less stiff and her expression lighter.

"What did you get me?" she asked, her voice carrying a hint of playfulness.

"Breakfast sandwiches, pastries, and coffee," Jake replied, setting the bag on the small table near the window. "Figured we could use a decent start to the day."

Julianna's eyes lit up, and Jake could hear the improvement in her voice. "You're a saint," she said, crossing the room to sit across from him.

They ate in companionable silence at first, the simple act of eating bringing a surprising amount of relief. The coffee was lukewarm but strong, and the sandwiches were far from gourmet, but neither cared.

"I'll admit," Julianna said, breaking the silence, "that shower helped. My wrist still feels like hell, but I'm not as stiff."

Jake nodded, taking a sip of his coffee. "Glad to hear it. I'm still piecing myself together, but at least we're in one piece." He paused, studying her over the rim of his cup. "You're tougher than most of the guys I've worked with, you know that?"

Julianna smiled, her expression softening. "Coming from you, that's high praise. But I couldn't have done any of this without you."

Jake shrugged. "We're a team. That's how it works."

They finished eating, and as the caffeine began to work its magic, their conversation shifted to the task at hand.

"Barstow," Julianna mused, her fingers absently tracing the rim of her coffee cup. "Is it a place, a person, or just another dead end?"

Jake leaned forward, his chin resting on his hand. "Could go either way. If it's a place, we're looking for a needle in a haystack. If it's a person… then we're chasing someone with a hell of a lot of influence." And then we've got to figure out the connection to Fred and the Aryan Circle."

Julianna nodded; her brow furrowed in concentration. "Fred said he needed to call someone back in the barn. That means whoever it is, they're important."

Jake sighed, leaning forward to rest his elbows on the table. "We'll start with what we know: get some rest, patch ourselves up, and hit the road. Barstow's not going to wait for us to get comfortable."

Julianna reached for her coffee; her movements slow yet purposeful. "You're right," she said softly. "We've come too far to back down now."

They spent the next hour tending to their wounds, the process slow and meticulous. They crawled back into bed, the sun was setting in the sky, and exhaustion quickly overtook them. Jake's last thought before sleep claimed him was a fleeting sense of gratitude for the woman beside him, and for the fragile alliance that had somehow become the most important thing in his life.

"Wake up, wake up," Julianna's voice cut through Jake's foggy dreams the next morning. Her tone was urgent but laced with excitement.

Jake groaned, rolling onto his side and squinting at her. "What is it?" he mumbled, his voice thick with sleep.

Julianna was perched on the edge of the bed, her laptop open beside her. "I think I know who Barstow is."

Jake groaned, rubbing the sleep from his eyes. "So, it's a *who* now? You're sure?"

She nodded, her eyes bright. "Yes!" she exclaimed, her voice sharp with excitement. "Back in Mexico, when we heard about a politician pulling the strings? I think this is him."

Jake's brow furrowed as he struggled to clear his mind. "That's right. I almost forgot about that."

Julianna smirked. "That foggy brain of yours again. Anyway, there's a Senator Barstow from Louisiana. He's been in office for years, and there have been rumors about him having ties to white supremacist organizations."

Jake's eyes widened slightly. "That has to be it," he said, the pieces falling into place.

"Exactly," Julianna replied. "It's a lead we can't ignore."

Moments later, they packed their bags, their movements quick yet deliberate. The stolen car sat in the parking lot across the street, a silent witness to their escape.

"We'll leave the car here," Jake said as they slung their bags over their shoulders. "No need to draw more attention to ourselves."

They flagged down a cab outside the motel, the driver's tired eyes barely noticing them as he pulled over. "Airport," Jake said, climbing into the back seat with Julianna.

The cab ride to the airport was cloaked in silence, tension weaving through the air like an unspoken pact. Julianna's gaze stayed fixed on the passing cityscape, her thoughts a tangle of possibilities and worst-case scenarios. Jake sat beside her, his jaw set and his eyes distant. They were a team, but the weight of their mission pressed heavily on both of them.

At the airport, they navigated the terminals with practiced ease, securing tickets to Washington, D.C., under a fresh set of aliases. As the plane ascended into the clouds, Jake turned his head toward Julianna, his voice low. "If this Barstow lead is right, we're not just walking into danger. We're running headlong into it."

Julianna locked eyes with him, her voice steady and certain. "We've come too far to stop. Whatever's waiting for us, we'll face it head-on."

Chapter 33: Let It Bleed

The Mexico City airport buzzed with activity, its terminals alive with the chatter of travelers and the hum of engines preparing for departure. Fred Alton emerged from the bustling arrivals hall, his shoulders stiff with tension. Flanking him were two burly Aryan Circle enforcers, their leather jackets adorned with faded insignias, a silent threat that promised violence to anyone foolish enough to challenge them. As they scanned the crowd, two of El Patrón's men emerged from the throng, dressed sharply in tailored suits that seemed out of place against the backdrop of weary travelers and fluorescent lighting.

"Señor Alton," one of them said, his tone curt but polite. "Por favor, follow us."

Without waiting for a response, the men turned and began weaving through the crowd. Fred's heart raced, but he kept his expression neutral. Behind him, the two Aryan Circle thugs exchanged wary glances but followed closely.

Outside, a gleaming white Escalade idled by the curb. Fred and his companions were quickly ushered inside. The air conditioning blasted them as the SUV pulled away from the airport, its tinted windows shielding them from the bustling chaos of the city. The ride was smooth but tense, the silence inside the vehicle broken only by the occasional crackle of a radio or the hum of the engine.

As they approached El Patrón's estate, the scenery shifted from urban sprawl to sprawling wealth. The mansion rose from the manicured landscape like a fortress of opulence. Its white stucco walls gleamed under the sun, the terracotta roof tiles lending a touch of old-world charm. High walls topped with razor wire encased the estate, while armed guards patrolled the grounds with the precision of soldiers on high alert, their weapons glinting in the afternoon sun.

The Escalade rolled through the gates and stopped near the entrance. Before Fred could gather his thoughts, he was ushered out of the vehicle and toward the house. The sound of raised voices drew his attention to the pool area, where El Patrón stood, yelling at two bound men kneeling at the edge of the water.

El Patrón's appearance was as striking as his reputation, a tall, broad-shouldered man with silver streaks in his slicked-back hair and an impeccably tailored suit. His gold watch gleamed in the sunlight as he gestured animatedly with a chrome revolver in hand. The two kneeling men were trembling, their faces pale with fear.

"¡Idiotas! ¿Cómo pudieron fallar tan miserablemente?" El Patrón's voice boomed, his anger palpable even from a distance. Without preamble, El Patrón raised the chrome revolver and fired, the deafening crack shattering the serene afternoon. The first man jerked violently before crumpling forward, his body plunging into the turquoise water with a muted splash. The second man's pleas were cut short as another shot rang out, the bullet finding its mark in his head. He too fell into the pool, the water quickly turning crimson.

Fred froze, his stomach churning as he watched the scene unfold. The two Aryan Circle thugs exchanged uneasy glances but said nothing. El Patrón turned, polishing his revolver with the end of his crisp white Cuba Vera shirt as he strode toward the house.

"You must be Fred Alton," El Patrón drawled, his voice carrying a deep, gravelly authority softened by the faintest trace of a cultivated Mexican accent. He stopped a few feet from Fred, his piercing eyes scanning him from head to toe. "As you can see, I am still cleaning up the mess that you and Manuel left me."

Fred swallowed hard; his mouth suddenly dry. "I'm very sorry, El Patrón. You know who I am by now, and my background. I knew Manuel from my DEA days, so, I thought I would deal with him directly."

El Patrón's lips curled into a sneer. "You mean you had leverage over him and decided to cut a deal that left me out of the equation?" He raised the revolver, pointing it directly at Fred's forehead. "Tell me, Señor Alton, were you and Manuel planning to set me up for the fall?"

Fred's knees threatened to buckle, but he forced himself to remain standing. "I swear, it was nothing like that," he said, his voice trembling. "He was the only contact I had, and I needed the muscle. And today I came here because I need your muscle. It will be very profitable for both of us."

El Patrón's expression didn't soften. If anything, his grip on the revolver tightened. "Profitable for both of us? You stand here in my home, after betraying me, and talk of profits?" He took a step closer, the revolver now inches from Fred's face. "The sole reason you still draw breath, Señor Alton," El Patrón growled, the revolver glinting under the sunlight, "is because I was curious to see the man foolish enough to think he could play me."

The Aryan Circle thugs shifted uneasily, their hands inching toward their weapons. El Patrón's men noticed immediately, their own hands moving to their holsters. The tension in the room was suffocating, the air thick with the potential for violence.

"Whether you leave here alive is still undecided," El Patrón continued, his voice low but menacing. "Now, tell me your plan, Señor Alton. And it had better convince me."

Fred nodded quickly, his mind racing. "El Patrón, the chaos in the southern U.S. cities is creating opportunities. I have connections and networks that can be leveraged. "Manuel's role was simple, muscle and logistics, but his greed derailed everything," Fred said, his words tumbling out in hurried precision. "I can stabilize the chaos he created. With your product and resources, El Patrón, we can carve out a stranglehold on these emerging markets."

El Patrón studied him for a long moment, his eyes narrowing. Slowly, he lowered the revolver but didn't holster it. "You have my attention, but understand this: one wrong move, and I will make an example of you so severe that your name will be cursed for generations. Do we understand each other?"

Fred nodded fervently. "Perfectly, El Patrón."

El Patrón turned to his men. "Take Señor Alton and his companions to the study. We will discuss this further." As they began to leave, he added, "And clean up the pool. It's starting to smell like cowardice."

Inside the study, El Patrón settled behind an ornate mahogany desk, its intricate carvings of jaguars and serpents gleaming under the light of a crystal chandelier. Behind him hung a massive portrait of a jaguar mid-pounce, its eyes burning with predatory intensity.

El Patrón leaned back in his chair, his expression unreadable as he studied Fred. "Ah, where are my manners?" El Patrón said with a cold, almost mocking smile. "You must be parched after your journey. Maria, fetch our guest a drink. Let us see, if tequila steadies his trembling hands."

A young woman appeared from a side door, carrying a tray with glasses of tequila and small bowls of lime and salt. She placed it on the desk and disappeared as quickly as she had come.

El Patrón picked up a glass but didn't drink. Instead, he swirled the liquid, his eyes never leaving Fred. "Señor Alton, before we get to these southern cities en Estados Unidos, I hear that you have been raising hell in Los Angeles and Las Vegas. What, pray tell, is that all about?"

Fred's throat went dry. He took a cautious sip of tequila, hoping it would steady his nerves. "That was all a big mistake," he admitted, his voice cracking. "Our eyes were bigger than our stomachs. We had hopes of taking these two large markets before we realized we'd bitten off more than we could chew."

El Patrón's lips curled into a sardonic smile. "I see by your metaphors," he interrupted, "that you are men with large appetites... no?"

Fred forced a weak laugh, but it sounded hollow. "El Patrón, with my connections in Washington and our distribution across the South, we are very capable of building a large organization. But to your point, we went too big too soon, and that was a mistake."

El Patrón's eyes darkened. "Tell me more about this present plan."

Fred nodded quickly, setting his glass down. "We have more resources across the South to handle distribution. We're already operating, or are about to, in Memphis, Kansas City, Birmingham, New Orleans, and Jacksonville. These are good-sized cities with plenty of poverty and potential customers, but they're not major hubs like Chicago or Los Angeles. If we dominate these secondary markets, the profits will exceed those of one or two larger cities. And as I said, we have more resources in these areas, as my two friends here can attest."

El Patrón's gaze shifted briefly to the Aryan Circle thugs before returning to Fred. "And what do you need from me, Señor Alton?"

Fred took a deep breath. "Long-term supply and short-term muscle to enter these markets."

El Patrón's smile vanished. He leaned forward, resting his elbows on the desk. "That is all very well, and I can supply you with whatever you need. You know my drugs are the best. But if I am going to commit my muscle, then tell me…" He paused. "Tell me, Fred," El Patrón said, his voice dropping to a venomous growl. "What stops me from cutting out the middleman, distributing my product myself, and leaving your corpse to rot on my doorstep?" The room fell silent, the air thick with tension. Fred's hands shook as he reached for his glass, but his voice held firm.

"Because, El Patrón," Fred began, his voice steady despite the sweat trickling down his temple, "your empire thrives on production. My network opens doors to places even you haven't breached. Together, we don't just profit, we dominate."

El Patrón leaned back, the faintest hint of a smile playing on his lips. "And you require my product. That is expected. But you also ask for muscle, which is a much larger commitment."

Fred hesitated, his pulse quickening. "Short-term muscle, El Patrón. Just enough to help us establish dominance in these markets. Once we're in, we won't need additional support."

El Patrón's smile faded. He placed the tequila glass down with deliberate care and fixed Fred with an unflinching stare. "I will supply you with the product you need, but there will be no muscle crossing the U.S. border. Before I agree to anything else," El Patrón said, his tone dripping with menace, "I want to look your politician friend in the eye. Bring him to me."

Chapter 34: Respectable

The Ritz Carlton in Washington, D.C., radiated quiet elegance, its marble floors gleaming beneath the glow of crystal chandeliers. The faint scent of fresh-cut lilies mingled with the polished oak and leather that infused the air with an air of refinement. Jake and Julianna had settled into a corner suite overlooking the courtyard, their vantage point offering an unobstructed view of Senator Barstow's Ritz Carlton residence, directly across the way. The room itself was a sanctuary of luxury, plush, cream-colored furniture, silk drapes framing the expansive windows, and Egyptian cotton sheets that Julianna had already praised more than once. But their focus remained fixed on the task at hand.

Three days into their surveillance, they had seen little of the senator. He came and went like a ghost, his movements frustratingly sporadic. It was only in the past few hours that the lights in his unit had come to life more consistently.

Julianna stretched out on the chaise lounge near the window, her wrist wrapped neatly and propped on a pillow. "I've got to hand it to you, Jake," Julianna said, her smirk teasing. "This might be the only stakeout where I'm debating caviar over lobster. Egyptian cotton sheets and baths big enough to swim in? I could get used to this." She stretched out and added, "Best way to heal our wounds, don't you think?"

Jake sat at the sleek mahogany desk, methodically cleaning the barrel of his handgun. His lips curved into a faint smirk as he glanced up. "Enjoy the five-star treatment while you can. Once Barstow makes his next move, this little vacation is over."

She sighed dramatically, casting a longing look at the room service menu on the coffee table. "Pity. I was hoping to try the caviar tomorrow."

Jake chuckled softly but kept his gaze trained on the courtyard, where lights flickered on in the senator's unit. A shadow moved across the window; Barstow's broad frame was unmistakable.

"Speak of the devil," Jake muttered. "Looks like he's entertaining tonight."

Julianna grabbed the binoculars from the coffee table and peered out the window. Her breath caught as a wiry man stepped into Barstow's unit. She passed the binoculars to Jake, her voice low. "Fred Alton. Looks like tonight's going to be interesting."

Jake nodded. "Let's see what these two snakes are up to."

From their vantage point, they could see Barstow's spacious living room illuminated in warm, golden light. Floor-to-ceiling windows revealed modern decor: sleek leather furniture, abstract art adorning the walls, and a fireplace crackling beneath a massive flat-screen television. Barstow sat in a high-backed chair; his posture relaxed but his expression stern as Fred paced in front of him. Unbeknownst to Barstow, a tiny listening device, discreetly planted by Jake during their first day of surveillance, broadcasted every word spoken in his suite. The signal fed directly to Julianna's laptop, its live audio providing a front-row seat to the senator's dealings. As they watched the interaction unfold, they also listened intently to the conversation through earpieces connected to their laptop.

Inside the residence Barstow leaned forward in his chair, his eyes narrowing with irritation. "Let's skip the dramatics, Fred. What did El Patrón say?"

Fred paced the room, his hand raking through disheveled hair. "Mexico was a damn nightmare," he admitted, his voice trembling just enough to betray him. "I didn't know if I'd make it back in one piece."

Barstow's brow furrowed. "I guess the fact that you're here, means we got what we need."

Fred hesitated, his face tightening. "Not exactly."

Barstow's jaw clenched, and he sat back in his chair, his fingers drumming against the armrest. "Explain."

"He's willing to supply us with whatever product we need," Fred began cautiously, his voice trembling. "But there are conditions."

"What kind of conditions?" Barstow snapped.

Fred swallowed hard. "He won't supply manpower inside U.S. borders. He says it's too risky for his organization. And he wants to meet you personally before finalizing anything."

Barstow's eyes narrowed, a flicker of irritation crossing his face. "Meet me? Why?"

"To establish trust, I suppose," Fred said with a shrug. "He's a man who values face-to-face dealings. Besides, he's still cleaning up the mess Manuel left behind. He wants assurances that this operation will be worth his while."

Barstow's lips pressed into a thin line. "And you didn't convince him?"

Fred raised his hands defensively. "I tried, Senator. But this man doesn't take anyone's word for it. He's cautious and calculating. I don't think we have a choice if we want his support."

Barstow leaned back, his gaze drifting toward the windows. The flickering light of the fireplace reflected in his eyes, making him look both contemplative and menacing. After a long silence, he said, "Fine. Arrange it. But let me be clear, this trip better be worth my time. If he thinks he can dictate terms to me, he's sorely mistaken."

Fred nodded quickly, relief washing over his face. "Understood. I'll set it up."

Barstow stood, signaling the end of the meeting. "Good. Now get out. I have other matters to attend to."

Fred hurried to the door. Barstow watched them leave; his expression unreadable.

Jake lowered the binoculars, his jaw tightening as he watched Fred's hunched shoulders and hurried steps. "Barstow's on edge. Whatever deal Fred pitched; it's not sitting well with him."

Julianna leaned against the window; her expression thoughtful. "Fred's practically sweating bullets. This operation must be massive, and risky."

Jake nodded thoughtfully. "The fact that El Patrón wants to meet Barstow himself? That's a power play. He's testing the senator, seeing how far he can push him."

"And Barstow knows it," Julianna added. She glanced at Jake, a glimmer of determination in her eyes. "We've got to figure out when and where this meeting's going down," Julianna said, her voice steely. "Getting El Patrón and Barstow in the same place…"

"…means we can cut off the head and the tail in one move," Jake finished his tone firm.

The two exchanged a knowing look, their silent resolve reaffirmed. Jake picked up his phone, scrolling through contacts. "Time to see if any of my old friends in D.C. can help us out."

Julianna smirked, leaning back. "And I'll see if our lovely front desk clerk knows anything useful. Sometimes all it takes is another Benjamin to grease the wheels."

Jake chuckled. "That charm of yours is deadlier than a sniper rifle, you know that?"

She winked. "I'll take that as a compliment."

Chapter 35: Money

The phone rang twice. Nikolai's deep, gravelly voice came through, unmistakable. "Jake," Nikolai's voice rumbled through the line, heavy with anticipation. "You've got something for me?"

"I do," Jake replied. He leaned against the small desk in their Ritz Carlton room, glancing at Julianna, who was sprawled across the bed with her laptop. "Barstow and Alton are working together; we know that for sure. Barstow's heading to Mexico to lock things in with El Patrón. I've got a plan to take them both down, but it'll have to wait until Barstow's back in DC. Timing is everything here."

Nikolai was silent for a moment, processing the information. Then he exhaled, the sound of satisfaction evident even over the phone. "Good. I expected nothing less from you. Barstow and Alton are linchpins, but while we wait for Barstow's return, I've got something else, something immediate."

Jake raised an eyebrow and switched the phone to speaker mode, motioning for Julianna to listen. "What kind of job?"

Nikolai's tone grew colder. "We've got problems with those Aryan Circle scum. Kansas City and New Orleans are crawling with them, holed up in fortified compounds. The locals want them gone, clean, precise, and permanent." They can't move on themselves; too much heat from the cops and FBI. Do you think you can handle it?"

Jake felt his pulse quicken. The thought of taking down those Aryan Circle scumbags brought a sharp edge to his voice. Jake muted the call, glancing at Julianna. "Nikolai's offering a job, three Aryan Circle compounds wiped off the map. What do you think?"

Julianna closed her laptop and sat up. Her brown eyes narrowed thoughtfully. "How much is he offering?"

"I haven't asked yet. But if it's Nikolai, it'll be worth our while."

Julianna leaned forward, her eyes flashing. "After everything they've put us through, this feels personal. I say we take it. But three compounds? That's serious firepower we're up against."

"I know," Jake admitted. "But if we're careful, we can handle it. We've faced worse."

She nodded, her resolve hardening. "Ask him how much. If it's good, we'll take it."

Jake unmuted the call, his tone steady. "What's the payday, Nikolai?"

Nikolai's voice remained steady, almost businesslike. "Six million if you can eliminate all three compounds," Nikolai said coolly. "Three as a deposit now, the rest after the job. No loose ends, Jake. You're ghosts, silent, clean, and final."

Jake leaned back in the chair, his mind racing. "Do you have the locations?"

"Yes," Nikolai said. "Say yes, and I'll send you everything you need."

Jake glanced at Julianna. She gave him a slight nod. "All right," Jake said into the phone. "We're in. But we will need some heavy artillery. Can we count on Kansas City and New Orleans to provide some hardware?"

"I will make sure you have everything you need," Nikolai replied. "I'll send the details and transfer the deposit immediately. Make sure you plan this carefully, Jake. These compounds are heavily fortified."

"We will," Jake assured him. "We'll be in touch once the job is done."

Nikolai hung up, leaving Jake and Julianna to sit in silence for a moment. Then Jake stood, running a hand through his graying hair. "Time to get to work."

Julianna smiled faintly, already pulling up maps on her laptop. "Looks like we've got some planning to do. Where do you want to start?"

Jake pulled a chair beside her and leaned over the screen. "First, we map the locations. Three targets mean three unique challenges. We'll need to prioritize and figure out how to hit fast without leaving a trace. Then we'll get into their security measures."

Julianna typed furiously, her fingers a blur on the keyboard. "We'll need to move fast between hits. Once we're spotted at one location, the others will be on high alert."

"Agreed," Jake said, his mind already mapping out potential routes. "This won't be easy, but if we hit them hard and fast, we'll stand a chance."

Julianna paused, glancing at him. "Six million is a lot of money. You realize we could disappear after this, right? Really disappear."

Jake met her gaze, a small smile tugging at the corners of his mouth. "Let's focus on the job first. If we get through this in one piece, then we'll talk about disappearing."

She nodded, a hint of a smile on her lips. "Deal."

For the next several hours, they pored over the intel Nikolai had sent. Satellite images, blueprints, and dossiers on the Aryan Circle leaders at each location. The compounds were spread out: one in the outskirts of Kansas City, another in the bayous near New Orleans, and the last in rural Mississippi.

Each location presented unique challenges. Kansas City was an industrial fortress, with high fences, watchtowers — the works. New Orleans was buried deep in the bayou, accessible only by water. Mississippi? A fortified farmhouse in open fields, complete with dogs. Three completely different setups, three nightmares.

"This isn't just about firepower," Jake said, tracing a finger over a map. "We'll need to hit them, when they least expect it. Take out their leadership first to throw them into chaos."

Julianna nodded. "And we'll need to be ghosts. In and out, before they know what hit them."

Jake leaned back, studying the plans they'd laid out. "We're looking at tight timelines and heavy resistance. It's risky, but it's not impossible. We get some rest now because tomorrow, the real work starts."

Julianna smirked, closing her laptop. "Another day, another impossible mission."

Jake chuckled, pulling her into a brief, almost protective embrace. "Wouldn't have it any other way."

Chapter 36: One Hit (To the Body)

Kansas City's outskirts were shrouded in an eerie stillness, the industrial complex looming like a graveyard of forgotten ambitions. The sprawling structure, with its cracked brick walls and rusting metal beams, looked like it had been abandoned for decades. Broken windows stared out like hollow eyes, while the faint tang of oil and decay clung to the crisp night air.

Jake and Julianna sat in their rental car, parked a block away in the shadow of a crumbling warehouse. The moon cast a silvery glow on the scene, but the compound's floodlights cut harsh beams across the perimeter. A few guards milled around, smoking cigarettes and chatting, their Aryan Circle insignias barely visible under their jackets.

Jake leaned in, his tone deliberate. "This place is a firetrap waiting for an excuse. We'll make it look like an accident. Quiet takedowns only, use your blade unless there's no other option. I'll spread the naphtha. You take point. Only use your gun if you absolutely have to."

Julianna smirked, checking her gear. "Got it. Silent and deadly, just the way I like it."

Jake chuckled softly. "Let's do this."

They slipped out of the car, moving through the shadows like ghosts. Julianna led the way, her movements fluid and deliberate. Jake followed close behind, a large canister of naphtha in one hand, his other ready to draw his knife if needed.

The industrial complex loomed larger as they approached, its hulking frame casting deep shadows. Julianna scoped out the first guard, a burly man leaning against a pillar, his cigarette glowing like a firefly. Julianna moved with predatory precision, closing the distance in a heartbeat. Her blade slid into his neck, the gasp dying in his throat as his knees buckled beneath him.

Jake crouched beside the body, sprinkling a thin trail of naphtha over the lifeless form. "One down," he murmured. "Let's keep moving."

Inside, the building was a labyrinth of narrow hallways and cavernous rooms filled with forgotten machinery. The wooden floors creaked under their boots, decades of varnish and grime making them slick. Jake dribbled naphtha along the baseboards and over the piles of old wooden crates stacked against the walls.

"This place might as well have kindling written all over it," Jake muttered, spreading more naphtha along the crates. "A single spark, and it'll go up like a damn bonfire."

Julianna nodded, her eyes scanning the dimly lit corridor ahead. As they exited one of the rooms, a guard appeared from around the corner, his eyes widening as he spotted them. Before he could react, Julianna lunged, her blade flashing as she closed the gap. The guard staggered, clutching his throat as he collapsed.

"Efficient," Jake muttered, sprinkling more naphtha. "Let's keep moving."

But their luck ran out a few minutes later. As they rounded another corner, a massive guard caught Julianna off guard, grabbing her and locking her in a crushing headlock. She struggled, her knife falling from her grip as she clawed at his arms, but his hold was unyielding. Without hesitation, Jake snatched a fire extinguisher from the wall, its metal handle cold in his hand. With a grunt of effort, he drove it into the guard's temple, the man's swastika tattoo momentarily visible before he crumpled like a felled tree.

"I totally had that," Julianna said, her voice mocking as she rubbed her neck. Then, with a grudging smile: "But fine, thanks for the save."

"Always here to help," Jake said, his tone light but his eyes serious. "Come on, let's finish this."

They worked quickly, moving through the rest of the building with practiced efficiency. Jake spread the remaining naphtha in strategic spots, ensuring the fire would engulf the entire structure. Stepping into the cool night air, they moved quickly toward the car. Each breath felt sharper, a grim reminder of the destruction left behind.

Jake pulled a small detonator from his pocket and handed it to Julianna. "Would you like to do the honors?"

She took the device with a mischievous smile. "Don't mind if I do."

She pressed the button. A soft *whoosh* echoed from inside the building. Within seconds, flames began licking up the walls, their orange glow casting eerie shadows across the surrounding area. The dry wood and decades-old varnish ignited almost instantly, feeding the hungry blaze.

As they hurried back to the car, the first explosion rocked the building, sending shards of debris into the air. By the time they were back on the road, the entire structure was engulfed, the flames visible in their rearview mirror.

Julianna glanced at Jake, her adrenaline still pumping. "That was... something."

Jake smirked; his hands steady on the wheel. "Not bad for a night's work. You did good back there."

She leaned back in her seat, letting out a deep breath. "You weren't so bad yourself, Mr. Firestarter."

They drove in silence for a few minutes, the glow of the fire fading behind them. Finally, Jake broke the silence. "One compound down. Two to go."

Julianna nodded, a determined look in her eyes. "Let's see how they like a little hellfire."

Now heading toward Mississippi, they stopped at the Memphis airport. Jake turned in the rental car while Julianna rented a sturdy black SUV. The transition was seamless; they needed to move quickly and quietly.

As they merged onto the highway, the city lights of Memphis faded in the rearview mirror, replaced by the dark, sprawling fields of the rural South. Julianna adjusted her grip on the wheel and glanced at Jake. "You think they're expecting us?"

Jake leaned back; his gaze fixed on the road ahead. "I don't think, they've had time to process what happened in Kansas City, yet. If we're lucky, they'll still be scrambling to figure out who's responsible."

Julianna smirked. "You think some of their Mississippi boys got called up to deal with the Kansas mess?" Julianna asked, her tone skeptical but hopeful.

Jake smirked; his tone sharp. "That's the plan. The fewer meatheads standing in our way tonight, the better."

Jake nodded, his lips curling into a faint grin. "Fewer guards at the compound tonight would be a nice bonus."

Julianna drummed her fingers on the wheel. "Let's hope you're right. I'd prefer not to get into another close-quarters fight if we can help it. My neck's still sore from that last guy."

Jake chuckled. "You handled yourself just fine. Besides, I had your back."

"Yeah, yeah," she teased, rolling her eyes. "Big hero with a fire extinguisher."

The banter eased the tension in the car as they drove deeper into the heart of Mississippi. The roads narrowed, flanked by tall pines that seemed to stretch endlessly into the night sky. The occasional flicker of headlights from oncoming cars was the only sign of life.

"This place is gonna be different," Julianna said after a long silence. "More isolated. Like they could hide an army out here, and no one would ever know."

Jake nodded, his expression turning serious. "That's exactly why they chose it. These guys thrive on being out of sight and out of reach. But we've been here before and we know what to expect."

As the miles ticked by, the duo fell into a comfortable silence, each lost in their thoughts. The road stretched ahead of them, dark and foreboding, but their resolve remained unshaken.

"One down," Julianna murmured, fingers drumming on the steering wheel. "Two left. No margin for error."

Jake glanced at her; his voice cold with determination. "Mississippi's next. And this time, we have a score to settle."

Chapter 37: Let It Rock

Two miles before the infamous dirt road, Jake and Julianna found a lesser-used path. It was barely a road, more like a Jeep trail, with uneven terrain and overgrown brush clawing at the SUV as they maneuvered through it. The trail paralleled the main dirt road leading to the compound and honky-tonk, offering them a discreet route to set up their operation.

"This is as far as we're going," Jake said, stopping the SUV in a small clearing. He shifted into reverse and expertly turned the vehicle around, pointing it back toward the trail for a quick getaway.

Julianna hopped out and popped open the hatch, her fingers quick and deliberate. "Let's see if they actually delivered," she murmured, her tone edged with doubt as she inspected the cargo. They unloaded two cases of what looked like hockey pucks. Each puck was an explosive device, one case filled with incendiary explosives and the other with high-powered charges.

"Looks like Santa's been busy," Jake said, hoisting one of the cases with a grunt.

Julianna smirked, grabbing the other case. "Trust me, they're going to remember tonight."

They also pulled out "Big Boy," a shoulder-fired rocket launcher with four extra rockets. Jake handed Julianna a high-powered rifle while strapping another to his back. They checked their handguns, ammunition, and gear, ensuring everything was ready before setting off toward the compound.

The trek was punishing, each step a deliberate effort under the weight of explosives and gear. The faint crunch of leaves and the occasional snap of a twig seemed deafening in the otherwise oppressive stillness.

They reached a high point overlooking the compound just as the last light of dusk faded into darkness. The compound sprawled below them, dimly lit by a few floodlights. The honky-tonk stood off to one side, its neon sign buzzing faintly in the distance. Guards patrolled lazily, their movements uncoordinated and routine.

Jake adjusted the scope of his rifle, his gaze sweeping the compound with surgical precision. "Not a lot of activity. Looks like they're understaffed tonight."

"Probably sent some guys to Kansas City," Julianna replied, setting down the cases and assembling her rifle. "Lucky us."

"Let's keep it that way," Jake said. He glanced at her. "Ready?"

She nodded, her expression steely. "Let's do this."

Taking turns, they stealthily made their way down to the compound. Each carried a mix of incendiary and explosive hockey pucks, placing them in strategic locations, under vehicles, near fuel storage, along structural supports, and inside key buildings. One of them always stayed back at the high point, covering the other with the rifle.

On one trip back, Julianna dropped to her knees beside Jake, her breathing quick but controlled. "I found their drug inventory," she said, pointing to a large warehouse near the center of the compound.

Jake lowered his rifle and looked where she indicated. "Did you set extra devices there?"

"Of course," she replied with a grin. "But, if we have an extra rocket, that's where it should go."

Jake nodded, a faint smile breaking his usual stoic expression. "Good thinking."

After two more trips down the hill, Jake returned and set the rifle down. "I think we're ready to rock and roll."

Julianna wiped the sweat from her brow and adjusted her gear. "I got the Big Boy," she said, hefting the rocket launcher onto her shoulder with ease.

Jake raised an eyebrow but chuckled. "All yours, babe. But let's start with the rifles first. We'll make some noise and see how they react."

They both settled into position, the cool night air bristling with anticipation. Jake peered through his scope, lining up his first shot. The muffled sound of the rifle cracked through the night, and one of the guards dropped silently. Julianna quickly followed, taking out another guard near the drug warehouse.

"Nice shot," Jake murmured, scanning for their next target.

"Not too shabby," Julianna teased, sliding another round into the chamber with practiced ease.

The compound roared to life, floodlights flickering on as voices barked frantic orders into the night. Guards emerged, weapons in hand, looking for the source of the disturbance.

"They're scrambling," Jake observed. "Time for phase two. Ready to light it up?"

"Let's crank up the volume," Julianna said, adjusting her stance as she hefted the rocket launcher onto her shoulder.

She aimed at the drug warehouse, her movements precise and deliberate. The rocket streaked through the air, slamming into the building with a deafening explosion. Flames erupted instantly, consuming the structure in a fiery blaze.

"Beautiful," Jake said, his voice tinged with admiration.

The compound descended into chaos. Guards shouted orders, some firing blindly into the darkness, others rushing to contain the spreading fire. Julianna loaded another rocket and aimed for the fuel storage. The second explosion shook the ground, sending a plume of fire and smoke skyward.

Jake picked off guards who ventured too close to their position, his shots precise and unrelenting. Julianna fired her remaining rockets, targeting vehicles and other key points, each explosion further plunging the compound into disarray.

As the final rocket was fired, Jake glanced at Julianna. "Now, for the grand finale."

Julianna pulled out the detonator for the hockey puck devices, her finger hovering over the button. She looked at Jake, a sly grin on her face. "Ready to make some real fireworks?"

"Do it," Jake said, his voice steady.

Julianna pressed the button, and a series of explosions rippled through the compound. The incendiary devices ignited with fierce intensity, sending walls of flame roaring through the buildings. The high-powered charges followed, erupting with deafening booms that shook the ground beneath them. Vehicles were tossed like toys, and the few remaining guards scattered in panic.

"That's how you light up the night," Julianna said, watching the chaos unfold.

"Damn right," Jake replied, a rare smile crossing his face.

"That's it," Julianna said, slinging the empty rocket launcher over her shoulder. "We've done enough damage."

Jake nodded, grabbing the cases and their gear. "Let's move. The cavalry will be here soon."

They retreated into the night, their path carefully planned to avoid detection. Behind them, the compound was a raging inferno, the glow of the fire visible for miles.

As they reached the SUV, Jake turned to Julianna, a rare smile crossing his face. "Not bad for a night's work."

Julianna chuckled, tossing the empty rocket launcher into the back. "Let's see how the Mississippi boys like a little hellfire."

Jake started the engine, and they drove off into the night, the roar of the flames fading into the distance.

Chapter 38: Connection

The air hung heavy and thick with the scent of tropical flowers as Senator Barstow and El Patrón sat by the shimmering blue pool at the cartel leader's opulent mansion. The expansive patio, lined with lush palm trees and marble statues, gleamed under the afternoon sun. A pair of Dobermans lounged nearby, their ears twitching at the faintest sound, while armed guards hovered at a respectful distance, their presence a constant reminder of the power dynamics in play.

El Patrón exuded command in his crisp guayabera and linen trousers and leaned back in his chair, a chrome revolver gleaming in the waistband of his belt. He sipped leisurely from a tall glass of some fruity concoction, the vibrant colors of the drink matching the flower arrangement on the table. "Across from him, Senator Barstow adjusted his tie and sipped his drink, the sheen of sweat on his brow betraying the discomfort of his substantial girth, and beneath the practiced veneer."

"You summoned me, El Patrón," Barstow began, his Cajun drawl breaking the tranquil stillness. "Mind telling me why you insisted I fly all the way down here?"

El Patrón set his glass down and leaned forward, his dark eyes piercing. "You see, Senator, I don't deal with middlemen. I deal only with the top dog. And I'm not yet convinced whether we should be doing business at all."

"Barstow paused, his grip tightening on his glass. "I was under the impression we already had a deal for supply. Am I mistaken?'"

El Patrón's lips curled into a faint smile that didn't reach his eyes. "I am a man of my word, Senator. When I say I will supply, I will deliver. But transportation? That is another matter entirely. If you want us to deliver on your side of the frontera, then we have much to discuss. And getting involved in your hostilities?" He shook his head slowly. "That is out of the question."

Barstow took a deep breath and a long sip of his drink. He wiped his brow with a silk handkerchief, the wheels in his mind clearly turning. "El Patrón," he began, his tone shifting to one of storytelling, "my daddy owned a small neighborhood grocery store in Slidell, just across Lake Pontchartrain from New Orleans. And when someone wanted to sell their product in Daddy's store, they would pay him a shelving fee for that privilege. Now, sir, we're risking a lot to open up new markets for you. It's only fair that we get a slice of the pie, and I'm not just talking about shelving fees. I'm thinking equity. After all, you wouldn't even *have* access without me."

Tension rippled through the air as El Patrón's expression darkened, his guards shifting almost imperceptibly in response. But then, to Barstow's relief, El Patrón threw his head back and laughed, the sound rich and commanding.

"'You've got cajones, Senator,' El Patrón said, his laughter fading as he wiped at the corner of his eye. 'Demanding my cooperation and then piling on favors… it's almost admirable.'" He leaned forward, his smile fading. "The question should be, what can you do for me? You are a politician, a man in Washington. How might you help my business?"

Barstow set his glass down carefully, choosing his words with precision. "El Patrón, you might run things down here, but up in Washington? That's my territory. You keep my operations running smoothly, and I'll make sure your name stays off the radar." He smirked, swirling his drink. "A man like me can make friends, or problems, faster than you'd believe."

El Patrón's dark eyes studied the senator intently, his fingers tapping a slow rhythm against the marble tabletop. "Information is valuable. But words are cheap. Can you deliver?"

"I wouldn't be here if I couldn't," Barstow replied firmly.

El Patrón leaned back, nodding slowly. "Very well. I will supply products directly to the cities you need. But let me be clear, Senator. I will not provide muscle. You must fight your own battles."

Barstow nodded, a small smirk forming. "And what about the premium goods? The young ones, boys, girls, don't matter. I've got plenty of buyers who'll pay top dollar, no questions asked." He chuckled as if discussing a harmless business opportunity.

El Patrón's expression hardened, his tone cold. "One step at a time, mi amigo. One step at a time."

Before the conversation could continue, Barstow's phone buzzed insistently on the table. He glanced at the screen, his irritation evident. "Excuse me," he said curtly, standing and brushing past a server without a glance. At the pool's edge, his voice dropped into a venomous hiss. "This better be important. I don't have time for your in-competence."

The voice on the other end delivered news that made the senator's face darken. "What? When did this happen? How many were lost?" He rubbed his temples, his frustration mounting. "I'll be there as soon as I can."

Barstow ended the call and took a moment to compose himself before returning to El Patrón, who watched him with a raised eyebrow. "Nothing serious, I hope?"

"I'm afraid it is," Barstow replied, his tone clipped. "I must return immediately. Thank you for your hospitality, El Patrón. I look forward to returning the favor next time you're in New Orleans."

El Patrón stood, his imposing presence undiminished. "Travel safe, Senator. And remember, in my world, loyalty is everything."

Barstow nodded curtly and hurried toward the waiting Escalade. As the vehicle sped away from the mansion, El Patrón watched the senator with thinly veiled contempt. The man was nothing but an opportunist in a suit, thinking himself untouchable. He had no loyalty, no honor, only greed. He took another sip of his drink, a pensive look crossing his face.

Chapter 39: Doom and Gloom

"Ever been out in the bayou before?" Jake asked, his voice flat, the question carrying a quiet edge. Julianna leaned back, her eyes scanning the endless stretch of water and gnarled trees. "No, but I've seen enough swampy horror movies to know how this ends." Her attempt at humor fell flat beneath Jake's silence.

Jake grunted. "Yeah, me too. Never had to use a boat for transportation on a job, though." His voice trailed off; his eyes glued to the road ahead as if the asphalt held answers to his unspoken worries. The silence between them thickened, heavier than the humid Louisiana air.

After a moment, Julianna broke the quiet. "This is going to be a hard one."

Jake nodded but didn't elaborate. His jaw was tight, and his hands gripped the wheel just a little too hard. The faint glow of the GPS lit his face as he followed its directions, weaving through the backroads. Eventually, they pulled into the gravel lot of a run-down motel about thirty miles from their destination. The flickering neon sign overhead buzzed faintly, casting jagged shadows across the peeling paint of the building.

Jake barely uttered a word as they checked in, and their room, with its sagging beds and the faint stench of mildew, seemed to close in on them. The lone window offered nothing but a view of swamp grass swaying under a low, oppressive sky. Jake's gaze lingered on the window for a beat too long, as if he expected eyes staring back.

Morning came too soon. Jake and Julianna were up before dawn, sipping weak motel coffee as they laid out their gear. The tension from the previous night was replaced with a grim determination. They knew what had to be done, and there was no turning back now.

By mid-morning, they were driving again, the landscape growing wilder with every mile. The swamp loomed on either side, its gnarled cypress trees clawing skyward, their roots twisting like skeletal hands into the water's black depths. Spanish moss-draped the branches, swaying like spectral veils, while the ceaseless buzz of cicadas filled the air like a warning.

Jake pulled into a dirt lot near the Atchafalaya River, where a weathered sign advertised an airboat for sale. The boat looked old but sturdy, its wide, flat hull designed to navigate the shallow, tangled waterways. It came with a recently new engine, a few pieces of fishing gear, and, most importantly, a spacious compartment that would easily hold their arsenal. Jake handed over a wad of cash to the owner without much haggling.

"Couldn't risk renting," Jake muttered, tightening the straps on their gear. "If the Aryan Circle has eyes in every bar and bait shop, they'd peg us before we even got on the water."

Julianna nodded grimly, her gaze flicking to the tree line as though she expected shadows to move. "This was the right call. Let's hope that they're as blind out here as they are dumb."

The airboat roared to life with a deafening growl, the oversized fan at the back churning the humid air. The airboat hummed through the water; its growl swallowed by the dense swamp pressing in on all sides. Vegetation clawed at the edges of the narrow channels, and every splash from unseen creatures sent ripples of unease through the humid air. It felt as if the swamp itself was watching, waiting.

"Hot and muggy doesn't even begin to describe this," Julianna said, wiping sweat from her brow. "How do people live out here?"

Jake smirked faintly. "Tough people live in tough places."

They followed the main river for miles, the oppressive heat bore down like a physical weight. The air was thick with the smell of decay and stagnant water, and dragonflies flitted around the boat in iridescent blurs. Eventually, they found a narrow turnoff that led deeper into the swamp. Jake slowed the engine to a crawl, the sound dying down as they navigated the twisting waterway.

When they saw signs of life ahead, faint lights through the trees, Jake cut the motor entirely. The airboat drifted silently to the bank, where they tied it off to a sturdy tree trunk. The swamp fell unnaturally silent as they approached, the usual cacophony of frogs and insects replaced by a suffocating stillness. Even the wind seemed to die, leaving only the faint hum of the distant generator and the weight of their own breathing.

"We're getting close," Jake whispered, his voice barely audible.

They grabbed their gear and moved on foot, treading carefully over the soft, muddy ground. The compound wasn't far, but the terrain was treacherous. Roots snaked across their path like traps, and every step was accompanied by the squelch of wet earth.

Julianna stopped abruptly, holding up a hand. Jake froze, following her gaze. A crude watchtower loomed in the distance, partially obscured by the dense foliage. A single guard stood inside, lazily scanning the area with a rifle slung over his shoulder.

"They've probably beefed-up security after our other assaults," Julianna murmured.

Jake nodded. "They'll be expecting us. Shock and awe won't work here. We'll have to be smart, careful."

"Think they've rigged traps?" Julianna whispered; her tone low but tight.

Jake scanned the undergrowth, his jaw clenched. "They're paranoid, and they've got a reason to be. Bet your life they've rigged every trail and doorway with something nasty."

They crouched low behind a cluster of trees, observing the compound. The buildings were ramshackle but fortified, surrounded by a makeshift fence topped with razor wire. A handful of guards patrolled the perimeter, their movements sluggish in the heat. Beyond the fence, they could see the faint glow of campfires and hear the muffled sound of voices.

Julianna wiped her brow once more and adjusted her grip on her rifle. "This is going to be one hell of a fight."

Jake's gaze remained fixed on the compound. "Let's make sure it's their hell, not ours."

They stayed until nightfall, mapping every detail of the compound and its defenses. When they finally made their way back to the airboat, the swamp seemed even darker and more foreboding than before. But despite the danger ahead, they felt a flicker of confidence. They had faced worse odds before, they told themselves, and they would again.

As the boat hummed back toward their base, the oppressive silence seemed to cling to them like the swamp's humidity. Julianna finally broke it, her voice soft but laced with forced levity. "If we make it through this, Jake, I'm not stopping at fancy sheets. I want a beach. Palm trees. Enough margaritas to forget this whole thing."

Jake let out a dry chuckle, barely audible over the engine's growl. "Survive tomorrow first. Then you can have all the margaritas you want, assuming you're still in the mood."

The tension between them eased, if only slightly, as they loaded the boat onto the trailer and pulled it back to the motel.

Chapter 40: Complicated

The compound loomed like a dark monolith against the predawn sky, its high fence crowned with razor wire glinting faintly in the pale starlight. The surrounding swamp was both its shield and its trap, a maze of muck and water offering no vantage point, only endless hazards. Jake and Julianna had come prepared, lugging an arsenal designed to break through the barriers and overwhelm the defenders. Beyond their standard rifles, handguns, and rocket launchers, they had brought extra rockets, two portable mortars with ample rounds, and an assortment of hand grenades. They had enough firepower to start a small war, and they were about to do just that.

Night cloaked them as they slipped through the dense underbrush, every rustle of leaves and snap of twigs heightening the oppressive quiet. The swamp seemed alive, its unseen eyes following their every step as they drew closer to the compound. The air was thick with humidity and the faint tang of decaying vegetation. Every snap of a twig underfoot made their hearts race, but they pressed on, each step bringing them closer to their carefully chosen positions.

Julianna crouched low on the west side of the compound, her breathing steady despite the tension in the air. She set up her mortar with practiced precision, the faint starlight glinting off the polished metal. Meanwhile, Jake worked on the southeast side, finding a spot nestled between the roots of a massive cypress tree. They had chosen positions that provided cover while avoiding the risk of friendly fire.

Jake's voice crackled softly in Julianna's earpiece. "You ready over there?"

"Locked and loaded," she whispered, her voice steady but edged with steel. "Let's wake them up the hard way."

They synchronized their watches, waiting for the exact moment. At 5:30 AM, the swamp exploded into chaos.

The first mortar round ripped through the silence, a banshee wail heralding its arrival. The ground shook as it detonated near the compound's northern edge, a column of fire and debris erupting skyward. It landed with a deafening explosion near the northern edge of the compound, sending a plume of dirt, wood, and metal skyward. A second round followed almost immediately, striking a guard tower and reducing it to splinters. Alarms blared, and the compound erupted into a frenzy of activity.

Julianna worked her mortar methodically, each round calculated to hit key targets. The explosions sent guards scrambling for cover as buildings burst into flames. Jake focused on the southern side, his mortar rounds punching holes in the fence and taking out a row of moored boats.

The defenders rallied quickly, returning fire with rifles and shotguns. Bullets zipped through the air, ricocheting off trees and tearing through the foliage. Jake ducked as a burst of gunfire struck the cypress trunk above his head, splinters raining down around him.

"They've spotted me," he muttered into his mic. "Switching to rockets."

He grabbed a shoulder-fired launcher and aimed at the main barracks, where defenders were pouring out to reinforce the perimeter. The rocket streaked across the compound, slamming into the building with a thunderous explosion. The structure buckled, flames licking at the sky as debris rained down.

Julianna had her own problems. The advancing guards' flashlights bobbed erratically, slicing through the murky darkness like searching eyes. Julianna's heart pounded as she fired off several rounds, buying herself precious seconds before yanking a grenade from her belt. She pulled the pin with a swift motion and hurled it into their path. The explosion sent bodies flying, and the remaining guards retreated, shouting in panic.

"They're trying to flank me," she reported, her voice steady but urgent.

"Hold tight," Jake replied. "I'll cover you."

He adjusted his aim and fired another rocket, this one targeting a watchtower overlooking Julianna's position. The tower disintegrated in a fiery blast, and the guards scattered. Julianna took the opportunity to reposition, moving to a new vantage point deeper in the shadows.

As the battle raged on, Jake and Julianna's coordinated assault began to overwhelm the defenders. Fuel tanks exploded, sending fireballs into the sky. Boats moored along the swamp's edge were riddled with bullets and engulfed in flames, their aluminum hulls crumpling like paper. One boat attempted to escape; its engine roaring as it sped down the narrow waterway. Julianna took aim with her rifle, firing a single shot that struck the engine. The boat sputtered to a halt, drifting aimlessly as its occupants jumped into the water.

By now, the compound was a war zone. Smoke billowed into the sky, casting an eerie orange glow over the swamp. The defenders' numbers were thinning, but the remaining guards were fighting with desperate tenacity. Jake and Julianna switched to their rifles, picking off targets with deadly precision.

Jake spotted a group of men trying to set up a machine gun on the roof of a warehouse. He took careful aim and fired, dropping the gunner before he could return fire. The others scattered, leaving the heavy weapon abandoned.

Julianna found herself in a close-quarters skirmish as a lone guard stumbled upon her hiding spot. He lunged at her with a knife, but she sidestepped and struck him with the butt of her rifle, knocking him unconscious. She quickly bound his hands and feet, leaving him as a potential source of intel.

"I've got one alive," she reported.

"Good," Jake replied. "We'll deal with him after we finish this."

With most of the compound's defenses neutralized, Jake and Julianna regrouped at their vantage points for one final strike. Jake readied the last of his rockets, aiming at the main fuel depot in the center of the compound. Julianna, meanwhile, loaded her mortar for a precision shot at the communications tower.

"On three," Jake said. "One… two… three."

The rocket and mortar round hit their targets simultaneously. The fuel depot detonated with a cataclysmic roar, the shockwave flattening everything within its radius. A mushrooming fireball illuminated the swamp, turning night into day for a brief, blinding moment. Flames licked hungrily at the sky as black smoke poured upward, choking the stars. The communications tower collapsed in a cascade of twisted metal and sparking wires. The remaining guards threw down their weapons and fled into the swamp, their morale shattered.

As Jake and Julianna began their retreat to the airboat, the sound of heavy footsteps and shouted commands echoed through the chaos. Jake turned just in time to see a group of guards closing in on him, and another group only a few feet from Julianna. She fired her rifle, taking two down, but another tackled her to the ground, and others then piled on.

"Julianna!" Jake shouted, raising his weapon and firing at the goons in pursuit of him.

"Go, Jake!" she screamed, her voice raw and desperate as she struggled against the guards pinning her down. "You can't save me if you're dead!"

Her voice crackled in his earpiece as Jake froze, torn between instinct and reason. His grip tightened on his rifle, his heart hammering with the impossible choice before him. Every second he lingered brought more guards closing in, and the gnawing realization sank in, if he tried to save her now, they'd both die. More guards were swarming the area, and the intensity of their firepower made survival impossible.

"Damn it," Jake hissed under his breath. He sprinted toward the airboat, the sounds of Julianna's struggle still ringing in his ears. "I'll come back for you," he whispered, his voice breaking.

The airboat roared to life beneath him, drowning out the chaos behind. But her voice pierced through the noise, faint and broken, yet resolute. "You better come back, Jake. You better."

Her words echoed in his mind as the boat sped down the channel, the glow of the burning compound fading behind him. The swamp seemed darker now, more sinister, and every ripple in the water carried the weight of her screams. He gritted his teeth, his knuckles white on the throttle. "I will," he muttered to no one, the promise cutting through his own doubt like a knife.

The roar of the engine drowned out everything else, but the memory of her screams stayed with him, a haunting reminder of what he had left behind.

Chapter 41: Baby Breaks It Down

Jake sped west on Interstate 10, his knuckles white as they gripped the wheel. The hum of the SUV barely registered over the storm raging in his mind. Every mile felt both a retreat and a betrayal, the road stretching endlessly toward nowhere. He wasn't sure where he was going, only that he needed distance, from the compound, from the screams echoing in his ears, from the fury that threatened to consume him. A green highway sign loomed ahead: **Houston 280 miles.**

His thoughts churned, a toxic brew of fury and guilt. Jake wasn't a man who wallowed in emotions; he'd buried those luxuries long ago. But now they clawed their way to the surface, raw and relentless, dragging Julianna's voice, her defiance, her screams, back into his mind. But Julianna was different. She had fought beside him, bled beside him, and now she was in the hands of a monster. Love? He wasn't sure. But loyalty? That he understood. And he would not abandon her.

The helicopter descended onto the compound's makeshift helipad, its rotors whipping the air into a cyclone of dirt and debris. Barstow stepped out, his polished shoes crunching against gravel as if the swamp itself bowed to his presence. His face was a mask of fury, and he barked orders well before his polished shoes even touched the ground.

"Where is the damn woman?" Barstow barked, his cold glare sweeping over the men as if their mere presence offended him.

"In the barn, sir," one of the guards replied nervously.

Barstow didn't wait for an escort. He strode toward the barn, barking orders over his shoulder. "Get the helicopter fueled and ready. I'm not staying in this godforsaken swamp any longer than I have to."

Inside the barn, Julianna was once again slumped against the post like she and Jake had been tied before. Her wrists were raw and bloody; her face bruised but defiant. When Barstow entered, she lifted her chin, meeting his gaze with unflinching determination.

"This is the infamous troublemaker?" Barstow sneered, his voice dripping with disdain as he circled her, a vulture sizing up its next meal. "You don't look like much to me."

Julianna held her tongue, meeting his gaze with a look so sharp it could cut. Her silence was a weapon, and she wielded it with surgical precision.

"Take her," Barstow ordered his men. "We're leaving."

The helicopter descended onto the manicured lawn of Barstow's Baton Rouge estate, a grotesque monument to wealth and arrogance. Its pristine white columns gleamed under the harsh glow of floodlights, the estate exuding a sense of suffocating grandeur, the manicured grounds patrolled by armed guards and sleek Dobermans. Inside, the decor was an exercise in ostentation: gold trim on every surface, heavy velvet drapes, and chandeliers that sparkled like diamonds.

Julianna was dragged into the mansion, her feet barely touching the marble floors. Barstow's staff scrambled like ants under his barked commands, their hurried steps echoing through the marble halls as they laid out a feast fit for a king or a tyrant.

"Bring her to my quarters. Tie her securely. And for God's sake, don't let her out of your sight."

The guards nodded, hauling Julianna toward the grand staircase. She fought against their grip, her every move a testament to her unbroken spirit. Barstow watched her struggle with a smirk.

At the dining table, Barstow sat alone, tearing into a steak as he took call after call. He berated his aides, threatened subordinates, and dismissed concerns about the escalating violence in Kansas City and Mississippi with contemptuous sneers.

"Handle it," he barked into the phone. "I don't care how you do it, just make sure it doesn't lead back to me."

As the night wore on, Barstow's mood darkened. When his plate was empty, he leaned back in his chair, staring into the middle distance. Finally, he rose, straightened his jacket, and ascended the staircase.

Julianna lay on a plush four-poster bed in Barstow's private suite, each wrist and ankle bound to a bedpost. The room was dimly lit, the flickering light from a nearby fireplace casting shadows across the walls. The air was thick with the scent of expensive cologne and cigar smoke.

The obese politician strode into the room, the click of his polished shoes slicing through the oppressive quiet. He set his drink down with deliberate precision, his lips curving into a smile that reeked of malice as he dabbed the beads of sweat from his face.

"You've made quite a mess, haven't you?" he said, his voice deceptively calm. "All that trouble in Los Angeles and Mississippi. And now Kansas City? I wonder, how much of that was your idea?"

Julianna's eyes burned with defiance, her silence a calculated act of rebellion that only seemed to feed his fury.

Barstow reached for a leather belt draped over a nearby chair, his fingers trailing along its length with a slow, predatory intent. "I can be very nice," he said, almost conversational. "Or I can be very mean. Which do you prefer?"

"Why don't you be nice and get the hell out of my sight?" Julianna shot back, her voice steady despite the pounding of her heart.

Barstow chuckled, a low, menacing sound. "You've got spirit. I'll give you that. But spirit won't get you far with me."

He leaned in close, his breath hot against her ear. "Tell me about your friend, Jake," Barstow said, his voice low and venomous. "Where's the rat running now? What pathetic plan has he cooked up to try and stop me?"

Julianna turned her head away, her lips pressed into a defiant line. Barstow straightened, his smile fading. He raised the belt, letting it fall onto the bed with a sharp crack that echoed through the room. The sound alone was enough to make Julianna flinch, though she refused to give him the satisfaction of a reaction.

"You think this is a game?" he growled. "You have no idea who you're dealing with. "When this is over, I'll send you to New Orleans," Barstow hissed, his tone dripping with venom. "You'll fetch a high price in my stable of girls. Maybe, I'll even give men a discount for your... spirit."

For the next hour, Barstow's interrogation continued, his threats growing viler with each passing minute. Julianna's resolve never wavered, her responses sharp and cutting despite her precarious position. Barstow's frustration grew, his mask of control slipping as he paced the room.

At last, Barstow stopped at the foot of the bed, his chest heaving, the mask of composure slipping from his face. "You're wasting my time," he growled, his voice laced with menace. "But don't worry. Time is something I have plenty of, and you're going to wish you didn't."

He turned and left the room, slamming the door behind him. Outside, he barked orders to the guards. "Take her to the basement and lock her in my special playroom. Do you hear me? And find me her phone!"

When the lock clicked shut, Julianna exhaled slowly, letting the tension bleed from her shoulders. Alone in the flickering light of the fireplace, her mind raced. She had survived worse, and she would survive this. Jake was coming, she clung to that thought like a lifeline. She stared at the flickering firelight, her mind racing. She was a survivor. And if she knew Jake, he was already planning her rescue.

Chapter 42: Driving Me Too Hard

Senator Robert Barstow, Bobby to those, who'd known him before he learned to weaponize his charm, had built his empire one blood-soaked brick at a time. The Cajun lilt in his voice and that warm, disarming smile weren't just tools; they were traps. Beneath that charm lay a man who had learned early that power wasn't given; it was taken.

Barstow wasn't lying when he told El Patron that folksy story about his daddy and the grocery store in Slidell, but he wasn't telling the whole story.

His father, George Barstow, was the kind of man who turned Slidell, Louisiana, into his personal hunting ground, a predator in a town too small to run from him. George ran the town's most ruthless loan-sharking operation, a web of debts that ensnared local business owners, desperate families, and unlucky gamblers. When debts went unpaid, George didn't just collect money. He collected dignity, stripping people of it piece by piece, leaving nothing but shame in his wake. Violence was his calling card, and repossessing homes, cars, or family businesses was just part of the game.

"Cross George Barstow," the locals whispered, "and you won't be able to cross the street."

George Barstow raised his sons on a diet of fear and violence. For Bobby and his older brother Joey, life was a constant reminder that there were no carrots, only sticks, and George swung them often. When Bobby was ten, his father handed him a switchblade and said, "If someone owes you, Bobby, you don't ask twice. You take, and then you take a little more for all your trouble."

Joey was the enforcer, the muscle, broad-shouldered, and quick to swing a bat. Bobby, on the other hand, had a sharp mind and an even sharper tongue. George saw the potential in his youngest son, but he didn't show favoritism, only contempt.

When the boys were old enough, George sent them out on collection runs. "Don't come back empty-handed," he'd warn. "If you do, I'll make sure you're the ones paying the price."

One job changed everything. They were sent to shake down a mechanic, who was behind on payments. Joey thought it would be simple: a few threats, maybe a black eye or two. But the mechanic had a gun. Joey never saw it coming. One shot to the chest, and he was gone.

Bobby froze, the scene burning itself into his memory: the hollow crack of the gunshot, the mechanic's ragged, panicked breaths, and the dark pool of Joey's blood creeping toward his shoes. When he finally stumbled back to his father, empty-handed and alone, George didn't console him. Instead, he beat him within an inch of his life.

"Joey's dead because you're weak," George spat. "Don't ever forget that."

Bobby didn't just remember, he seethed. Grief twisted into rage, and rage hardened into something colder: ambition. He carried the weight of Joey's death and his father's wrath like an anchor, channeling it into something darker: ambition. Over the years, he used George's reputation and influence to build his own power base. By his mid-20s, Bobby had his own crew. By 30, he was running a successful racket that extended beyond Slidell. He diversified into real estate scams, money laundering, and eventually politics.

Politics, Bobby realized, was a game for men like him, bigger bribes, sharper suits, and bloodless violence waged through whispers and legislation. The same rules applied: take what you can crush anyone who stands in your way. He traded baseball bats for campaign slogans, but the ruthlessness remained the same.

Now, as Senator Robert Barstow, he sat at the pinnacle of power, a king atop a crumbling throne. The higher he climbed, the sharper the fall waiting for him at the bottom. The FBI had been circling him for years, sniffing around his money-laundering schemes. They didn't have anything concrete until a few months ago, when his longtime bookkeeper, Agnes Grady, flipped. Agnes had been with Bobby since the early days, managing his accounts with meticulous precision. She knew where every dollar came from and where every cent was buried. Now, she was in an FBI safe house, singing like a canary.

Bobby knew the ax was about to fall. He'd spent the past weeks in a state of barely contained panic, lashing out at everyone around him. At his Baton Rouge mansion, the staff bore the brunt of his fury.

"Where's my goddamn coffee?" he roared, his voice echoing through the cavernous hall. When the maid trembled and muttered an apology, he hurled the porcelain cup at her feet, watching it shatter. "If you can't even do that right, why are you still breathing?"

His chief of staff wasn't spared, either. "Are you completely useless?" he snarled into the phone, his knuckles whitening as he gripped the receiver. "I don't pay you to screw up, I pay you to make sure I don't have to clean up your messes!"

In public, Bobby was the picture of Southern charm, shaking hands with constituents, grinning for cameras, and waxing poetic about "family values" and "the American dream." But behind the polished facade lurked a man unraveling, his desperation sharpening every cruel edge, and now he was silently unraveling.

One evening, he sat alone in his office, a tumbler of whiskey in hand. The room was dark except for the glow of his laptop screen. FBI Director David Harris's face stared back at him from a news article.

"BREAKING: FBI Probe into Senator Barstow's Financial Dealings Gains Momentum."

The headline made his stomach churn. He downed the whiskey in one gulp and slammed the glass onto the desk. His mind raced. He thought about Agnes. He'd trusted her. She'd been like family. But in the end, everyone betrayed him.

"She had the nerve to betray me?" he hissed, his voice low and venomous. "Agnes won't live long enough to watch me fall; she'll be the first to go."

Even as Bobby plotted his next move, he knew time was running out. The FBI's case was airtight, the net drawing tighter around him. But fear didn't soften him; it hardened him. He became crueler, more reckless.

At his next rally, he smiled and waved, shaking hands with constituents who believed his every word. But behind that polished exterior was a man desperate to stay ahead of the storm.

"I clawed my way out of the gutter for this," he thought, his gaze sweeping over the adoring crowd. "And I'll wade through a river of blood before I let anyone take it from me."

Chapter 43: Hate to See You Go

Jake wasn't anywhere near Houston yet, but he had crossed the state line into Texas before pulling off of the highway. The rest area was dimly lit and sparsely occupied, the kind of place where you could lose yourself in your thoughts, or drown in them. He killed the engine and leaned back in the driver's seat; his eyes drifting shut as he tried to make sense of the chaos swirling in his mind.

Jake knew he could finish the job without Julianna. He'd been trained to shove emotions into a locked box, to focus only on the mission. But the thought of moving forward without her was a gnawing rot, eating away at the resolve he'd spent a lifetime building. The job came first, always. But as he sat there, the thought of moving forward without her gnawed at him.

For the first time, Jake questioned the purpose of it all. What was the point of victory if it came without Julianna? Without her sharp wit, her fearless fire? The thought was as foreign to him as hope, and twice as dangerous. Jake realized he didn't just want to finish the job; he wanted to ride into the sunset with her. The realization felt foreign, like wearing a suit that didn't quite fit.

He knew this feeling could make him reckless. His professional side warned him to bury it, to focus, but his heart wouldn't let it go. Eventually, his heart overruled his better judgment. He opened his eyes, reached for his phone, and dialed the number he had memorized but never thought he'd call.

It rang twice before being picked up. The voice on the other end was smooth, dripping with disdain.

"Well, well, Jake," Barstow drawled, his voice oozing mockery. "What a pleasant surprise. You're the topic of the hour over here. Isn't that funny?"

Jake's grip on the phone tightened. "You have something of mine, Barstow. I want her back. Unharmed."

Barstow's laughter echoed through the line, cold and mocking. "Unharmed? Oh, Jake, you're such an optimist," Barstow sneered. "Let's just say, Julianna and I have been getting… acquainted. She's a tough one, but even the toughest bends eventually. Some just need more persuasion."

Jake's jaw clenched so hard it felt like his teeth might shatter. "If you've hurt her, I swear…"

"Swear what, Jake?" Barstow interrupted, his tone a razor-sharp taunt. "You burn my businesses to the ground, kill my men, like they're nothing, and now you think you can *demand* something from me? Do you even know who you're dealing with?"

Jake's voice was low, controlled, but brimming with rage. "I'm the man who's going to take you down, if anything happens to her."

Barstow's amusement returned, darker now. "Oh, Jake, you sound so desperate. You know, it's adorable. Desperation suits you." He paused as if savoring the moment. "But let's be honest. You're not in a position to make threats. I am."

"What do you want?" Jake ground out.

Barstow let the question hang in the air for a moment, reveling in his control. "I'll tell you what I want," he said finally. "Agnes Grady."

Jake's stomach dropped. "The bookkeeper?"

"Ah, so you've heard of dear Agnes," Barstow purred, his voice dripping with malice. "She's cozy in an FBI safe house right now, spilling all my dirty little secrets like the turncoat she is. She's a liability, Jake. One I need you to… eliminate."

"You really think I'd take you at your word?" Jake asked, his voice was ice-cold as his grip tightened on the phone.

"Of course not," Barstow admitted with a smug chuckle. "Trust is irrelevant. The real question is, do you love Julianna enough to do what I want or don't you? Or don't. But I'll tell you this, Jake: she won't last long if you refuse. And her suffering will be… extensive."

Jake's knuckles whitened as he gripped the steering wheel, his mind racing. Jake knew Barstow was dangling bait laced with poison — that the man's word was worth less than the air it traveled through. But Julianna's voice haunted him, raw and desperate: *Go, Jake. Just go… but come back for me.*

"Fine," Jake said, his voice like steel. "I'll do it. But if you harm her any further, there's no corner of this earth where you'll be safe from me."

Barstow's laughter was chilling. "I'll keep that in mind. Good luck, Jake. You'll need it."

The line went dead. Jake sat in the silence of the SUV, his breathing heavy, his thoughts darker than they'd ever been. He knew Barstow would double-cross him. He knew Julianna's life hung by a thread. And he knew that if he was going to save her, he'd need to play this game smarter, deadlier, and more ruthlessly than ever before. But above all, Jake needed to stall. Julianna wasn't just a hostage; she was a pawn in Barstow's twisted game. And pawns didn't last long unless the board changed.

He started the engine and pulled back onto the highway, his jaw set, his eyes hard. He didn't know where Agnes was yet, but he'd find her. He'd do what needed to be done to keep Julianna alive. And when this was over, Jake promised himself one thing: Barstow wouldn't just lose his empire, he'd lose everything, including his life.

Chapter 44: Sparks Will Fly

Jake leaned against the hood of his rented SUV, the oppressive Louisiana heat wrapping around him like a vice. The setting sun bled orange over the bayou, casting long shadows that stretched across the endless, still waters. The air clung to him, heavy with humidity and the faint metallic tang of the swamp. It soaked into his skin and dragged at his thoughts like quicksand. He wiped the sweat from his brow and stared at the GPS tracker on his phone. The blinking red dot on Jake's phone traced Special Agent William Carter's car, parked like a beacon of frustration outside the Federal Attorney's office in downtown New Orleans. His jaw tightened as he considered his next move.

This has to be it, he thought. The Feds were too predictable, always sticking close to their procedural playbook. If Carter hadn't left the city, then Agnes had to be somewhere nearby. And with the frequent trips to a Chalmette neighborhood close to the St. Bernard Parish Hospital, it all pointed to one thing: a safe house. The thought frustrated him but it also fueled his determination.

Jake's mind raced as he pieced together what he'd learned over the past two grueling days of surveillance. Carter's movements were consistent: the Federal Attorney's office, the FBI field office, his hotel downtown, and Chalmette. There was no doubt in Jake's mind now. The safe house was in that residential neighborhood.

But how to breach it? That was the question that loomed largest.

He climbed into the SUV and started the engine, letting the faint rumble ground his thoughts. Earlier, as Jake had cruised the streets of Chalmette, the neighborhood struck him as maddeningly serene. Modest single-story homes with American flags fluttering on porches and potted plants arranged with care painted a picture of unbroken normalcy. But beneath that calm exterior, Jake knew, lay a fortress. It was a neighborhood that seemed untouched by the chaos of Jake's world, a facade of normalcy masking the presence of a federal safe house. He gripped the steering wheel tightly.

The thought of Agnes hiding behind federal protections while Julianna suffered in Barstow's grip churned Jake's stomach. Fury bubbled beneath his skin, threatening to boil over, but he forced himself to focus. Anger was useless if it wasn't controlled. *Focus, he commanded himself, gripping the steering wheel so hard his knuckles turned white. Emotions get you killed. Regret buries you next to the people you couldn't save.*

Jake left the SUV two blocks away, tucking it into the shadows between an overgrown fence and a line of low trees. As he slipped into the neighborhood on foot, the humid air pressed close, muffling his movements as if the swamp itself conspired to keep him hidden. The faint glow of porch lights and the flicker of televisions inside homes cast shadows across the sidewalks. Jake moved like a ghost, his boots barely brushing the concrete as he glided through the shadows. His sharp eyes scanned for the tiniest anomaly, a car that didn't belong, the faint rustle of curtains, the cold glint of a surveillance camera lurking in the dark.

A nondescript house caught his attention, a dark sedan crouched in the driveway, its government plates barely visible in the dim, flickering glow of a nearby streetlamp. Bingo. Jake circled the block, noting the angles and possible entry points. The house itself was unassuming, blending perfectly with the rest of the neighborhood. But there were small details that betrayed its purpose, a reinforced front door, no mailbox, and curtains drawn tight in every window.

As he walked back to the SUV, Jake's thoughts churned. The stakes were higher than ever, and the timeline was unforgiving.

Julianna's out there, counting on you, he reminded himself. *You can't afford to make mistakes.*

He climbed into the driver's seat and pulled out a small notebook, jotting down everything he'd observed: the layout of the neighborhood, the comings and goings of Carter, and the details of the house. Jake had walked into dangerous situations before, but never with stakes like this. It wasn't just a mission, and it wasn't just survival. It was Julianna, his anchor, his reason to keep breathing.

Jake stared at the page, his pen hovering as he let out a frustrated sigh. Jake had built a career on detachment, treating every mission as a puzzle to solve, every obstacle as a calculation. But this time, the lines blurred. This wasn't a puzzle; it was personal. He'd thought about walking away more than once, abandoning the chaos for a quiet life somewhere far away. But as much as he tried, he couldn't shake the image of Julianna's face.

"She kept me alive when I had no reason to be," Jake muttered to himself, his voice barely above a whisper as if the words themselves were fragile. The silence in the SUV pressed against him, broken only by the faint hum of the engine. "If I lose her, I…" He couldn't finish the thought. The idea of a world without Julianna felt like a weight he couldn't bear.

As the night deepened, Jake turned his focus to forming a plan. A frontal assault was out of the question; it would be nothing short of suicide. The Feds weren't amateurs, and a wrong move here wouldn't just get him killed, it would seal Julianna's fate. He needed to draw them out, and create a diversion. Maybe even exploit Carter's routine. But how? And could he do it without leaving a trail? It wasn't just the Feds he had to outmaneuver. Barstow's men were out there, lurking in the shadows, watching for any sign of a misstep. Jake could feel their invisible eyes, waiting for him to falter.

His phone buzzed, pulling him from his thoughts. It was an encrypted message from one of his contacts in D.C.

Carter's been running solo. No extra protection detail. Safe house confirmed in Chalmette. Be careful.

Jake smirked grimly. At least he was on the right track. He sent a quick reply: **Appreciate it. Stay available. This one's personal.**

As he leaned back in the seat, staring at the notes in his notebook, the outline of a plan began to take shape. He didn't have all the answers yet, but one thing was clear: he wasn't leaving without Agnes. And once he had Agnes, there would be no more games, no more negotiations. Jake would rain hellfire on Barstow, and the man wouldn't just lose, he'd burn for every moment Julianna had suffered.

The thought steadied him, his resolve hardening like steel. Julianna's voice echoed in his mind, urging him forward. *Go, Jake. Go and come back for me.*

Chapter 45: Dirty Work

By midday, Jake's Sedan idled a block from the suspected FBI safe house, his grip on the wheel ironclad as his eyes locked on the dark sedan pulling out of the driveway. Each second felt like an eternity as his heart hammered against his ribs, the weight of what came next pressing down on him. He followed the car as it headed down the quiet suburban street. He followed at a cautious distance, his heart pounding in anticipation of what lay ahead.

The sedan pulled into a small, nondescript restaurant. Jake waited until the driver disappeared inside before stepping out. With deliberate movements, he approached the parked sedan and, after a quick scan of the surroundings, crouched down to plant an explosive device underneath it. He retreated quickly, his pulse steady, and slid back into his car to resume the tail.

Jake trailed the sedan back to the safe house, his distance calculated, his eyes never leaving the target. The tension in his chest coiled tighter with every turn, every stop, every flicker of a brake light. The agent got out of the vehicle, a brown paper bag of food clutched in one hand, and entered the house. Jake drove past, noting the layout and finding a spot half a block away where he had a clear line of sight.

Over the next several hours, Jake observed the comings and goings of the agents. Around 5 PM, a shift change took place: three agents left the house, and three replacements arrived. Jake's jaw tightened. He had faced far worse odds, but the stakes had never been higher. As the sun dipped below the horizon, he rehearsed the steps of his plan in his mind, steeling himself for what was to come.

At 10 PM, one of the agents stepped out onto the front stoop for a cigarette. Jake watched as the orange ember flared in the darkness before the man disappeared around the back of the house to continue his rounds. At 11 PM, as the same agent made his way to the rear of the house again, Jake seized his chance. He moved quickly and silently across the lawn, slipping into the backyard undetected.

Scaling the house with practiced ease, Jake hauled a duffle bag over his shoulder. He reached the roof and positioned himself near the chimney, his sniper rifle already loaded with tranquilizer darts. His pistol, also loaded with tranq. rounds, rested snugly in his waistband. He took a deep breath; his nerves were calm but his senses were razor-sharp.

"Ready, Jake," he muttered to himself. His finger hovered over the detonator's button.

The night erupted in chaos. The explosion tore through the silence, a sharp, deafening crack followed by a fiery bloom that consumed the sedan in a hellish blaze. Flames licked hungrily at the air, casting flickering shadows across the front of the house and illuminating the panic of the agents within. Jake's lips tightened into a grim line as two of the agents burst out of the house, their hands instinctively moving toward their weapons. They never had the chance. Jake's rifle hissed twice, the tranquilizer darts slicing through the chaos with lethal precision. The agents barely had time to register the threat before crumpling to the ground like marionettes with their strings cut.

Jake anticipated the third agent's instinct to protect Agnes, and he moved before hesitation could creep in. Grabbing the rope he'd secured earlier, he swung silently through the second-floor window. Glass shattered around him in a cascade of jagged edges, the crash muffled by the roar of the fire outside. The glass shattered as his boots struck it, sending shards cascading into the darkened bedroom. Agnes let out a startled scream, but Jake was quicker. He fired a dart into her shoulder before she could make another sound.

The door burst open, and the remaining agent stormed in, gun drawn. Jake remained in the shadows; his breath steady. As the agent scanned the room, Jake fired two darts in rapid succession. The man staggered, dropping his weapon before slumping to the floor.

Jake didn't hesitate. He slung Agnes over his shoulder in one fluid motion, his steps swift and deliberate as he navigated the house. The heat from the burning car outside cast flickering shadows on the walls, adding to the chaos of the moment. Jake exited through the back door, crossed a neighbor's yard, and reached his getaway vehicle. He dumped Agnes unceremoniously into the truck and climbed into the driver's seat.

The engine roared to life, and Jake sped away into the night. His hands clenched the wheel, his mind racing faster than the vehicle. He glanced at the rearview mirror, watching the glow of the fire fade into the distance.

Jake's thoughts swirled in the quiet hum of the SUV. The mission was a success, on paper. But the hollow ache in his chest told him otherwise. Each mile put more distance between him and the burning wreckage, but it couldn't dull the sharp image of Julianna's face, battered and defiant, or the sound of her voice calling out to him. The image of Julianna, bound and at the mercy of Barstow, gnawed at him. Jake's jaw tightened with resolve. Whatever it took, whatever lines he had to cross, he would get her back. For now, he pushed those thoughts aside and focused on the road ahead, disappearing into the night.

Jake switched vehicles to a fresh SUV that he had stashed, placing Agnes, still unconscious, gently into the bench seat directly behind him. Jake adjusted the rearview mirror, his eyes flicking to Agnes slumped unconscious in the backseat. He gripped the wheel tighter, the hum of the highway beneath the tires doing little to drown out the storm raging in his head. As soon as he was clear, he dialed Julianna's number.

"Tell me, Jake," Barstow purred, his voice thick with venom. "Is my little problem… resolved?"

Jake's jaw tightened. "First, let me talk to Julianna. I need proof of life."

There was a pause, and Jake could hear muffled voices in the background before Barstow spoke again, irritation creeping into his tone. "Wait a moment," Barstow said, irritation bleeding into his tone. Jake could hear the faint rustle of movement and the muffled voices of Barstow's men. The senator's footsteps echoed faintly; each one a reminder of the fragile line Jake was walking.

Jake could almost visualize Barstow descending from his posh, upper-floor suite to the grim confines of the basement where Julianna had been kept. Barstow's footsteps echoed faintly, followed by the groan of a heavy door swinging open. The air inside the makeshift cell was thick and stagnant, and Julianna sat slumped in the corner, her wrists bound but her spirit unbroken.

Barstow put the phone on speaker and held it out toward her. "Talk," he commanded.

Julianna's voice was faint but defiant. "Is that you, Jake?"

Jake's grip on the steering wheel tightened. "Yeah, babe, it's me. Are you okay?"

Her tone sharpened, fueled by both fury and desperation. "Jake, you hear me?" Julianna's voice cracked, raw with fury and desperation. "Kill him! Kill this sick bastard!"

Before Jake could respond, Barstow snatched the phone back, muting Julianna's protests as he stepped out of the cell and locked the door behind him. He spoke into the phone, his voice now cold and measured. "Well, Jake, what do you have for me? Did you kill her?"

Jake's voice was steady but laced with anger. "Not yet," Jake said, his tone cold, calculated. "She's in my trunk, alive, for now. So, what's it gonna be, Barstow? You want her back, or should I deliver her gift-wrapped to the nearest courthouse?"

There was a sharp intake of breath on Barstow's end, followed by a hiss of frustration. "The deal was for you to kill her! You have to finish the job!"

Jake smirked, though there was no humor in it. "Now, why would I do that? If you want her dead, you can do it yourself, or I can do it for you, after I have Julianna."

Barstow's silence was telling, a mix of fury and reluctant calculation. Finally, he spoke, his voice dripping with venom. "Fine," Barstow hissed, his facade cracking for a brief second. "Name the place. Yours or mine?"

Jake's smirk deepened. "Your place," Jake said, his voice laced with quiet menace. "And don't bother trying to play coy. I know your address better than your damn mailman."

Barstow's voice faltered for just a moment before regaining its edge. "Bring her to me. And Jake? Don't try anything stupid."

Jake ended the call without replying, tossing the phone onto the passenger seat. His hands gripped the steering wheel as a wave of determination surged through him. This was no longer just about Julianna. It was about taking down the monster who had dared to hurt her. The SUV growled beneath him as Jake pressed the accelerator, his gaze fixed on the dark road stretching ahead. This wasn't just about Julianna anymore. It was about justice, delivered cold, brutal, and without mercy.

Chapter 46: Low Down

Barstow sat in his study, the crystal glass of bourbon in his hand catching the light from the grand chandelier above. The room's opulence, with its dark mahogany walls and gold-accented furniture, seemed almost suffocating, a veneer of control masking the chaos swirling in his mind. Jake and Julianna were irritants, thorns he could eventually pluck. But Agnes, Agnes was a noose cinching tighter with every breath, her betrayal threatening to choke the life out of everything he had built. She knew too much, and if Jake was audacious enough to keep her alive, it only escalated Barstow's urgency to end this once and for all.

Jake's sole focus was Julianna, her safety, her freedom. His own life, even Agnes', faded into insignificance. Every decision, every move, was a step toward one goal: getting her out alive. As he drove the SUV toward Barstow's sprawling mansion, his thoughts were a chaotic mix of desperation and strategy. Agnes was collateral. Jake had long made peace with what might happen to himself. But Julianna? She wasn't just part of the mission. She was the mission. She *had* to make it out alive, no matter the cost. She was his anchor in this storm, and he would do whatever it took to ensure she made it out alive.

When Jake reached the mansion's wrought-iron gates, he dialed Barstow's number. The line clicked immediately. "I'm here," Jake said, his voice steady despite the storm raging in his chest.

"Drive in slowly," Barstow replied, his tone dripping with smugness. "We're ready for you."

The gates creaked open with deliberate slowness, the driveway stretched ahead, taut with danger, like a fuse waiting to ignite. Manicured lawns framed the path, and the towering sycamore trees lining both sides of the driveway seemed to stretch toward Jake like grasping fingers. The sun cast long shadows across the grounds, and Jake's sharp eyes scanned the grounds, noting the guards stationed in the shadows of the trees. Their stances were relaxed but ready, their rifles glinting faintly in the fading light. The mansion loomed ahead, a sprawling structure of stone and glass. In the center of the driveway's cul-de-sac stood a grand fountain, its cascading water glinting in the fading light.

Jake rolled the SUV forward at a crawl, his knuckles white on the steering wheel. His mind cataloged every detail: the guards' positions, the lack of cover, the looming tension. The mansion's massive double doors swung open, and Julianna stepped out, her hands bound tightly in front of her. Her face was pale, her hair disheveled, but her eyes burned with defiance, a fire Barstow hadn't managed to extinguish. Behind her, a guard pressed a gun to her head.

Jake slammed the SUV into the park and stepped out, keeping his hands visible. "Everybody, stay cool," he called out, his voice cutting through the still evening air.

He moved deliberately around to the passenger side, opening the back door to reveal Agnes, still unconscious. In her arms, concealed by her body, was a silenced handgun. Jake lifted Agnes carefully, cradling her limp form as if she weighed nothing, his every motion deliberate and controlled. The silenced handgun now concealed beneath her body pressed reassuringly against his palm. As he carried her up the steps, the tension in the air was electric.

Barstow watched from the shadows of an exterior balcony; his lips curled into a smug smile. "You're playing your part nicely, Jake," he called out.

Jake didn't respond. He reached the top step, where the guard held Julianna. The man's grip tightened on her arm, and the barrel of the gun pressed against her temple.

"Let her go," Jake said, his voice calm but firm.

The guard hesitated, glancing up toward Barstow, who gave a small nod. With one swift motion, the guard released Julianna and reached out to take Agnes from Jake. It was the moment Jake had been waiting for.

In one fluid motion, Jake shifted his hold on Agnes, drawing the silenced handgun from beneath her body and firing. The guard didn't have time to react; the shot was clean, precise, and fatal. The man's body crumpled, and Jake caught Agnes before she could hit the ground. In the chaos, Julianna bolted toward the SUV.

Jake didn't hesitate. He tossed Agnes into the back seat, his voice cutting through the cacophony of gunfire. "Julianna, move!" he commanded. Bullets pinged off the SUV's reinforced body, each impact ringing out like a war drum. The guards among the trees opened fire, bullets ricocheting off the SUV's armored exterior and pinging against the stone steps. Jake dove into the driver's seat, slamming the door shut as the windshield cracked under the barrage.

"Julianna!" he yelled. She was already in the passenger seat, her hands now free, reaching for the stash of weapons at her feet. She grabbed an explosive, yanked the pin, and lobbed it toward the nearest guard. The grenade exploded with a deafening roar. Dirt and shrapnel ripped through the guards' formation, leaving chaos in its wake. The gunfire faltered, replaced by shouts of confusion and pain.

"Hang on," Jake said, gripping the wheel with one hand and before he hit the gas, he pulled out a small detonator from his pocket with the other. With a grim smile, he pressed the button.

A chain of explosions ripped through the pristine lawns, the shockwaves tearing ancient sycamore trees from their roots and hurling guards through the air like ragdolls. The manicured perfection of Barstow's estate disintegrated into a scene of fiery ruin. The garage, where Jake had planted several charges days earlier, went up in a fiery blast, consuming Barstow's prized car collection. Flames licked at the edges of the mansion, smoke billowing into the twilight sky.

"Jake!" Julianna shouted, snapping him back to the present as another wave of bullets slammed into the SUV. Jake slammed his foot onto the accelerator, the tires screeched against the gravel. The SUV shot forward, bullets ricocheting off its reinforced frame as flames licked at the edge of the driveway. Guards scrambled to take aim, but Julianna kept them at bay, firing off rounds from a rifle she had grabbed.

"Hit the gate," she yelled, her voice hoarse but fierce.

The SUV barreled into the wrought-iron gates, the impact sending them shuddering off their hinges in a screech of twisting metal and flying sparks. In the rearview mirror, the mansion stood engulfed in flames, a crumbling monument to Barstow's hubris. Smoke billowed into the night sky, the glow of the inferno staining the horizon. But the night was far from over. Jake's grip on the wheel tightened, his eyes scanning the dark road ahead. The real fight was just beginning.

Chapter 47: I'm Free

"They're gaining on us," Julianna snapped, her eyes darting to the convoy of headlights piercing through the smoke and chaos behind them.

Jake's jaw tightened; his focus locked on the winding backroad ahead. "Keep them off us," he said, his voice low but urgent.

Without hesitation, Julianna leaned out the passenger window, rifle in hand, and began firing. Tires blew out, vehicles swerved off the road, and explosions lit up the night as she lobbed grenades at their pursuers.

"We're not out of this yet," Jake muttered, gripping the wheel tighter as he pushed the SUV to its limits.

In the chaos of the chase, one thing was clear: Barstow had underestimated them, and Jake wasn't stopping until Julianna was safe and Barstow was buried. The fight was far from over.

The SUV tore through the narrow Louisiana backroads, its engine growling like a beast unleashed. Each sharp turn sent rocks flying, the vehicle skidding dangerously close to the edge of the gravel. Gunfire erupted from the pursuing convoy, a barrage of bullets peppering the SUV. One round punched through the rear windshield, shattering it in a cascade of jagged glass that glittered in the dim moonlight. Julianna instinctively ducked, cursing under her breath as she fumbled with a grenade from the stash at her feet.

"Hold it steady, Jake!" she shouted, yanking the pin and tossing the explosive out the window.

Jake veered left sharply, the SUV tilting precariously before righting itself. The grenade detonated with a thunderous roar, lighting up the night like a flash of hellfire. The lead car swerved too late, flipping end over end before slamming into a ditch, engulfed in a plume of flames and twisted metal.

"Nice throw!" Jake called, gripping the wheel tightly.

Julianna smirked, adrenaline pumping. "Thanks, but we're not done yet!"

In the rearview mirror, two more cars emerged from the dust cloud, their headlights bouncing on the uneven terrain. The second car was closing fast. A sharp turn loomed ahead, and Jake timed it perfectly, pulling the emergency brake and spinning the SUV 180 degrees. The screeching tires sent up a haze of smoke, and as the pursuing car came into view, Julianna leaned out the window, her rifle aimed and ready.

"Lights out," she muttered, squeezing the trigger. The pursuing car's front tire blew, sending it careening into a tree with a sickening crunch.

The final vehicle remained relentless, its driver weaving to avoid obstacles and closing the gap. Ahead loomed a narrow wooden bridge, its planks weathered and creaking under the weight of time. Jake's eyes narrowed. It was their only shot. He punched the gas, gripping the wheel tightly as they barreled across. The bridge groaned under the weight, the wooden planks rattling beneath them. As the pursuing car reached the bridge, Jake slammed the brakes, wrenching the SUV into a fishtail. The tires screeched in protest, sending gravel and debris flying in a blinding cloud.

Julianna lobbed another grenade onto the bridge behind them. The explosion sent splinters of wood flying, and the final car skidded wildly as the grenade blast tore the bridge apart behind them. Wood splintered and groaned before the vehicle veered off course, plunging nose-first into the murky bayou with a resounding splash.

Jake exhaled sharply, the tension releasing slightly as they finally left their pursuers behind. He eased up on the accelerator, and the SUV hummed steadily down the open road.

"She still breathing?" Julianna asked, her voice sharp as she glanced at Agnes slumped like a rag doll in the backseat.

Jake's eyes flicked to the rearview mirror. "Still out. She's tough, though. She'll wake up pissed, with a headache to match."

As they approached the outskirts of Baton Rouge, Jake pulled the SUV into a dark side street. "We need to switch vehicles," he said, scanning the area.

Julianna nodded, her gaze locking onto a shiny sedan parked under a flickering streetlight. Without missing a beat, Julianna slipped out of the SUV, her movements precise and practiced. In less than a minute, the sedan's lock clicked open, and the engine roared to life under her deft touch

"Let's go," she said, motioning to Jake. They transferred their gear and Agnes into the stolen car before speeding off into the night.

Hours later, they pulled into the parking lot of a brightly lit shopping plaza just outside New Orleans. The lot was mostly empty, save for a handful of late-night shoppers and employees heading home. A large grocery store dominated the plaza, its neon sign flickering intermittently.

"This will do," Jake said, pulling into a shadowy corner. He turned to Julianna. "You ready?"

Julianna nodded and opened the back door. Jake lifted Agnes out gently, cradling her as though she were a sleeping child. They carried her to the line of shopping carts near the store entrance and laid her down carefully.

Julianna took a deep breath, smoothed her hair, and then screamed at the top of her lungs, "Help! Please, someone, help!" Julianna screamed, her voice raw and desperate as she waved frantically at the few patrons in the lot. "This woman needs an ambulance!"

Her voice echoed across the lot, drawing nearby patrons' attention milling about. A grocery store manager, a wiry man with thick glasses and a concerned expression, rushed out.

"What's going on?" He asked, his voice trembling slightly.

Julianna turned to him, tears brimming in her eyes. "We found her like this! She's barely breathing! Please, call 911!"

The manager's face turned ashen, and his hands fumbled as he yanked his phone from his pocket. "An ambulance is on the way," he assured her, glancing nervously at Agnes. "Do you know her name?"

Julianna shook her head dramatically. "No! She was just lying here when I arrived!"

As a small crowd gathered around the commotion, Jake slipped away, motioning discreetly to Julianna. She nodded, wiping away her feigned tears before turning back to the manager. "Thank you," Julianna gasped, her voice trembling as if on the verge of tears.

Moments later, Jake and Julianna melted into the shadows, disappearing into the night.

Minutes after the ambulance arrived, two paramedics knelt beside Agnes, checking her vitals. "She's coming around," one of them said, shining a flashlight into her eyes. "Ma'am, can you hear me? What's your name?"

Agnes groaned, her eyelids fluttering as she slowly came to, her eyes bleary but filled with groggy defiance. "Agnes," she rasped, her voice barely audible.

As the paramedics rolled up her sleeve to administer an IV, they froze. Scrawled in bold marker on her arm were the words:

"Please return me to the FBI. Call Special Agent William Carter – (504) 555-1212."

The two paramedics exchanged stunned glances. One of them pulled out his phone and dialed the number.

"Special Agent Carter," came a gruff voice on the other end.

The paramedic hesitated, still staring at the message on Agnes's arm. "Uh, are you missing a little old lady named Agnes?"

There was a pause, followed by a sharp intake of breath. "Where is she?" Carter demanded.

"In an ambulance heading to Mercy General in New Orleans," the paramedic replied. "She's alive, but…you might want to come get her."

Agnes, now slightly more alert, chuckled weakly. "Told you," Agnes rasped, a ghost of a smirk tugging at her lips. "I'm a VIP."

As the ambulance sped toward the hospital, Jake and Julianna vanished into the night, the glow of the city on the horizon. Their mission wasn't over, but their resolve burned brighter than ever.

Chapter 48: I'm Alright

"You holding up, babe?" Jake asked, his voice hoarse with exhaustion but edged with quiet concern.

Julianna glanced over at him from the passenger seat, her face illuminated by the passing glow of highway lights. She shifted in her seat, brushing her hair back. "I'm fine," Julianna replied, her voice quieter than usual. She paused, pushing the memory away. "Barstow roughed me up a bit that first night. Left some marks." Her words wavered for a moment before her jaw tightened. "But I knew you'd come back for me. I never doubted it."

Jake's lips twitched into a faint smirk. "Leaving you with that bastard? Not in this lifetime."

Julianna shook her head, a mix of admiration and exasperation. "But seriously, Jake," Julianna said, her tone equal parts admiration and disbelief. "What the hell was that? Charging into Barstow's mansion like some action hero with a death wish? You're either the smartest or luckiest man I've ever met."

Jake chuckled dryly, keeping his eyes on the road. "Maybe I'm a little crazy," Jake admitted with a shrug. "But leaving it to fate's never been my style. I'd rather take my chances with a half-baked plan than sit around waiting for miracles."

She crossed her arms, tilting her head. "Half-baked? That's an understatement. You're lucky they didn't have more guys posted at the gate. And what if Barstow had set a better trap?"

"Then I'd have sprung it and improvised," he replied with a shrug, glancing at her briefly. "Worked out okay, didn't it?"

Julianna's lips twitched into a smile despite herself. "You're impossible. You know that?"

Jake opened his mouth to retort when Julianna's sharp gasp cut him off. "Jake!" Julianna's eyes widened at the dark stain spreading across his jeans. "You're bleeding! Why didn't you say anything?"

Jake glanced down, his brows furrowing as he noticed the blood pooling beneath him. "Huh," he muttered, almost dismissively. "Guess I got clipped back there. Didn't think it was that bad."

"Not that bad?" Julianna's voice rose, sharp with disbelief. "You're practically marinating in your own blood!" Pull over, now."

Jake hesitated but then saw the determination in her eyes and relented. A sign for a small roadside motel loomed ahead, with a Walgreens visible across the street. He pulled into the lot, parking near the far end where it was shadowed by the streetlights.

The room was small but clean, with faded floral wallpaper and a faint smell of bleach. Jake tossed the keys onto the table while Julianna grabbed her wallet.

"I'll be back," she said, pointing toward the Walgreens. "Stay put and don't you dare bleed out while I'm gone."

Jake grinned faintly, though his face was pale. "I'll try to keep it together."

A short while later, Julianna returned with a bag full of medical supplies. She dumped them onto the bed, pulled Jake into the bathroom, and made him sit on the closed toilet lid.

"Alright," Julianna said, snapping on a pair of gloves. "Let's see the damage. Pants off."

Jake arched a brow, smirking despite himself. "Didn't think you'd make the first move, Jules."

She smirked, pulling a pair of scissors from the bag. "Trust me," Julianna quipped, brandishing scissors with a flourish. "This is strictly business."

With a wince, Jake unbuckled his belt and slid his pants down far enough to reveal the wound. The bullet had torn through the fleshy part of his backside, leaving a ragged hole.

"Well," Julianna said, examining the injury. "It went straight through. Lucky for you, nothing vital was hit."

Jake groaned. "Yeah, lucky me. Just make it quick, okay?"

She cleaned the wound with antiseptic, ignoring Jake's sharp intake of breath. "Wow, for a guy who charges mansions and dodges bullets, you're awfully sensitive," she teased, dabbing the wound with antiseptic.

"Let me shoot *you* in the ass, and we'll compare notes," Jake grumbled, wincing.

Julianna laughed her first real laugh in days. "Oh, trust me, I won't tell anyone you got shot in the butt. Wouldn't want to ruin your tough-guy image."

Jake managed a chuckle despite the pain. "It's not funny. If this gets out, I'll never hear the end of it."

"Who am I going to tell, Jake?" she said, threading a needle. "It's not like I'm posting this on social media."

Jake's laugh turned into a wince as she began stitching the wound. "Geez, could you be a little gentler?"

"Nope," she said with a grin. "Consider this payback for scaring me half to death back at Barstow's."

Jake fell silent, his sharp retort dying on his lips as he watched her work. The precision of her hands, the determination in her eyes, she was steady, even after everything they'd been through. And damn, he was grateful for her. Her humor, her resilience, even her gentle hands, all reminded him why he couldn't let her go.

Once she was finished, Julianna stepped back, peeling off the gloves. "There. Good as new."

Jake stood carefully, testing his weight. "Thanks, Doc," he said with a small smile.

She tilted her head, smirking. "Just don't make a habit of this, okay? You're not invincible, Jake."

Later, as they settled onto the bed, the tension between them eased for the first time in days. Jake reached for her hand, squeezing it gently. "Thanks for having my back out there," he said quietly.

"Always," Julianna replied, her voice soft but firm. "Just promise me one thing," Julianna said, her voice quieter now, the humor slipping away. "Don't make me go through that again, Jake."

Jake's lips curved into a tired smile. "I can't promise that, babe. But one thing's for sure, I'll always come back for you."

Chapter 49: Angie

Special Agent in Charge William Carter leaned against the wall of the hospital room, his arms crossed tightly over his chest. His eyes scanned the various machines connected to Agnes. Tubes and wires snaked across her bed, their steady beeps a reminder that she was alive, despite her calm demeanor, which suggested a weekend spa retreat rather than a high-stakes abduction.

Agnes propped up with pillows, her silvery hair neatly combed despite the ordeal, looked entirely at ease. Her lips curled into a sly smile as she met Carter's concerned gaze.

"Agent Carter," Agnes said with that maddening mix of calm and amusement, "you've got that look again like someone just told you recess is canceled. Relax, honey. I'm fine."

Carter's jaw tightened; his tone clipped. "Fine? You were kidnapped from a secure safe house, my men were neutralized, and you're sitting here acting like it's a Sunday brunch. How the hell are you this calm?"

Agnes tilted her head, her smile growing. "Well, darling, it seems someone needed my company for the night. And lucky for you, they returned me in one piece. Been a long time since I spent an evening with a gentleman." Her eyes twinkled mischievously. "Longer still since I had a night that I couldn't remember what happened."

The agents stationed around the room exchanged quick glances, their lips twitching as they fought, and mostly failed, to stifle their grins. One of them couldn't hold back a chuckle, which quickly turned into a stifled cough as Carter shot him a withering glare.

"Agnes," Carter said, his tone exasperated, "this isn't a joke. You could've been killed."

"But I wasn't," Agnes replied smoothly, patting the edge of her blanket. "Seems to me whoever did this wasn't out for blood. And if you ask me, you should be glad I'm still breathing. You've got your case, don't you? Or is it me that's holding it together for you?"

Carter sighed, rubbing a hand over his face. She wasn't wrong. His case against Senator Barstow was as solid as ever, thanks to Agnes and the detailed ledgers she'd kept for decades. But the attack still didn't add up. If this had been Barstow's doing, there would've been carnage at the safe house. Barstow didn't leave loose ends.

"Fine," Carter muttered. "You're alive, and the case is intact. But that doesn't mean we're brushing this off. From now on, we double security. Two agents on your door at all times until you're ready to leave. No exceptions."

Agnes gave him an amused look. "Oh, honey, if they're anything like the last team, I should be guarding them."

A burst of laughter escaped one of the younger agents stationed by the window. He quickly covered his mouth, his face turning red as Carter shot him a look that could've cut through steel.

"Out. Now," Carter barked, his finger stabbing toward the door. The agents filed out, some muttering apologies, others exchanging grins.

In the hallway, Carter turned on his team with a glare that could rival a storm cloud. "Explain this to me," Carter snapped, his voice like a whip. "We're supposed to be the best. But someone sneaks past you, takes out three agents, kidnaps our star witness, and you don't fire a single damn shot. How does that happen?"

The agents stood stiffly, their faces reddening under Carter's tirade. One finally mustered the courage to speak. "Sir, we didn't hear or see anything until the explosion. By the time we got out there, it was chaos."

"Chaos?" Carter repeated, his voice rising. "Chaos is what happens when you're asleep at the wheel," Carter growled. "You should've had eyes on every angle of that house. And now I have to explain to my superiors how the star witness in our biggest case was kidnapped and then dropped off at a grocery store like a package!"

Another agent piped up hesitantly. "To be fair, sir," one agent muttered hesitantly, "at least they gave us a return label."

Carter's eyes narrowed dangerously, and the agent quickly looked away.

"From this moment forward," Carter growled, "there's zero margins for errors. Two of you on that door at all times. Rotate every four hours. And if she, so much as sneezes without a tissue, I want to know about it. Are we clear?"

"Yes, sir," they replied in unison.

Back in the room, Agnes chuckled softly as she watched Carter through the window. The poor man looked like he was about to pop a vein. She shook her head, a small smile tugging at her lips.

"Men," Agnes muttered, settling back into her pillows with a faint smirk. "Always convinced the world will fall apart without them."

As Carter reentered the room, she glanced at him, her expression softening slightly. "William," Agnes said, her tone softening just enough to tease, "You're a good man. But you need to loosen up before stress turns you into a patient next to me. And trust me, I'm much better company than you'd be."

Carter sighed; the weight of the day etched into his face. "Agnes, I swear, if you weren't so damn important to this case, I'd lock you in a bunker just to keep you out of trouble."

Agnes muttered under her breath, "If I were twenty years younger..."

Carter turned sharply. "What was that?"

She flashed him a grin, her eyes twinkling. "I said, 'And miss all this excitement? Not a chance.'"

Carter shook his head, the ghost of a smile tugging at his lips despite himself as he dragged a chair closer to her bedside. For all her wit and sass, Agnes was right. The case was still solid, and that was the most important thing. As Carter's gaze flicked to the steady beeps of the monitors, a grim certainty settled over him, he couldn't shake the nagging certainty: they'd need to find her a safer place, and soon.

Chapter 50: I'm Going Down

Senator Robert Barstow paced the narrow confines of his reinforced safe room, the polished toes of his leather shoes scuffed against the cold tile with each agitated step. The room, a fortress of steel and surveillance screens, suddenly felt more like a cage than a sanctuary.

Barstow nursed his third, or was it his fourth? Glass of whiskey, the amber liquid barely calming the rage simmering beneath his sweaty brow. His usually well-groomed silver hair was disheveled, and his expensive suit was rumpled, stained with a splash of the whiskey he had sloshed in his agitation.

"Damn idiots!" Barstow snarled, slamming his glass onto the steel desk so hard the amber liquid sloshed over the rim where a small stack of classified documents lay scattered. The valet, wiry and perpetually wary, stood near the door, wringing his hands.

"Sir," the valet began cautiously, his voice trembling, "the perimeter is secure now. Perhaps, it's safe for you to step out and... assess things?"

Barstow whirled on him, his bloodshot eyes narrowing. "Safe?" Barstow roared, jabbing a trembling finger at the surveillance monitors. "Does this look *safe* to you? Those idiots couldn't protect a doghouse, let alone my estate! You think I'm just going to waltz out there like nothing happened?"

The valet hesitated but stood his ground. "It's been over an hour, sir. Most of the men you hired are still on the property. They've secured the exits and are conducting patrols. I assure you; the threat is gone."

Barstow grunted, downed the remainder of his whiskey in one gulp, and tossed the glass onto the desk, where it rolled precariously but didn't fall. "Fine. But if anything happens to me, you'll wish you were the one they came for."

When Barstow finally stepped out of the safe room, the sight that greeted him was one of utter devastation. His once-pristine mansion, a symbol of his power and wealth, now bore the scars of the night's chaos. Bullet holes pocked the walls, shattered glass crunched beneath his loafers, and smoke still lingered in the air. His remaining security personnel snapped to attention as he stormed into the main hall, his face twisted in fury.

"You call this security?" Barstow thundered, his voice ricocheting off the marble walls like a gunshot. "Look at this place! My home, a goddamn war zone because of your incompetence!"

A burly man in tactical gear stepped forward, trying to explain. "Sir, we did the best we could. The attack was coordinated…"

"Coordinated?" Barstow cut him off, his voice dripping with sarcasm. "Coordinated? My seven-year-old niece could've coordinated a better defense than you clowns!"

The man clenched his jaw but said nothing.

Barstow continued his words slurring slightly from the whiskey. "You're all useless! Get out of my sight! And if I ever see your faces again, it'll be in a courtroom suing you for breach of contract!"

The security team dispersed, muttering under their breath, while Barstow marched to his office, his mind racing. He couldn't stay here. The walls of his once-impenetrable fortress now felt as fragile as glass.

Barstow tore through his office, yanking open drawers and rifling through their contents with frantic urgency. The dark mahogany-paneled walls seemed to press in on him, the unused shelves of law books now mocking relics of his fabricated legacy. His thumb pressed against the biometric scanner, the safe opening with a soft, mechanical hiss that felt louder in the tense silence.

From inside, he pulled out a thick stack of hundred-dollar bills, a forged passport under a false name, a sleek Beretta pistol, and a manila folder filled with sensitive documents. He tucked everything into the satchel, his movements methodical despite the urgency.

Once packed, he stepped into the garage, surveying the damage. Most of his cars were riddled with bullet holes, their sleek exteriors ruined.

Only a battered black SUV remained unscathed. He climbed in, tossed the satchel onto the passenger seat, and gunned the engine.

The drive to his hunting cabin in Arkansas stretched endlessly, each mile a cruel reminder of how far his empire had fallen. The hours dragged as the SUV sped down desolate highways, the countryside gradually swallowing the urban sprawl of Baton Rouge. Barstow gripped the steering wheel tightly, his knuckles white. His mind was a storm of anger, paranoia, and desperation.

"They think they can humiliate *me*?" Barstow muttered, venomous, gripping the steering wheel until his knuckles whitened. The glow of the dashboard cast eerie shadows on his face. "Jake, Julianna, those damn Russians, every last one of them will pay. And the FBI? They'll wish they'd never heard my name."

As he crossed the state line into Arkansas, the scenery grew darker, towering pine trees loomed on either side of the highway, their gnarled branches intertwining to form a suffocating canopy that swallowed the faint moonlight. He veered onto a dirt road, the SUV's tires crunching over gravel as the cabin came into view.

The hunting cabin was a rugged, two-story structure buried deep in the woods, its weathered facade blending seamlessly into the oppressive darkness of the forest. It was surrounded by towering oaks and dense underbrush, the nearest neighbor miles away. Barstow had built it as a retreat, a place to unwind, or so he claimed. In truth, it was a hideout, stocked with enough supplies and ammunition to outlast a siege.

He parked the SUV under a camouflaged tarp and entered the cabin, flipping on a single lantern that cast flickering light across the room. The interior was Spartan: a worn leather armchair, a cast-iron stove, and walls lined with mounted animal heads. A dusty bottle of bourbon sat on the wooden table next to a hunting knife and a loaded shotgun.

Barstow dropped heavily into the worn leather armchair; the satchel clutched against his chest like a lifeline. He pulled out the bourbon, taking a long swig straight from the bottle.

"They think they've got me cornered," he growled, the flickering lantern casting jagged shadows across his face, his voice low and venomous. "But I didn't claw my way to the top just to let a bunch of amateurs take me down."

He glanced at the manila folder on the table, his mind already plotting his next move. Barstow knew he couldn't stay here long, but for now, the isolation of the woods felt like the safest place on Earth.

"And when the time's right," he growled, his fingers tightening around the bottle, "I'll make them all regret the day they crossed Senator Robert Barstow."

Barstow stared at the flickering lantern, his mind churning with thoughts of revenge and survival. He leaned back in the armchair, the bourbon bottle resting against his thigh as he reached for the burner phone in his satchel. The cheap plastic felt out of place in his manicured hands, but it was a necessary tool for situations like this, untraceable and disposable.

He thumbed through the pre-programmed contacts until he reached "Fred Alton." Pressing the call button, he brought the phone to his ear and listened to the line ring.

"Senator," Fred answered, his voice tense. "I was just about to…"

"Spare me the pleasantries, Fred," Barstow snapped, his voice coiled with fury. "Just shut up and listen." Barstow snapped. "I don't care what you were about to do. We've got a situation, and I need it handled. Now."

Fred hesitated. "What kind of situation?"

"The kind where two people who should already be dead are still breathing," Barstow snarled. "Jake and his damn woman," Barstow spat. "They stormed my estate, wiped out half my security detail, and turned my home into a war zone. I want them gone."

Fred whistled low. "That's bold. Didn't think anyone had the stones to come after you directly."

Barstow clenched the bottle until his fingers ached. "Now you see just how bold they've gotten," Barstow snarled. "Which is why I need you to do your damn job. I need them eliminated, cleanly, quickly, and completely. I don't care what it costs or who you have to call. Get it done."

"And Agnes?" Fred asked cautiously.

"We'll deal with her later," Barstow snapped. "Right now, Jake and Julianna are the priority. They're the ones lighting fires under our operation. Get rid of them, and we can regroup. Fail, and I'll make sure you're the next target."

Fred's voice dropped an octave. "Understood, Senator. I'll reach out to my contacts and make the arrangements. You'll have your hitmen."

"Good," Barstow growled. "Call me when it's done. And Fred?"

"Yes, Senator?"

"Don't screw this up. If you do, you'll wish Jake and Julianna found you before I did."

Fred swallowed audibly on the other end. "I won't. You have my word."

Barstow hung up without another word, tossing the phone onto the table beside the manila folder. He took another long swig of bourbon and stared at the mounted buck's head above the fireplace. Its glassy eyes seemed to mock him as if it could sense the crumbling empire he was trying to hold together.

"They think they can outmaneuver me," Barstow muttered, his voice a venomous growl as his bloodshot eyes fixated on the flickering lantern. "But they don't know who they're dealing with."

He leaned forward, his shadow stretching across the dimly lit room. "Nobody crosses Robert Barstow," he whispered, his tone dripping with malice. "And lives to regret it."

Chapter 51: Let Me Go

Fred Alton thrived in the shadows. Years in the DEA had sharpened his instincts into a weapon, and while his body had softened with time, his mind remained razor-sharp, always two steps ahead. Organizing manhunts wasn't just his skill, it was his art. Though his body had grown soft with time and comfort, his mind remained sharp. He wasted no time putting together a plan. Twelve operatives, handpicked and ruthless, were already stationed at key airports across the southeastern United States. Each carried grainy photos of Jake and Julianna, instructions to shoot on sight, and the unspoken promise of a fat paycheck for a clean kill.

In Tampa, one of Fred's men, a nondescript figure with a nondescript name, spotted the pair just as they left the ticketing area. They moved casually, blending into the busy crowd, but the hitman's trained eye caught them. He trailed them from a distance, watching as they split up to head into their respective restrooms.

The hitman leaned casually against the sinks. His trained eyes locked on the stall Jake had entered. His demeanor was calm, but his fingers toyed with the silencer in his pocket, readying it like a predator stalking its prey. Once the last innocent bystander exited, he moved quickly to the entrance and hung a "Closed for Cleaning" chain across the door. With a glance back to ensure no one was watching, he began screwing the silencer onto his pistol, his every movement deliberate.

Inside the stall, Jake's senses were on high alert. The faint scuff of boots on tile and the unnatural pause outside, all screamed danger. Years of survival instincts kicked in, and Jake knew he wasn't alone. He'd ditched his weapons before arriving at the airport, so he was unarmed and vulnerable. But instinct told him he was being hunted. Years of survival had honed his reflexes, and he wasn't about to be caught off guard.

Jake eased himself out of the stall, locking the door from the inside as a decoy. Moving silently, he slipped behind the second row of stalls, his belt already sliding free in his hand, a makeshift weapon in the absence of anything else.

The hitman moved swiftly, his boot slamming into the stall door with a sharp crack. The door swung open, his silenced pistol raised, the muzzle sweeping the empty space inside. Finding the stall empty, he froze, momentarily confused. That pause was all Jake needed.

From behind, Jake snapped the belt across the hitman's wrist, sending the silenced pistol skidding across the floor. Before the man could react, Jake looped the belt around his neck, pulling tight. The hitman gagged, clawing at the belt as Jake planted his feet and heaved, lifting the man off the ground in a deadly chokehold.

The man thrashed, his boots scraping against the tile. With a desperate burst of strength, he twisted free, collapsing to the floor and scrambling for the gun near the handicapped stall.

Without hesitation, Jake grabbed the stall door and drove it into the hitman's head with savage force. The first blow staggered him; the second sent blood spraying against the white tile. By the third, the man crumpled like a marionette with its strings cut. Blood smeared the door as the hitman slumped to the floor, unconscious.

Jake grabbed the hitman's gun, tucking it into the waistband of his jeans and covering it with his jacket. His heart pounded, adrenaline surging through his veins, but his voice was calm as he tapped his earpiece.

"Julianna," Jake muttered into his earpiece, his voice tight. "You there?"

Julianna's voice crackled through the line, laced with sarcasm. "Yeah, I'm here. You're not about to tell me I can't pee in peace, are you?"

Jake interrupted her. "We've been made. We gotta go, right now!"

"Dammit, Jake," she muttered, exiting the stall and then stepping out of the women's restroom.

Jake scanned the halls in both directions as he stepped out of the men's room, casually pulling the "Closed for Cleaning" chain back into place. His calm movements belied the adrenaline surging through his veins. Julianna emerged moments later, her eyes narrowing at his urgency.

Without a word, Jake grabbed Julianna's hand and pulled her into the throng of travelers, their pace quick and deliberate. Blending in was their best chance now.

They moved quickly, weaving through passengers and airport staff toward the baggage claim. Jake scanned the area constantly, his sharp eyes searching for any more threats. Julianna kept pace beside him, her hand gripping his tightly.

"Barstow must have sent him," Jake said under his breath as they hurried outside. "If there's one, there are probably more."

Julianna's jaw clenched. "Great. Just what we need."

Outside, they spotted a rental car shuttle idling at the curb. Jake ushered Julianna onto the rental car shuttle, his eyes scanning the terminal behind them for any sign of pursuit. Their breaths came fast and shallow, adrenaline still pumping. As the shuttle pulled away, Jake leaned closer and whispered, "Stick to the story: delayed flight, rental mix-up. Just act normal."

Minutes later, they were heading north on Interstate 275 in a rented sedan. Jake kept the sedan at a steady speed, his eyes darting between the road ahead and the rearview mirror, watching for headlights that lingered too long.

Julianna leaned back in her seat, exhaling slowly. "That was too close," Julianna said, her voice softened now. She glanced at Jake, her brows knitting with concern. "Are you okay?"

Jake grunted; his knuckles white against the wheel. "I'm fine," he said, though the tension in his voice told a different story. "But this? This is just the start. They know where we are now."

Julianna turned to look out the window, her expression hardening. "Then we need to get ahead of them. No more running blind."

Jake nodded; his jaw set with determination. "Agreed. But first, we put some distance between us and Tampa. They're not getting a second shot."

As the city lights faded into the distance and the highway stretched before them, the weight of the chase began to settle. Jake's mind churned with plans, but one thought rose above the chaos: Julianna was still beside him. For now, the only thing that mattered was that Julianna was still beside him. But Jake knew better than to believe the reprieve would last.

Chapter 52: Moonlight Mile

The tires droned endlessly against the asphalt of I-75, the road stretching into the dark like a black ribbon unraveling beneath their headlights. Atlanta was still hours away, and exhaustion clung to them like a second skin, but neither dared let their guard slip. It had been too close in Tampa, and both of them knew Barstow wasn't finished yet.

Julianna's eyes flicked to the green glow of a highway sign overhead: Atlanta, 320 miles. "Hey, Jake, we still have that gear we stashed in Atlanta, don't we?"

Jake gripped the wheel, his knuckles pale against the dark leather, and nodded. "Yeah, I remember. I was pretty foggy at the time, but I didn't forget."

Julianna shifted in her seat, her body aching from their relentless pace. "We should go there, grab the gear, swap cars, and keep moving."

Jake considered her plan, his brow furrowing slightly. "That sounds like a good move. And I have a place in mind where we can lay low for a day or two."

The miles to Atlanta dragged like a weight, but as the faint glow of dawn crept over the horizon, the city skyline emerged, a jagged silhouette against the bruised sky. The streets were uncharacteristically still, the usual cacophony of city life replaced by an eerie calm. Yet, the occasional hum of a passing car or distant footsteps served as a reminder that the world moved on, blissfully ignorant of the storm chasing them.

They pulled into the dimly lit parking garage, the air thick with the metallic tang of oil and exhaust. Their stash was hidden in a rusted storage locker wedged between crumbling concrete pillars, forgotten by everyone but them. Julianna crouched by the storage locker, her fingers deftly working the lock. Jake stood a few steps away, his sharp gaze sweeping the empty garage for any sign of trouble. Inside were two duffel bags stuffed with clothes, nonperishable food, basic medical supplies, a couple of handguns, ammunition, and a wad of cash.

"Funny how a stash of weapons and canned beans can feel like old friends," Julianna said, slinging a duffel over her shoulder with a wry smile.

Jake smirked. "Let's not get too sentimental. We still need to swap cars and throw off any tails."

They found a sedan parked a few levels down, its unlocked door and outdated alarm system practically inviting theft. Within minutes, Julianna had the car running. At Hartsfield-Jackson Atlanta International Airport, they parked the rental in a long-term lot, tucking it between two SUVs. It was a subtle move, but if Barstow's men were tracking them, the decoy might buy them some time.

"Hopefully, anyone tracking us will think we skipped town on another flight," Jake said as they walked back to the stolen car.

Julianna nodded. "Smart move. Let's hope they fall for it."

As the towering skyscrapers of Atlanta gave way to rolling hills and dense forests, the tension in the car began to ease. The air felt lighter here, the kind of calm that only the mountains could offer. The trees pressed closer, their shadows stretching across the winding road. The air turned crisp, carrying the faint scent of pine and earth, as the suffocating weight of the city faded into the serene embrace of the mountains.

Julianna, her head resting against the window, spoke up. "So, what's the plan now? We can't just keep running forever."

Jake glanced at her, his eyes momentarily softening. "How are you at riding motorcycles?"

Her brows lifted in surprise. "I grew up on dirt bikes and motocross. Didn't do much street riding, though. Why?"

Jake chuckled, a rare sound in the chaos of their lives. "Well, I've got a surprise for you. Just trust me."

The journey brought them to the edge of North Carolina, where Deals Gap lay nestled at the foot of the Smoky Mountains. The village of Deals Gap was a speck on the map, a cluster of rustic cabins and mom-

and-pop shops dwarfed by the looming Smoky Mountains. At its heart stood the legendary Deals Gap Motorcycle Resort, a haven for bikers drawn to the infamous Tail of the Dragon, an 11-mile stretch of road with 318 curves.

Jake pulled the car into the gravel lot of the resort, the crunching sound under the tires cutting through the stillness of the night. The resort was a weathered wooden lodge with a wraparound porch where gleaming motorcycles stood like sleeping beasts, their chrome catching the faint glow of the porch lights.

Inside, the desk clerk, an older man with a kind face, greeted them with a tired smile. "Late night, huh? You folks passing through or staying awhile?"

"Three nights," Jake replied, sliding cash across the counter.

The man handed them a key and gave them directions to a room tucked at the back of the resort. "Breakfast is at seven, but no one's going to judge if you sleep in. You look like you've earned it."

The cabin-style room was modest but tidy, its twin beds neatly made with thick quilts that carried the faint scent of cedar. A small window overlooked the dark expanse of the forest, where moonlight filtered through the trees in ghostly beams. Julianna dropped her bag unceremoniously onto the floor and sat heavily on one of the beds.

"I swear, I've never been this tired in my life," Julianna muttered, kicking off her boots before collapsing onto the bed, not even bothering to pull back the covers.

Jake chuckled softly, dropping his bag in the corner. "You and me both, babe."

As Jake's eyes drifted closed, the sound of crickets and the cool mountain air lulled him into uneasy sleep. The Dragon's winding roads and looming dangers could wait for tomorrow. For now, they had the moonlight mile behind them.

For the first time in days, the weight pressing down on them eased. The Smoky Mountains offered a temporary reprieve, a chance to breathe, if only for a little while.

Chapter 53: Ride 'Em on Down

Julianna sat on the porch in the cool morning air, the steam from her mug curling lazily upward, mingling with the early mist clinging to the trees of the Smoky Mountains. The world around her was still, save for the rustle of leaves in the breeze and the occasional trill of a bird hidden in the dense forest. She had brewed the coffee using the ancient Mr. Coffee machine in their room, the faint hum of its machinery now replaced by the gentle clink of her mug against the wooden railing.

The Smoky Mountains stretched out before her, draped in a veil of mist that caught the pale light of dawn, painting the forest in hues of gray and green. It was the kind of quiet that felt sacred, as though the world itself was holding its breath. The quiet serenity was something she hadn't experienced in years, and despite her longing for action, she found herself appreciating the calm.

A few minutes later, Jake emerged, his hair a mess of unruly waves, a steaming mug in hand. He leaned against the porch railing with a satisfied sigh, letting the crisp air wash over him. "Middle of nowhere's got its charm," Jake said, his voice rough with sleep. He took a sip of coffee, his eyes scanning the mist-shrouded trees.

Julianna gestured to a tree near the parking lot. "Check this out," Julianna said, gesturing toward a gnarled tree near the parking lot, its branches weighed down with broken motorcycle parts. "They call it the Tree of Shame. Every piece on it belongs to someone who thought they could tame The Dragon."

Jake chuckled and shook his head, taking another sip of his coffee. "It's a monument to overconfidence. Bet every single one of those people thought they were invincible."

She smirked, turning to face him. "You've probably already noticed there's no Wi-Fi or cellphone signal here, right?"

"Oh, I noticed," Jake replied, raising an eyebrow. "How long do you think you can survive without contact with the rest of the world?"

Julianna let out a dramatic sigh, rolling her eyes. "I'll manage. Barely."

Jake gave her a playful nudge. "No contact is how we stay alive right now, so work with me, alright? Now, let's go get some breakfast or lunch, I guess."

"Yeah, it's more like lunchtime now, but I'm starving for breakfast," she said, setting her mug down and stretching.

The café was a cozy roadside spot, its wooden beams darkened with age and walls adorned with vintage motorcycle posters and faded photographs of riders who'd either conquered or been conquered by, The Dragon. The air was thick with the smell of coffee, frying bacon, and maple syrup. Locals filled a few tables, their conversations a mix of weather talk and stories about The Dragon. Jake and Julianna found a corner booth and ordered a carb-heavy breakfast: pancakes, bacon, biscuits, and eggs.

As the food arrived, Julianna leaned back, savoring the aroma. "This is the kind of breakfast that makes you think life might actually be okay," Julianna said, tearing into a biscuit. She paused, her tone shifting. "But seriously, Jake, what's next?"

Jake swallowed a bite of pancake and glanced out the window. "First, we need a couple of motorcycles. Did you see that house we passed about a mile back? The one with a few bikes for sale in the yard?"

She tilted her head. "Didn't notice, but let's check it out after we eat."

They polished off their meal and paid their bill, leaving a generous tip for the waitress who had kept their coffee cups full.

The house was modest, with a gravel driveway and a few motorcycles parked on the lawn. A middle-aged man wearing bib overalls, a pair of Doc Martens, and no shirt stepped onto the porch as they pulled up. He shaded his eyes with one hand and shouted, "Can I help you?"

Jake stepped out of the car; his stance casual but his tone firm. "We're looking for a couple of bikes. Fast, sharp handling, good tires, and no mechanical headaches. Got anything that fits the bill?"

The man scratched his stubbly chin and nodded. "Got a couple of sport bikes over here that might be what you're lookin' for."

He led them over to a sleek red Yamaha R6 and a black Kawasaki Ninja 650. Julianna swung a leg over the red Yamaha R6, gripping the handlebars and settling into the seat. "Feels just right," she said, her feet planted firmly on the ground.

Jake ran a hand over the black Kawasaki Ninja 650, his fingers brushing the throttle. "Yeah, this one's solid. It'll do the job." He glanced at Julianna. "These bikes are really fast. You good with that?"

She grinned. "Oh, I can handle it. The real question is, can you?"

Jake chuckled, shaking his head. "Alright, smartass."

After some negotiation, Jake bought both bikes, a fully enclosed trailer, and two helmets. He threw in some extra cash for good measure and had the man deliver everything to the Deals Gap Motorcycle Resort. The man's grin stretched ear to ear as he pocketed the wad of cash, giving Jake and Julianna a cheerful wave before driving off with his truck rattling under the weight of their trailer.

The rest of the day and the following one were spent on the bikes, exploring the winding roads of the region. They started with the Cherohala Skyway, an open stretch of road that offered breathtaking views of the mountains and valleys. The sweeping curves of the Cherohala Skyway were a perfect warm-up, the smooth pavement stretching out like an open invitation. The cool mountain air whipped past them as they leaned into each turn, the world below unfolding in breathtaking layers of green and blue.

Julianna sped ahead; her laughter carried by the wind as Jake struggled to keep up. "What happened to all that talk about me being the one who had to catch up?" she teased through her earpiece.

"Wait until we hit The Dragon," Jake shot back, his tone playful but challenging. "That's where the real fun begins, and where I leave you in the dust."

The following day, they tackled the legendary Tail of the Dragon. The tight, twisting turns tested their skills and nerve, but both of them handled the challenge like seasoned riders.

"Jake," Julianna said, breathless as they pulled over at a scenic overlook. "This road is absolutely insane. It's like it dares you to mess up."

Jake grinned, while taking off his gloves. "Yeah," Jake said, now pulling off his helmet and grinning. "There's nothing else like it. Every curve, every drop — it's pure adrenaline."

By the end of the second day, their confidence in the bikes was sky-high. They returned to the resort, exhausted but exhilarated, and collapsed into chairs on the porch.

Julianna turned to Jake, her windblown hair catching the faint light from the porch. "You know," she said softly, "this has been... good. For a little while, it almost feels like we're just two normal people on a road trip."

Jake leaned back, a rare smile on his face. "That's the idea, babe. Just for a little while."

The stillness of the Smoky Mountains wrapped around them like a protective cocoon, offering a fleeting taste of freedom in a world that seemed intent on hunting them down. For now, it was enough.

Chapter 54: Can't You Hear Me Knocking

Morning broke over the Smoky Mountains, with the sun casting its first golden rays through the lingering mist. The air was crisp, carrying the faint scent of pine and damp earth, a stark contrast to the heavy tension that hung between Jake and Julianna as they packed the Suburban. Jake and Julianna were up early, packing their gear into the almost new Chevy Suburban parked outside their cabin. The trailer, loaded with its two sport bikes, sat neatly hitched and ready for the long journey ahead.

As Jake double-checked the trailer hitch, he looked over his shoulder at Julianna, who was tightening the straps on the bike covers. "I guess it's time to get back to civilization, babe," he said, his voice carrying a reluctant tone.

Julianna paused, brushing her hair back from her face. "Copy that," she replied. "We need to locate Barstow and Fred so we can finish this thing."

Jake paused, his gaze sweeping over the mountains, their peaks shrouded in wisps of morning fog. For a fleeting moment, he savored the calm, knowing it wouldn't last. "And we need to bring Nicolai up to speed," he added. "He owes us for the compounds. Time to collect."

With the last of their bags stowed in the Suburban, they climbed into the vehicle. As they rolled out of the parking lot of the Deals Gap Motorcycle Resort, Jake slowed to a stop, both of them gazing back at the place where, for a brief moment, they'd found a sliver of peace.

"I hate leaving this behind," Julianna murmured, her voice barely above a whisper, as though speaking louder might shatter the fragile peace they'd found.

Jake nodded. "Me neither." He lingered for a moment longer before pressing down on the gas pedal. "But peace doesn't pay the bills, or keep us alive," Jake said, his tone hardening as he pressed the gas pedal, steering them into the chaos waiting beyond the mountains.

As they merged onto Interstate 81, the tension began to creep back in. The further they got from the mountains and the closer they got to the grid, the more they could feel the invisible eyes watching. Every road sign, every car that lingered too long in the rearview mirror, became a potential threat.

By late afternoon, near Leesburg, Virginia, they turned onto a gravel driveway framed by weathered fence posts and dense trees, the crunch of tires on stone breaking the heavy stillness. At the end of the path stood a weathered farmhouse, its white paint peeling but sturdy, with a steel barn looming beside it like a silent sentinel. The house was large and weathered, its white paint chipped in places, but still sturdy and secluded. A steel barn sat adjacent to the house, big enough to house the Suburban, trailer, and bikes. The nearest neighbor was a mile down the road, and the dense tree line surrounding the property provided ample privacy.

"This'll work," Jake said, stepping out of the Suburban and scanning the property with a practiced eye. His hand instinctively rested on the grip of his handgun as he took in the isolation and the dense tree line surrounding the house.

Julianna followed him, her hands resting on her hips. "Not bad. Plenty of space to lay low and plan."

They rented the property for the month, paying cash and ensuring the landlord asked no questions. As they unloaded their gear, Jake swept the farmhouse for bugs or hidden cameras, just to be safe. Satisfied it was clean, with no cameras, and no listening devices, they settled in. But the silence of the farmhouse wasn't comforting; it was the kind of quiet that sharpened your nerves instead of dulling them.

The farmhouse was their sanctuary, but Tysons Corner was where the real work awaited. Nestled in the anonymity of a nondescript high-rise, their flat was perfect, unassuming, forgettable, and close enough to the pulse of the city to stay informed. It would serve as their base for electronic surveillance and communication.

As they set up their equipment in the flat, Julianna sat at the desk, unpacking laptops and signal jammers. "It feels like we're on borrowed time," she said.

Jake leaned against the counter; arms crossed. "We are. The moment we turn these on, Barstow's people could find us."

"That's why we're using this place instead of the farmhouse," she reminded him.

Jake nodded. "We run this tight," Jake said, firmly. "Short transmissions, clean lines. If anything is suspicious, we shut it down and relocate. No risks."

With the equipment up and running, Jake called Nicolai using a secure line. After a few rings, the Russian mob boss's deep, gravelly voice came through. "Jake, my friend. Tell me you've got good news."

Jake leaned back in the chair; his face grim. "We hit the compounds. Kansas City and Mississippi are done. The bayou one was messy, but it's handled."

There was a pause on the other end of the line. "Messy?" Nicolai's tone was sharp, like the crack of a whip. "Jake, I don't like messy. Messy leaves trails and trails lead to problems."

Jake sighed. "Let's just say Barstow didn't appreciate the loss. He's got button men on us, and it's slowed us down. Finishing this job might take longer than expected."

Nicolai's tone grew sharp. "You understand how important it is to wrap this up. This isn't just business anymore," Nicolai growled. "It's personal. My men, my name, my family, all of it is tied to this. You don't get the luxury of delay."

Jake's jaw tightened. "I understand better than anyone, but you don't just kill a US Senator and expect to walk away. This has to be done just right, and I expect you to hold up your end when we do."

A moment of silence passed before Nicolai spoke again, his tone softening slightly. "You've always delivered, Jake. That's why I trust you. But don't mistake my trust for patience. You know what's at stake," Nicolai continued, his voice dropping to a deadly calm. "If Barstow walks away, we both lose more than money."

Jake glanced at Julianna, who was watching him intently. "We'll get it done," he said firmly.

Nicolai's voice carried a note of finality. "You'll find three million waiting in your offshore account," Nicolai said. "Consider it a reminder that failure isn't an option. The rest comes when Barstow and Fred are no longer breathing."

"Understood," Jake replied.

As the call ended, Jake leaned forward, resting his elbows on his knees. Julianna walked over, placing a hand on his shoulder.

Julianna crossed her arms, her eyes narrowing. "So, what's next, Jake? How do we play this?"

Jake looked up at her, a flicker of determination in his eyes. "First, we take stock. Then we go hunting."

Julianna nodded, a small smile playing on her lips. "That's the Jake I know."

Back at the farmhouse that night, Jake and Julianna sat on the porch, the faint chirping of crickets filling the silence. The stars were out in full force, casting a gentle glow over the dark countryside.

"This place," Julianna said, leaning back in her chair as her eyes wandered to the horizon, "it's almost enough to make you believe the world's not falling apart."

"Almost," Jake echoed, his voice low, his eyes scanning the tree line as if expecting the danger, they'd left behind to materialize out of the darkness.

They sat in comfortable silence for a while before Jake finally stood. "Get some rest, babe. Tomorrow, we go back on the offensive."

Julianna watched him disappear into the house, a wave of determination washing over her. She knew the storm wasn't over, not even close. But as long as Jake was beside her, she could face whatever came next.

Chapter 55: It Won't Take Long

Fred Alton sat hunched in a dimly lit motel room outside Tampa, the stale scent of takeout and cigarettes clinging to the air. The blinds were drawn so tight that even the relentless Florida sun barely seeped through, leaving the room cloaked in a dull, suffocating gloom. His laptop hummed on the scratched wooden table, surrounded by half-eaten takeout containers and scattered files. He had been at this for days, poring over every lead, contact, and scrap of information he could find to locate Jake and Julianna. Yet, nothing had panned out.

The burner phone on the table buzzed violently, and Fred knew who it was before he even picked it up. He braced himself.

"We seem to have lost them, sir," Fred said cautiously.

On the other end of the line, Senator Barstow's voice exploded with rage. "You incompetent moron! I am surrounded by morons!"

Fred winced, holding the phone slightly away from his ear.

Barstow continued; his voice laced with venom. "Do you have any idea how much is at stake here? My career, my freedom, my *life,* all of it hangs by a thread, and I have to rely on *you*! You had better find them, and find them fast, or I will kill you myself!"

Before Fred could stammer out a response, the line went dead.

Fred hurled the phone onto the cluttered table, muttering curses under his breath. Beads of sweat trickled down his temple as he rubbed his face with shaking hands. "This is getting worse by the damn minute," he muttered to himself, glancing at the growing pile of cigarette butts in the ashtray.

In New Orleans, Special Agent William Carter sat in his office at the FBI field office, staring at the chaotic whiteboard in front of him. The whiteboard in office looked like the web of a desperate spider. Photos of Barstow, Fred Alton, and Agnes were pinned haphazardly, red strings crisscrossing between them like veins in a dying organism. Two glaring question marks at the bottom labeled "Unknown Assailants" taunted him, a reminder of how little they knew about Jake and Julianna.

One of his men burst into the office, holding a printout. "Sir, we intercepted part of a phone message the Senator made to Alton."

Carter raised an eyebrow. "What did it say?"

The agent smirked. "Well, he threatened to kill Alton if he doesn't find the targets soon."

Carter leaned back in his chair, stroking his chin thoughtfully. "Barstow's cracking," Carter murmured, his eyes narrowing at the chaotic board. "Desperation makes people sloppy. Let's make sure we're ready when he slips. Can you get a location on him?"

The agent shook his head. "We're trying, but he's bouncing his signals all over the place. It's tough to pin him down."

Carter tapped his pen absently against the desk. "If you can't locate him, we'll see if he shows up back in Washington when the Senate reconvenes next week. He won't be able to hide forever."

The agent nodded and left the room, leaving Carter alone with his thoughts.

Meanwhile, in their flat in Tysons Corner, Julianna pushed her desk chair back triumphantly and declared, "Voila! I've cracked it!"

Jake, leaning against the kitchen counter with a mug of coffee, raised an eyebrow. "What did you crack?"

Julianna turned to him; her eyes gleaming with excitement. "Two things," Julianna said, swiveling her chair toward Jake with a triumphant grin. "First, I've hacked into Barstow's texts. Not only can we see what he's sending and receiving, but we can also send messages that look like they're straight from his phone."

Jake set his coffee down and walked over, impressed. "And the second thing?"

"I've reprogrammed our phones to make it look like we're anywhere we want. If someone's tracking us, they'll think we're in Timbuktu while we're sitting right here."

Jake's lips curved into a slow, rare smile, the kind that only Julianna ever got to see. "Have I told you I love you today?"

Julianna tilted her head, pretending to be surprised. "Why, Jake, I don't think you've ever used the L word before."

Jake smirked and headed back to the kitchen, hiding his face as he casually said, "Okay, just checking."

Julianna laughed and bolted from her chair, chasing after him. She jumped onto his back, wrapping her arms around his neck in a playful, loving embrace.

She kissed the side of his head and whispered in a sultry tone, "How about we take this celebration somewhere more… private?" Julianna whispered, her breath warm against his ear, her voice laced with playful seduction.

Jake chuckled, turning his head slightly to meet her gaze. "Good idea," he said, his voice low.

He carried her toward the bedroom, their laughter filling the small flat.

The bedroom was small yet inviting, with the muted afternoon light spilling through sheer curtains to cast golden streaks across the bed. For once, the chaos of their lives felt far away, replaced by an unexpected, fleeting sense of normalcy. The bed was neatly made with crisp white sheets, a small victory in their chaotic lives.

As they fell onto the bed together, Jake cupped Julianna's face gently, brushing a strand of hair behind her ear. His voice softened in a way it rarely did. "Do you even know how incredible you are?"

Julianna smiled, her brown eyes sparkling. "Don't you forget it?"

For a while, the world outside didn't exist. The danger, the enemies, the mission, all of it faded into the background. For now, they had each other, and that was enough.

As the afternoon wore on, the soft hum of city life outside mingled with their whispered words and quiet laughter. For a few stolen hours, the world outside ceased to exist. The danger and desperation waiting for them melted into the background, leaving only warmth, whispered promises, and the fragile hope that maybe, just maybe, they could outrun the storm.

As the light outside began to fade, Jake lay awake, staring at the ceiling. Julianna was curled against his side, her breath soft and even in the quiet. He let his hand rest on her shoulder, his fingers brushing against her bare skin as if grounding himself in the reality of her presence.

But his mind was miles away. Barstow wasn't going to stop. And as much as he wanted to stay in this moment, he knew it wouldn't last.

He exhaled deeply, his resolve hardening.

"Soon," he whispered into the darkness. "This all ends soon."

Chapter 56: It Must Be Hell

The morning sun was just beginning to rise as Jake and Julianna pulled into the desolate industrial zone near Lorain, Ohio. The crumbling brick buildings, broken windows, and overgrown weeds exuded decay. It was the kind of place no one cared about, except for those about to die there.

Jake stepped out of the car, surveying the area with his binoculars. "This will do," he said, nodding toward a small warehouse that looked like it hadn't seen activity in decades.

Julianna got out of the car, her boots crunching on the gravel. "I don't love the idea of being bait, but I trust you."

Jake turned to her; his blue eyes sharp. "We don't have a choice, babe. This is the last of our ammo and weapons. If this doesn't work, we're screwed."

They spent the next several hours rigging the building with traps. Jake placed explosive charges along the entrances, while Julianna set up makeshift tripwires rigged to grenades. Every corner of the warehouse was a deathtrap waiting to be sprung.

When the sun dipped below the horizon, they retreated to two sniper nests in nearby buildings. Jake set up in a crumbling office building across the street, while Julianna chose an old grain silo with a perfect line of sight to the warehouse.

Over the next 24 hours, they made two phone calls designed to be intercepted. Jake pretended to be in Boston, calling Julianna with fabricated plans. "I miss you," he said, laying it on thick. "I can't wait to see you again."

Julianna matched his tone. "Me too, babe. Just a couple more days, and we'll be back together. Stay safe."

Jake smirked after hanging up. "That should be enough to bait the hook," he said to himself.

At 2:00 AM, Jake lay prone in a crumbling office building across the street, his rifle scope fixed on the warehouse entrance. The silence was absolute, broken only by the faint hum of a nearby transformer. Then he saw it, a black van creeping into the lot, its headlights cutting through the darkness.

He adjusted the scope, his pulse steady as he counted the figures climbing out of the van. Six men, all armed, moved with practiced efficiency. At the back of the group was Fred Alton, looking jumpy and out of place.

"They're here," Jake said into his earpiece, his voice low and controlled.

Julianna, stationed in a grain silo across the street, responded immediately. "Copy that. I've got eyes on them. Let me know, when."

Fred barked orders, his voice carrying through the still night. The men fanned out, circling the warehouse like predators closing in on prey. Through the scope, Jake tracked their movements, noting their formations and weapons.

"Looks like Fred hired some professionals," he muttered. "Too bad, it won't matter."

As the last man stepped into the warehouse, Jake gave the signal. "Now."

Julianna didn't hesitate. She pressed the detonator.

The explosion ripped through the warehouse with a deafening roar, sending flames and debris skyward. The fire lit up the industrial park, casting long shadows against the surrounding buildings. Jake watched as two men blown backward out of the doors, their bodies engulfed in flames before they hit the ground. Another stumbled out with his hands over his ears, his face twisted in pain. His pants caught fire, and he dropped to the dirt, rolling to extinguish the flames.

"Direct hit," Julianna said, her voice tight but satisfied.

Jake watched it all through his scope, his jaw set. "Good hit," he said into the earpiece.

The van screeched into reverse, its tires kicking up dirt as it tried to flee the scene.

"Pick off these last few guys while I go after Fred," Jake instructed.

"Copy that," Julianna replied.

Julianna adjusted her scope, aiming at one of the remaining men. She squeezed the trigger, and he dropped instantly. Another tried to crawl away, but she caught him with a clean shot to the back of the head.

Jake jumped into the car, peeling out after the van. His tires screeched as he turned onto the main road, the van's taillights glowing like two red targets in the distance.

Fred's driver was erratic, swerving wildly to avoid gunfire. Jake leaned out of the window, firing a few rounds that shattered the van's rear windshield.

The van veered onto a side street, nearly hitting a lamppost. Jake followed, his tires skidding on the slick pavement. The two vehicles weaved through narrow alleys and empty streets, the roar of their engines echoing in the night.

Fred's driver tried to shake Jake by turning onto a dirt road, but Jake stayed close, his car bouncing over the uneven terrain. He fired another shot, hitting one of the van's tires. The van fishtailed but managed to stay on course.

"Come on," Jake growled, his knuckles white on the steering wheel.

The chase reached a fever pitch as the van turned back onto a paved road. Jake was gaining ground when Fred's driver suddenly slammed on the brakes. Jake swerved to avoid a collision, his car skidding off the road and smashing into a tree.

The impact jolted him forward, his airbag deploying with a loud *whoomp*. Jake groaned, shaking his head to clear the dizziness.

Through his cracked windshield, he saw the van speeding away into the night.

"Damn it!" he shouted, slamming his fist against the steering wheel.

Julianna's voice crackled in his earpiece. "Jake? Are you okay?"

Jake exhaled sharply; his frustration evident. "I'm fine, but Fred got away."

There was a pause before Julianna replied. "We'll get him, Jake. He's running out of places to hide."

Jake leaned back in his seat, staring at the road ahead. "Yeah," he said, more to himself than to her. "We'll get him."

As the adrenaline subsided, Jake climbed out of the wrecked car, already thinking about their next move. The war wasn't over, not by a long shot.

Julianna always had to have the last humorous word so she added, "I wonder how Fred's other team is doing in Boston…"

Chapter 57: Doo Doo Doo Doo Doo

(Heartbreaker)

The night pressed down heavily as Julianna eased the sedan into the quiet suburban cul-de-sac, her headlights cutting through the darkness. Jake limped toward her, his torn clothes and rigid posture a testament to the night's chaos.

Sliding into the passenger seat, Jake winced as he sank into the cushion, his exhaustion almost palpable. "You're a sight for sore eyes," he muttered.

Julianna smirked, but her gaze lingered on his bandaged leg, the blood seeping through. "Funny, I was about to say the same thing. You're not falling apart on me, are you?"

"Not yet," Jake replied, his tone thick with frustration. "But we've got bigger problems. Fred got away, and we're running on fumes, literally and figuratively. No gas, no ammo, no plan."

He glanced at her. "We need a fresh arsenal. And a lead on Barstow."

Julianna tightened her grip on the wheel, her knuckles whitening. "Alright. What's the play?"

Jake let out a heavy sigh, leaning his head back against the seat. "I know a guy in Philly, Marco. He deals in everything: guns, ammo, explosives. If anyone can set us up, it's him."

"Philly it is," Julianna said, pressing down on the accelerator. The car surged forward, the highway stretching east toward Pennsylvania.

The drive across Pennsylvania was long and uneventful, giving them plenty of time to reflect on their precarious situation. The mountainous terrain of the state loomed around them, the road winding through dense forests that stretched endlessly into the horizon. Small towns dotted the landscape, their lights flickering like fireflies in the dark.

"This place is kind of beautiful," Julianna said, her voice almost wistful.

"Don't let it fool you," Jake replied, watching the tree line blur past. "There's danger everywhere. We can't let our guard down."

Julianna glanced over at him, her brow furrowing. "A little dramatic don't you think? You always this paranoid?"

Jake smirked. "You call it paranoia; I call it staying alive."

By the time they reached Philadelphia, the first light of dawn broke over the city skyline. Julianna navigated the early morning traffic with precision, her eyes scanning for anything out of the ordinary.

The rendezvous point was a gritty street corner in South Philly. The dealer, a wiry man with thinning hair and a nervous energy, approached their car and climbed into the back seat.

"Jake, my man." Marco said, extending a hand. "It's been a while."

"Too long, Marco," Jake replied, shaking his hand. "Still in business, I see."

Marco grinned. "Business is booming. Pun intended."

Julianna turned in her seat, raising an eyebrow. "Booming? In a place like this?"

Marco shrugged. "Philly's always been hot. Gangs, mafia, you name it. They keep me busy."

As they exchanged pleasantries, Marco gestured for them to follow his directions. "Warehouse is in Allentown. Not far. Let's get you what you need."

Julianna smirked. "Allentown? Like the Billy Joel song?"

Marco and Jake turned to her in unison, their expressions deadpan. "Of course," Marco said dryly.

The warehouse was tucked away in an industrial area, surrounded by rusting fences and broken-down trucks. Inside, the air smelled of gun oil and sawdust, and the walls were lined with racks of weapons that gleamed under the harsh fluorescent lights.

"Come on in," Marco said, leading them toward his office in the back. "Let's have some coffee and figure out what you need."

Julianna and Jake followed him into the cramped office, where Marco slid behind his desk. The desk was cluttered with papers, coffee mugs, and a half-empty bottle of whiskey.

As Jake and Julianna took their seats, Marco leaned back, his hands resting on his lap. "So, what's it gonna be? Rifles, shotguns, grenades? I've got it all."

Before Jake could answer, Marco leaned forward, reached beneath the desk, and a deafening *boom* erupted. A shotgun blast tore through the desk, slamming into Jake's right shoulder and sending him sprawling backward.

"Son of a bitch!" Jake roared, clutching his bleeding shoulder.

Marco smirked; his face twisted with malice. "You've pissed off the wrong people, Jake."

Instinct took over. Jake braced his feet against the desk and shoved it forward with all his strength, pinning Marco against the wall.

"Julianna!" Jake shouted, his voice a mix of pain and urgency. "Find a weapon!"

Julianna sprang into action, diving behind a nearby table and grabbing a handgun.

Meanwhile, Jake vaulted over the desk, his good arm swinging hard. His fists connected with Marco's face again and again, each punch fueled by rage and betrayal.

"Who sent you?" Jake growled, his knuckles slick with blood. "Who sent you, you bastard?"

Marco sputtered; his words incoherent through his broken teeth.

"Jake!" Julianna's voice cut through the chaos. "Step back!"

Jake turned just as Julianna leveled the handgun at Marco's head. With both hands steady, she pulled the trigger. The shot rang out, and Marco slumped lifelessly against the wall.

Jake staggered back, blood dripping from his shoulder. "He set us up," he muttered, his voice tight with rage and disbelief.

Julianna grabbed his uninjured arm, pulling him toward the door. "We need to get out of here. Now."

Jake nodded; his face grim. "You're right. But we're not leaving empty-handed."

They moved quickly through the warehouse, grabbing what they could: rifles, handguns, ammo, and grenades.

"So many guns, so little time," Julianna muttered, stuffing a duffel bag with bullets.

Jake glanced out the window, his jaw tightening. "Make it quick. We don't know who else is coming."

Minutes later, they were back in the car, speeding away from the warehouse as the late morning sunlight broke through the receding clouds.

Julianna looked over at Jake, her face pale. "We're running out of people we can trust."

Jake's grip on the wheel tightened. "No kidding. The circle's getting smaller by the minute."

"So, what do we do now?"

Jake glanced at her; his expression hard but determined. "We regroup. Back to the farmhouse. We'll figure this out."

As they drove, the weight of their situation pressed down on them. The world was closing in, and the stakes had never been higher. But if there was one thing Jake and Julianna knew how to do, it was to survive.

Chapter 58: 19th Nervous Breakdown

The silence of the old farmhouse was broken by only Jake's sharp intakes of breath and Julianna's muttered curses. She had spread a clean towel across the kitchen table, where Jake sat shirtless, leaning forward to expose his wounded shoulder.

"I swear, Jake," Julianna muttered, her voice sharp with concentration, "if you keep getting yourself blown up, I'm switching to duct tape and calling it a day."

Jake smirked, though pain flashed briefly across his face. "Wouldn't be the first time duct tape saved my ass."

She rolled her eyes but didn't respond, focusing instead on removing a particularly stubborn piece of shrapnel lodged just below his collarbone. The tweezers slipped for a moment, and Jake winced.

"Sorry," she muttered, genuinely. "Almost got it."

Jake gave a shaky laugh. "You know, you're pretty handy with a pair of tweezers. Maybe when this is all over, you should think about med school."

"Sure, Jake," Julianna said dryly, dropping another bloody fragment into the metal bowl beside her. "Because I'm dying to spend my golden years poking at more bullet wounds."

Jake chuckled, then winced again as her tweezers found another shard. "You could specialize in idiots who run into gunfire for a living. I hear there's a market for it."

She smiled faintly but didn't take the bait. "You're done," she said finally, pressing a clean bandage over the wound and securing it with medical tape. "Try not to rip this one open, okay?"

Jake rotated his shoulder experimentally, grimacing at the stiffness but nodding. "I'll do my best."

As Julianna cleaned up, Jake leaned back in the chair, exhaustion creeping over him. "We need to figure out if Barstow is coming to Washington next week. If he stays in hiding, all our plans are shot."

Julianna finished wiping her hands and turned to face him. "There's been little activity in his text messages. Nothing that screams D.C. yet."

Jake grunted, his eyes narrowing in thought. "He can't stay holed up forever. The Senate is back in session next week. If he skips out, someone's going to notice."

Barstow paced the hunting cabin, a whiskey glass in one hand and his phone in the other. The cabin, a rustic but well-appointed retreat, was adorned with hunting trophies, deer heads, bear skins, and an impressive display of rifles on the wall. The Senator, however, was anything but relaxed. His usual composed demeanor had given way to a jittery frustration.

He called his aide at the Senate office. "Anything suspicious going on?" he asked sharply, his Southern drawl sharper than usual.

"No, sir," the aide replied. "Everything seems normal. No visits from the FBI, no subpoenas, nothing out of the ordinary."

Barstow hung up and immediately dialed a trusted contact within the FBI. "Any activity I should know about?" he asked, his tone feigning casualness.

"Nothing, Senator," the agent replied. "No warrants, no investigations. You're in the clear, for now."

Barstow exhaled slowly, some of the tension leaving his shoulders. "Good. Keep it that way."

He booked a flight from Little Rock to Washington, D.C., for Monday morning and sent a text to his aide: **Arrange transportation from the airport to my residence at the Ritz**.

The notification came in almost immediately. An analyst burst into Carter's office, holding a printout. "We intercepted a flight reservation for Barstow. He's booked for D.C. Monday morning, and he texted his aide about a ride to the Ritz."

Carter's brow furrowed. "He's coming out of hiding. Good. Set up 24-hour surveillance the moment he lands. I want eyes on him at all times."

The analyst nodded. "Yes, sir."

Julianna burst into the living room where Jake was cleaning one of the rifles they'd picked up in Allentown. "He's coming back," she said, her tone triumphant.

Jake looked up sharply. "To D.C.?"

She nodded. "Text messages show he's booked for Monday. He'll be back at the Ritz."

Jake let out a slow breath, setting the rifle down. "Good. That gives us time to prepare." He paused, his expression hardening. "This thing has to go perfectly. There are a lot of moving parts."

Julianna sank into a chair across from him, her expression equally serious. "Not the least of which are the guys chasing us and the FBI all over Barstow."

Jake nodded grimly. "And Barstow himself. He's not going to make this easy. We need to be ready for anything."

They spent the next few days in a flurry of preparation. Julianna fine-tuned the motorcycles, ensuring they were in peak condition for what they both knew could be a high-speed escape. Jake went over their arsenal, cleaning and testing each weapon meticulously.

In the evenings, they sat at the farmhouse's old wooden table, poring over maps of Washington, D.C., and discussing potential scenarios.

"What if the FBI gets to him before we do?" Julianna asked one night.

Jake shook his head. "They won't. They're watching him, not protecting him. He's their case, but they don't care if he gets taken out before they can arrest him."

Julianna leaned back in her chair, her fingers tracing the edge of the map. "And what about Fred? Do you think, we can get him too?"

Jake's jaw tightened. "You know what to do with Alton. He'll finally get what he deserves."

As Monday was approaching, the tension in the farmhouse was palpable. Both knew the risks, but neither voiced their fears. Instead, they focused on the task at hand, their unspoken resolve binding them together more tightly than ever.

"We'll be ready," Jake said late Sunday night, as they loaded the last of the gear into the Suburban.

Julianna nodded, her eyes meeting his. "We have to be."

Chapter 59: Cool, Calm & Collected

The farmhouse was silent as Jake and Julianna rolled the Suburban into the barn, securing it for a quick getaway if needed. The late afternoon sunlight cast long shadows across the dusty floor, and Jake took a moment to survey the scene before pulling the barn doors shut. "That should do it," he said, dusting his hands off on his jeans.

Julianna leaned against a support beam, typing a message. She showed it to Jake before hitting send.

It read: **I NEED TO SEE YOU AT MY WASHINGTON RESIDENCE AT 7:30 TOMORROW NIGHT. DON'T BE LATE.**

"Looks good," Jake said with a nod. "If he buys it, Fred will show up like a good little soldier."

Julianna hit send, then pocketed her phone. "He'll buy it. Barstow's been barking orders at him since this whole thing started. Fred will assume that it's business as usual."

They moved back to the farmhouse to go over their checklist one last time. Rifles? Check. Silenced handguns? Check. Tactical knives, communication devices, and backup plans for backup plans? Check.

As they adjusted their motorcycle gear, Jake handed Julianna her helmet. "You think we're ready?" he asked, his voice tinged with a mix of confidence and apprehension.

Julianna slid the helmet over her head, her voice slightly muffled. "We're as ready as we'll ever be. Besides, we've got a room waiting for us at the Ritz, and you've got the key cards, right?"

Jake patted the breast pocket of his motorcycle jacket. "Right here. Let's ride."

The ride to Washington, D.C., was unusually calm for a Sunday. The roads were clear, the late autumn air crisp and invigorating. The trees lining the highway had mostly shed their leaves, and the golden hues of the remaining foliage were muted under the overcast sky.

Julianna rode ahead, her form graceful and confident on her bike. Jake followed close behind, his thoughts darting between the task ahead and the woman leading the way.

"It'd be a nice ride," Julianna said over their comms., "if we weren't gearing up for war."

Jake smirked. "Maybe after this, we'll take a real ride. Somewhere quiet. No bugs, no guns, no hit lists."

"Deal," Julianna replied. "But first, let's take out the trash."

They pulled into the Ritz Carlton's parking garage just as dusk was settling over the city. The air smelled faintly of exhaust and rain, the kind of urban aroma that seemed to cling to D.C. no matter the season.

Jake parked his bike beside Julianna's near the employee entrance on the garage's bottom level. They grabbed their duffel bags, each laden with gear, and headed toward the side entrance of the hotel.

Inside, the Ritz was as opulent as they remembered. Marble floors gleamed under crystal chandeliers, and the faint aroma of fresh flowers mingled with the rich scent of polished wood. The staff barely glanced at them as they headed their suite.

The room was a mirror of their previous stay: spacious, with cream-colored walls, plush furniture, and a large window overlooking the courtyard and Senator Barstow's residence. They had also secured the adjoining room under a different name, its purpose purely tactical.

Julianna dropped her bag on the bed and looked out the window. "Same view, same target," she said softly.

Jake joined her, peering out at the Senator's residence. The curtains were drawn, and no lights were on yet. "Familiar, but different," he said. "This time, we finish it."

They spent the remaining daylight hours setting up. Bugs in Barstow's residence were checked and confirmed operational. Communication lines were tested, and weapons were cleaned and loaded. Julianna checked the vent covers, ensuring they hadn't overlooked anything.

As the sun dipped below the horizon, they explored the hotel, mapping out escape routes and planting small stashes of gear in strategic locations. A silenced handgun in the laundry room. Extra ammo behind a maintenance panel on their floor. Most importantly Julianna hacked the security cameras to show looped video on Barstow's floor that could be activated with a device that looked like a simple key fob.

When they returned to their suite, they were exhausted but focused. They each took a few hours of sleep, the weight of the coming confrontation pressing down on them like an invisible force.

The next morning, room service arrived with a breakfast spread that seemed almost laughably luxurious considering the circumstances. Fluffy omelets, crisp bacon, fresh fruit, and steaming cups of coffee adorned the small dining table by the window.

Julianna poked at her food, her mind clearly elsewhere. "You think… he'll come here or head to his office first?"

Jake took a sip of coffee, his gaze fixed on the Senator's residence across the courtyard. "Probably here. He'll want to check in, change clothes, and make sure everything seems normal, before he comes home tonight."

Julianna nodded. "And that's when we make our move."

Jake set his coffee down, leaning forward. "This has to go perfectly, Jules. No surprises. No mistakes. There are too many variables already. If we don't do this right, we will be on the run the rest of our lives or worse."

She reached across the table, resting a hand on his. "We've got this, Jake. We've come too far to screw it up now."

He gave her a faint smile, his fingers closing over hers. "You're right. Tonight, it ends."

They sat in silence for a moment, the weight of their mission hanging heavy in the air. Beyond the window, Washington hummed with its usual rhythm, oblivious to the storm taking shape inside the Ritz Carlton.

Chapter 60: Don't Stop

Senator Barstow stepped off the plane at Reagan National Airport, his steps purposeful yet hurried. He carried his leather briefcase in one hand and used the other to adjust his tie, its knot just slightly loosened during the flight. His tailored suit was disheveled, and his face betrayed the strain of the past week. The Senator's once confident demeanor had been replaced with a kind of paranoia.

The FBI agent spotted the moment he entered the baggage area. To the untrained eye, he was just another politician moving with the deliberate air of someone accustomed to power. The agent tailing him noticed the little tells: the way Barstow looked over his shoulder twice, the slight hitch in his step as if he expected someone to call out his name and the way his fingers tapped a rhythm on the handle of his briefcase.

The agent radioed the description and license plate number of the black town car that picked him up at the curb. "Black limo, plate Bravo-X-ray-2-3-7-1. Target in the vehicle, heading east," the agent said, keeping his voice steady.

"Copy that," another agent responded from his sedan parked nearby. The handoff was seamless, the second car sliding into traffic several lengths behind the limo.

The Senator's limo pulled into the porte-cochère of the Ritz Carlton. A valet rushed forward, offering a warm, practiced smile. "Welcome back, Senator. Is there anything you need?"

Barstow waved him off with a quick gesture, his eyes scanning the area. He saw nothing out of the ordinary but couldn't shake the feeling of being watched. As he strode into the marble-floored lobby, the familiar scent of fresh flowers and leather upholstery filled his nostrils. He walked past an FBI agent seated in an armchair near the concierge desk, completely oblivious to the man's watchful eyes.

The elevator ride to his suite was solitary. When he stepped inside his residence, he felt a brief wave of relief. Everything was just as he had left it. The curtains were drawn, and the faint woody aroma lingered in the air. He walked to the bathroom, peeled off his travel-worn clothes, and stepped into the shower. The hot water cascaded over his broad shoulders, washing away the tension that had built up over the past week.

When he emerged, he donned an expensive navy-blue suit, a crisp white shirt, and a red silk tie that practically screamed power. Standing in front of the mirror, he adjusted the tie, ran a comb through his thinning hair, and smirked. He looked like a man who couldn't be touched, a man who was once again in control. Confidence surged through him as he returned to the limo waiting outside to take him to Capitol Hill.

Meanwhile, somewhere high above Cleveland and Pittsburgh, Fred Alton sat in a window seat on a plane bound for Washington. His forehead glistened with sweat as he gripped the armrests. The turbulence jolted the plane again, causing his drink to slosh in its plastic cup.

He looked out the window at the rolling clouds and wondered if this was a sign. Maybe he should take the money he had and disappear, skipping the country entirely. But he hadn't been paid his full cut yet, and Barstow wouldn't take kindly to being abandoned.

Fred exhaled slowly, his mind racing. *Stay the course,* he told himself. *Finish the job, get the money, and then disappear.* He reached for his drink and downed the last of the whiskey, hoping it would steady his nerves.

As Barstow carried out his duties in the Capitol, the FBI was quietly tightening its net around him. They had planted agents in key locations.

Bravo 1 sat in the Ritz Carlton lobby, casually reading a newspaper and sipping coffee. Another, Bravo 3, was stationed in a car parked across the street, his eyes darting between the hotel entrance and a laptop displaying surveillance feeds. The most crucial agent, however, was Bravo 2, on the roof of the Ritz, armed with high-powered binoculars and a direct line to Special Agent Carter. They wanted to know Barstow's every move, ready to pounce the moment a warrant came through.

Across the courtyard in their Ritz suite, Jake and Julianna were just as busy. Their room was a hub of preparation, weapons, and tools laid out methodically on the coffee table. The room's luxurious decor contrasted sharply with the grim purpose of their work.

Julianna adjusted her disguise in the mirror, pulling her hair back into a tight bun, taping her breasts as flat as she could, and applying a modest amount of makeup that would make her look like a young man working for a courier service. "How's this?" she asked, turning to Jake.

Jake glanced up from the duffel bag he was packing. "You look great. No one will suspect a thing."

Julianna pulled the baseball cap down to cover her eyes and smiled faintly, then returned to the mirror, her expression hardening. "I hope you're right. What about you?"

Jake shrugged into a tailored jacket and adjusted his tie. "I'll blend in. Just another suit in a sea of politicians."

They paused for a moment, exchanging a glance that spoke volumes. The tension in the room was palpable.

"This has to go perfectly," Jake said, his voice low and steady.

Julianna nodded, her eyes narrowing with determination. "It will. We've got everything planned to the last detail."

Jake walked to the window, looking out at the Senator's residence. Evening shadows stretched across the courtyard. "Once he's back from Capitol Hill, we move. No mistakes."

Julianna joined him at the window, her voice soft but firm. "No mistakes," she repeated.

The two stood in silence for a moment, the gravity of the mission settling over them like a storm cloud. As the city buzzed below them, they knew the calm wouldn't last.

Chapter 61: Get Off of My Cloud

The Senator's mood was uncharacteristically cheerful as he stepped out of the limo in front of the Ritz Carlton, at 6:30 PM. He tipped the valet generously and even managed a faint smile as he waved at the front desk clerk. After a day spent wheeling and dealing, using his influence to secure backroom promises and leverage favors, Barstow felt like himself again, large and in charge.

The elevator ride to his penthouse was smooth, and he hummed a tune under his breath as he made his way down the hallway. His expensive leather loafers echoed against the marble floors as he reached his apartment door, already loosening his tie in anticipation of a quiet evening.

At the same time, Julianna, dressed as a courier for a well-known delivery service, entered the Ritz lobby. She wore a crisp uniform with the courier's logo on the front pocket, a pair of work boots, and a baseball cap pulled low over her face. Slinging a messenger bag over her shoulder, she approached the concierge desk with a delivery envelope in hand.

"I've got a delivery," she said briskly, deliberately avoiding eye contact.

The concierge looked up. "For whom?"

She shook her head and smirked. "I know where to go." Without waiting for a response, she headed toward the elevators.

The concierge paused briefly before shrugging. Delivery workers came and went all the time.

As Julianna stepped into the elevator, Jake, wearing a tailored suit that helped him blend in with the upscale clientele, casually slipped in behind her. Julianna activated the security loops for the cameras while the two said nothing, their silent coordination speaking volumes.

Julianna stepped out on the penthouse floor and made her way to the Senator's door, the soles of her work boots muffled by the plush carpeting. Jake hung back at the corner of the hallway, keeping an eye on the corridor.

Julianna rang the doorbell, a deliberate series of sharp, quick presses. "Delivery!" she called out, her voice loud and flat, the perfect tone of disinterest.

Moments later, the door opened. Barstow, standing there in his robe, stood in the doorway. His eyes narrowed as he took in the clipboard she thrust toward him, a pen dangling from a string attached to it.

"What's this?" he grumbled, grabbing the clipboard.

She remained silent, just stood there with a blank expression. Barstow clicked the pen, which jabbed into his thumb.

"What the…" he began, but his words trailed off as the neurotoxin took hold. His body stiffened, his legs buckled, and he began to slump forward.

Julianna caught him under the arms, her movements smooth and practiced, and guided him back into the apartment. Without making a sound, she walked him to his favorite chair near the fireplace and eased him into it, arranging his body as if he had just sat down to relax.

Jake slipped into the apartment behind her, closing the door softly. He moved with precision, sweeping the room with a small electronic device to check for bugs.

"All clear," he said after a few minutes, pulling the bugs they had planted earlier from their hiding places. He held them up to Julianna. "We don't need these anymore."

Julianna smirked and placed her messenger bag on the floor. Both wore latex gloves, their movements efficient and deliberate.

Barstow's mind screamed in terror, but his body betrayed nothing. He could see everything, hear everything, but he couldn't move. He was trapped, a prisoner in his own body, as the two intruders worked around him.

Julianna began searching the apartment, opening drawers and cabinets with quick, precise movements. "Here it is," she said, pulling a sleek black handgun from the pocket of the Senator's silk robe. She held it up, inspecting it.

Jake turned to look. "That's a beauty."

Julianna pulled a small package from her bag, unwrapped it, and revealed a brand-new silencer. "I bought you a little present, Senator," she said, her voice dripping with mock sweetness.

Barstow's internal panic reached a fever pitch as Julianna screwed the silencer onto the gun, the metallic clicks echoing in his ears like the tolling of a death knell.

Julianna moved behind the chair, standing directly behind the Senator's slumped form. She leaned in close, her breath warm against his ear. "You know," she said softly, "if I had my way, this would be slow. Very slow."

Jake stepped in front of Barstow, crouching slightly to meet his eyes. His tone was calm, almost conversational. "Senator, you're probably wondering what's going on. Let me explain. That little jab you felt? Neurotoxin. You can see and hear everything, but you can't move a muscle. Kind of poetic, don't you think? You've spent your life paralyzing people with fear and corruption, and now here you are."

Julianna ran her fingers over the gun in her hand, her voice turning cold. "You know, Jake, I could end this right now. One shot. Quick, clean."

Jake shook his head, his gaze never leaving the Senator's frozen face. "Not yet. We're waiting for one more guest."

The Senator's eyes darted wildly, the only part of him that could move. He tried to will his body into action, to scream, to fight, but the toxin held him in its cruel grip.

Julianna leaned into his line of sight, tilting her head as she studied him. "You look scared, Senator. Good. You should be."

Jake stood, his voice calm but steely. "Don't worry, Senator. You'll get what's coming to you. It's just a matter of time."

As the two continued their grim preparations, while the Senator's mind raced with desperation, knowing that his time was running out and there was nothing he could do to stop it, Julianna turned off the security loops.

Chapter 62: Heart of Stone

Agent Carter sat stiffly in one of the lobby's overstuffed leather chairs, his eyes fixed on the main entrance. Next to him, another agent posed as a casual guest, glancing periodically toward the revolving doors. The radio crackled softly in Carter's earpiece.

"This is Bravo 1," said the agent in the lobby, his voice calm. "I see Fred Alton coming through the lobby right now."

Carter shifted in his seat and glanced sideways. Sure enough, there was Fred Alton, walking with a forced air of confidence, a leather briefcase in one hand.

"Bravo 2 here," came the voice of the rooftop agent. "I can't see anything. Curtains are still closed."

Bravo 3 chimed in from the car across the street. "If they both come out, who do I follow?"

Carter leaned into his mic, issuing instructions with precision. "Bravo 1, stay here and keep an eye out for Alton. Bravo 2, make your way down and prep a vehicle, in case we need to follow Alton. Bravo 3, you only follow the Senator, do not lose him under any circumstances. Copy?"

"Copy," came the chorus of voices.

Fred made his way to the elevator bank and disappeared inside. Carter's jaw tightened. "Stay sharp, everyone. Let's see how this plays out."

Fred took a deep breath as he stood outside the Senator's door. He had spent the entire flight to D.C. debating whether to flee or stay the course. Now, his heart raced as he knocked on the door.

The door opened swiftly, and Fred froze. Jake stood there, his gun mere inches from Fred's forehead.

"Come on in, Mr. Alton," Jake said coolly, gesturing with the barrel. "We've been waiting for you."

Fred swallowed hard and stepped inside, his legs trembling. Jake motioned to the couch. "Take a seat."

Fred sank into the plush cushions, gripping his briefcase as though it could shield him. Julianna leaned casually against the back of Barstow's chair, her silenced pistol resting on the armrest of the Senator's chair.

"Well, well," Julianna said, her voice dripping with sarcasm. "Fred Alton in the flesh. You don't look so brave without a dozen goons surrounding you."

Jake reset the apartment's alarm system, ensuring no interruptions, and Julianna turned the security loops back on. He turned to face Fred, his expression dark. "You know, Fred, I hate people like you, men with no code, no honor. Just rats scurrying from one dark corner to the next."

Fred opened his mouth, but Jake cut him off. "Save it. I'm not here to listen. I'm here to deliver justice."

Julianna moved in closer, crouching next to Barstow, who was still paralyzed in his chair. She rested her gun on the armrest, aiming it squarely at Fred.

"Jake, remind me," she said, her voice mocking. "What's the sentence for being a cowardly scumbag?"

"Death," Jake replied without hesitation.

Fred's eyes widened as Julianna pulled the trigger twice in quick succession. The silencer muted the shots, but the impact was unmistakable. One bullet struck Fred square in the chest, and the second ended with a clean shot to his temple. Fred slumped over, his briefcase falling to the floor with a dull thud.

Jake had stepped back, avoiding the blood splatter. Julianna calmly placed the gun in Barstow's limp hand, pressing his fingers around the grip.

"Here's how this is going to go, Senator," Jake said, his voice low and menacing. "That gun now has your fingerprints on it. In a moment, we're going to inject you with something to counteract the neurotoxin.

You'll be feeling much better in five minutes. But as we leave, your security alarm will be triggered. The authorities will be here in no time."

Barstow's eyes darted wildly, the only part of him that could move. Jake leaned in closer. "Your choices are limited. You can explain all this and hope they believe you, or, if you've got any shred of decency left, you can take yourself out before they get here. Personally, I think the second option suits you better."

Julianna prepped the syringe and injected Barstow in the arm. "Good luck, Senator," she said with a chilling smile.

Jake and Julianna moved swiftly to the freight elevator, disappearing into the depths of the building. Julianna pressed the button one last time, which would turn the security loops off and restore the security cameras to regular operation, as they descended.

In the lobby, the hotel's security desk lit up with alerts as the Senator's alarm system triggered. The head of security grabbed his key card and motioned to the police officers stationed nearby. "Something's going on upstairs."

Carter, still seated in the lobby, stood immediately. "Let's move," he said, motioning for the lobby agent to follow.

They took the main elevator to the Senator's floor. The head of security used his key card to unlock the door, then stepped back as armed police officers moved in.

Barstow was slumped in his chair, his hand twitching as he raised the gun. "No!" he croaked, his voice hoarse.

One of the officers, seeing the movement and the gun, reacted instinctively. A single shot rang out, striking Barstow center mass. He gasped, the life draining from his eyes as he slumped further into the chair.

Carter entered cautiously, taking in the scene. His gaze lingered on Fred's lifeless body and the gun in Barstow's hand. "Call it in," he said grimly.

As the room filled with agents and forensic teams, Carter couldn't believe that two years of investigation would end like this.

Chapter 63: Driving Too Fast

The elevator doors slid open into the basement of the Ritz Carlton. Jake and Julianna stepped out casually, blending into the flow of employees and staff moving through the labyrinth of the basement corridors. Both carried themselves with deliberate calm, their gear concealed in the nondescript messenger bag.

Julianna kept her voice low. "You think the FBI is onto us?"

Jake adjusted the strap on his bag. "If they are, we'll know soon enough. Just stay cool."

They followed the EXIT signs to the employee entrance. Their motorcycles awaited just a few yards away, waiting like loyal steeds. They slipped on their riding jackets and helmets with the ease of seasoned pros. Jake tapped his earpiece. "Check your comms."

"Loud and clear," Julianna responded.

The sound of the bikes roaring to life was like music to their ears. They swung their legs over the seats, gave a quick glance around, and rolled out of the garage at a controlled, inconspicuous speed. The streets of Washington bustled with the usual evening chaos, and Bravo 2 and 3, focused on the building, never noticed them weaving into the traffic.

The city traffic thickened, but Jake led the way, cutting deftly through gaps between vehicles. Julianna followed close behind, her smaller frame allowing her to maneuver effortlessly. The rumble of their engines was a subtle harmony under the din of horns and sirens.

As they hit the open highway, the tension of the last few hours began to ease, the wind whipping past them like a cleansing force. But the reprieve didn't last long.

"Jake," Julianna's voice crackled in his earpiece. "I've got movement. Unmarked SUVs merge onto the highway from the on-ramp behind us. Three of them."

Jake glanced in his side mirror, his jaw tightening. The SUVs were closing fast, their blacked-out windows gleaming under the streetlights.

"They're running tight formations," he said. "That's definitely not a coincidence."

"What's the move?" Julianna asked, her voice calm but sharp.

Jake checked the lanes ahead. "Hold tight. Let's see what they do."

The SUVs gained ground quickly, one moving into their lane and creeping closer to Jake's rear tire. He could feel the weight of their intentions like a physical force.

"Yeah, they're onto us," he said. "Time to show them what these bikes can do."

Without warning, Jake twisted the throttle, his bike surging forward. Julianna followed, matching his speed as they darted between lanes, their movements precise and fluid.

The SUVs accelerated, their engines growling as they gave chase. Jake led them into the HOV lane, the narrow corridor forcing the bulky vehicles to fall into single file.

"Let's lose them in the city," Jake said. "Exit coming up. Stay close."

He veered sharply onto the off-ramp, the tires of his bike skidding slightly before gripping the asphalt. Julianna mirrored his move, her body leaning low over her bike as they descended into a maze of side streets.

The SUVs followed, their bulk making it harder to keep pace. Jake glanced over his shoulder, a small smirk tugging at his lips. "They're slower than I thought."

"Don't get cocky," Julianna warned.

The streets narrowed, the bikes zipping through alleys and sharp turns that forced the SUVs to slam on their brakes to avoid collisions. Jake spotted an open pedestrian walkway and swerved onto it, the roar of his engine echoing off the brick walls.

"Shortcut," he said.

Julianna grinned behind her visor. "Show-off."

As they exited the walkway, the SUVs reappeared, cutting them off at a four-way intersection. Jake cursed under his breath, yanking his bike into a hard left.

"They're smarter than they look," Julianna said, following close.

The chase intensified as they sped into the industrial district. Jake spotted a construction site up ahead and an idea struck. "Jules, follow me. We're about to go off-road."

He veered into the site, the bikes kicking up clouds of dirt as they wove through stacks of lumber and idle machinery. The SUVs followed, their tires struggling for traction on the uneven ground.

Jake spotted a partially constructed ramp and gunned his engine. "Trust me!" he shouted into the comm.

Julianna's laugh crackled through the earpiece. "I hate you!"

Jake hit the ramp at full speed, his bike soaring over a wide trench before landing hard on the gravel. Julianna followed without hesitation, her bike skidding slightly on the uneven surface.

The SUVs screeched to a halt at the edge of the gap, their drivers unwilling to risk the jump. Jake glanced back, a triumphant grin spreading across his face.

"Looks like they're not as brave as us," he said.

"Or as stupid," Julianna shot back, though her voice carried a hint of exhilaration.

They sped away from the site, weaving through more back roads until they were sure they had lost their pursuers.

As the familiar outline of the farmhouse came into view, Jake exhaled slowly, tension easing from his shoulders.

Pulling into the barn, they killed their engines and dismounted. Jake turned to Julianna, his grin still in place. "That was one hell of a ride."

Julianna pulled off her helmet, her hair tousled but her eyes shining. "I'll give you that. But next time, let's avoid the death-defying stunts, okay?"

Jake smirked, tossing his helmet onto the seat of his bike. "Where's the fun in that?"

Julianna rolled her eyes but couldn't suppress a smile. They were alive, and for now, that was enough. Without warning, she buried her head against his chest. He wrapped his arms around her, pulling her into a protective embrace.

"Is it all over?" she asked, her voice muffled against him.

Jake rested his chin on the top of her head. "I think so. Who else is left to kill?" He let out a dry chuckle. "Unless the FBI decides we're their next priority, I think we're in the clear."

She looked up at him, her brown eyes searching his face for reassurance. "What do we do now?"

He shrugged. "We lay low. Take a breath. Figure out what's next. But for now, we rest."

The two stood in the quiet barn, the tension of the past few weeks finally beginning to melt away. But in the back of their minds, they both knew: that peace was a fleeting thing in their line of work.

Chapter 64: Living in a Ghost Town

Special Agent William Carter arrived at the FBI field office two days later, the weariness in his eyes matching the dark circles beneath them. The corridors hummed with agents moving briskly between cubicles. Carter straightened his tie as he entered the debriefing room, where a panel of his superiors waited. The room smelled faintly of coffee and disinfectant, heavy with anticipation.

"Special Agent Carter," the senior official greeted, gesturing to a chair across from the table. "Thank you for joining us. Let's get started."

Carter nodded, taking his seat, his posture rigid. He had anticipated this grilling, and though his nerves were steady, he wasn't sure where this would lead.

"Let's begin with the officer-involved shooting," one of the panel members said, adjusting his glasses. "Do you believe the officer acted appropriately?"

"Absolutely," Carter replied without hesitation. "The Senator raised his weapon. The officer had no choice but to neutralize the threat. Standard procedure. Clean shoot."

Another member of the panel flipped through a file. "The autopsy report confirmed traces of a neurotoxin in Barstow's system. Any theories as to how it got there?"

Carter leaned back slightly, choosing his words carefully. "Unusual, I'll admit. But with Barstow's connections and his paranoia, it's not hard to imagine he might have been dabbling in something... unconventional. Could've been self-administered or part of his... dealings. Hard to say for sure."

The room was silent for a beat before a woman at the end of the table spoke. "The forensic evidence aligns with witness statements. Alton was shot dead, the Senator holding the gun. It all points to a fallout between two criminals. Would you agree?"

Carter hesitated. He could feel the weight of the question pressing down on him. "On the surface, yes. That's exactly what it looks like."

"On the surface?" the woman pressed.

Carter exhaled slowly, his brow furrowing. "If I'm being honest, I have my doubts. Something about this doesn't sit right."

The panel exchanged glances before another official leaned forward. "What does your gut tell you, Special Agent?"

Carter stared at the table for a moment, the words caught in his throat. Finally, he met their gazes. "My gut says there's more to this. We never identified who kidnapped Agnes. We chalked it up to Barstow, but the logistics never made sense. Barstow didn't operate that cleanly. Whoever grabbed her was precise, and professional. And there's no trace of them left behind."

The senior official tapped a pen against the table. "Based on your instincts and the evidence, what are your recommendations?"

Carter paused, the room growing heavier with each passing second. "Honestly, I can't prove my gut feelings. Even if I could, I'm not sure if there's anything to chase. Whoever they were, they didn't leave us much to work with. And… they did us more favors than harm. Aside from bruising my ego, I don't see the point in pursuing ghosts."

The panel whispered amongst themselves before the senior official nodded. "Thank you, Agent Carter. That will be all."

Carter rose from his seat, his jaw tight. He could feel their eyes on him as he left the room, their curiosity burning, but their hands tied by the lack of concrete evidence.

As he walked down the corridor, one of his colleagues, Agent Daniels, fell into step beside him.

"How'd it go?" Daniels asked.

Carter gave a humorless chuckle. "They're letting it go. Just like I figured."

"You think they'll come back to it?"

Carter stopped, glancing out the window at the bustling street below. "Not unless someone gives them a reason to. And whoever these people are, they don't leave reasons lying around."

Daniels smirked. "Ghosts, huh?"

"Yeah," Carter said quietly, his gaze distant. "Ghosts. But damn effective ones."

He walked away, his thoughts swirling. He had no proof, no leads, and no idea if he'd ever cross paths with the elusive figures responsible for Agnes's disappearance and Barstow's downfall. But something deep inside him told him he hadn't seen the last of them.

The morning sun filtered through the gaps in the barn's old wooden walls, casting golden beams across the Suburban and trailer. Dust motes danced in the light as Jake hoisted the last duffle bag into the back. The air was fresh, and for the first time in weeks, there was a lightness between Jake and Julianna.

As Julianna rolled the motorcycles up the ramp and into the trailer, she said, "Nicolai deposited the money this morning. We're rich! We can go anywhere, do anything." She paused, wiping her brow with the back of her hand, and turned to Jake with a playful grin. "Where should we go first? Vegas?"

Jake raised an eyebrow, leaning against the trailer. "For the casinos? Or wedding chapels?"

Julianna laughed, the sound echoing in the barn. "Somebody likes me, he really likes me," she teased, batting her eyelashes dramatically.

Jake chuckled, stepping closer to her. He rested his hands on her hips, pulling her in gently. "You know I do," he said, his voice soft but steady.

Julianna leaned her forehead against his, closing her eyes for a moment. "Well, if that's true, then I guess I'll keep you around for a while," she said, her lips curling into a smirk.

Jake stepped back, mock-serious. "A while, huh? I guess, I'll take what I can get."

Julianna shook her head, laughing again as she moved to secure the bikes in the trailer. "Why don't we load the bikes and just see, where the wind takes us?"

Jake grinned, watching her tighten the straps with practiced ease. "Now, that sounds like a plan."

With everything packed and double-checked, Jake tossed the keys to Julianna. She caught them with one hand and raised an eyebrow. "Oh, so I'm the chauffeur now?"

"Yup," Jake said, climbing into the passenger seat. "I'm retired. You're driving."

Julianna climbed into the driver's seat, shaking her head. "Retired, huh? From what exactly? Being bossy?"

Jake smirked, reclining his seat slightly. "From saving the world, obviously. Now, I'm just here to enjoy the ride."

The Suburban roared to life, and Julianna guided it out of the barn. As they pulled onto the gravel driveway, the crunching of the tires matched the rhythm of their shared heartbeat, a steady, unspoken understanding that, for the first time in a long time, they were free.

The road stretched ahead of them, winding through the countryside, flanked by trees still dressed in autumn colors. The sunlight danced on the windshield, and Julianna reached over, lacing her fingers with Jake's for just a moment before returning her hand to the wheel.

"Any requests, co-pilot?" she asked, glancing at him with a grin.

Jake pretended to think, rubbing his chin theatrically. "Hmm, how about somewhere with good coffee? You know, priorities."

"Priorities," she echoed, rolling her eyes. "You're lucky you're cute."

"And you're lucky I'm so charming," Jake shot back, winking at her.

The Suburban hummed along, towing their future behind it in the trailer. As they drove, the tension of the past weeks seemed to melt away. For the first time in what felt like forever, they weren't running, they were simply moving forward. Together.

"Vegas is still on the table, you know," Jake said after a while, breaking the comfortable silence.

Julianna glanced at him, a playful glint in her eye. "I want to find some great twisty roads for the motorcycles."

Jake shrugged, his smirk widening. "Have you ever ridden through Bear Tooth Pass? Now that's a motorcycle road!"

Julianna laughed, her voice filling the car with warmth. "Let's see where the wind takes us first," she said. "For the first time in a long time, we've got nowhere we need to be. And I want to take advantage of that."

Jake chuckled, leaning back in his seat and watching the trees blur past. "Wherever the wind takes us, babe."

And with that, the Suburban disappeared down the winding road, leaving behind the farmhouse, the barn, and the ghosts of their past, as Jake and Julianna drove toward an open horizon full of endless possibilities.

Outro: You Can't Always Get What You Want

When it comes to my line of work, some people love it too much. They get off on the chaos, the blood, the fear they see in someone's eyes, right before it's lights out. Not me. I'm not here for the thrill. I'm here because I'm good at it. Cold, calculated, efficient, that's my currency. I don't savor it I don't draw it out, does that make me a monster?

I know you're disappointed. I can almost feel it. You wanted the Senator on his knees, begging. You wanted to see me carve his sins into his flesh, make him feel every ounce of pain he dished out. You wanted to watch me turn the monsters into prey and drag them into the same hell they built for everyone else. But that's not me. I told you from the start, I am a professional, I don't play with my food. Torture is for the sadists. Payback is for amateurs. And I'm not the Devil. Perhaps you are.

Because if you're here, if you've followed me through every kill, every explosion, every game of cat and mouse, what does that make you? You're still reading, aren't you? Still watching from the shadows, hoping I'll give you the vengeance you crave. You say you want justice, but what you crave is blood.

Don't get me wrong, I'm not judging you. Maybe you have a point. Maybe someone needs to be the Devil, to hold the mirror up to the scum of the earth and show them what true darkness looks like. But that's not who I am. I'm a soldier, plain and simple. A tool for hire.

I told you before, this world is twisted. There are no heroes here, no white knights riding in to save the day. Just people like me, doing what needs to be done. Call me a killer if you want. Call me cold, ruthless, whatever helps you sleep at night. But don't you dare pretend you're not complicit. You've been here for the whole ride.

I'm here because there's always one more job, one more mess to clean up — one more loose end to tie. Judge me if you want, I don't care. Just remember, in a world this broken, someone like me isn't the problem. Someone like me is the solution.

Today, they call me Jake. Tomorrow? Who knows? But for now, this is my story. Take it or leave it.

Author Bio – Skip Williams

Skip Williams is the author of three other books, dozens of published articles, and over three hundred blog posts, primarily in the business advice genre. Now, he turns his expertise in strategy and precision to fiction with his debut novel. Semi-retired and living at 10,000 feet in the mountains of Utah, Skip enjoys traveling and exploring the outdoors, when he's not at his computer crafting his next story.